TRAIL OF OBSESSION

THE PREDATOR / PREY THRILLER SERIES
BOOK 1

VALERIE BRANDY

EMERALD LION
PRESS

Published by: Emerald Lion Press

23901 Calabasas Rd., Ste 2088, Calabasas, CA 91302

emeraldlionpress@gmail.com

ISBN 978-1-964161-01-3

Cover designed by Stuart Bache. Copy Editing provided by Sharon Lennon-Mehlschau and Linda Triol. Photo of the author by David Mueller.

Printed in the United States of America.

Yosemite National Park is a public space visited by 4 million people each year, located in Central California. Specific landmarks mentioned may be visited by contacting the National Park Service. For more information, visit: nps.gov.

Visit the author's website at: www.valeriebrandy.com

❀ Created with Vellum

For my Mom,
who taught me to bite back—

-- and for all the girls
who are finding their fangs.

CONTENTS

FACT

The myth of alpha males leading wolf packs is entirely false. Wild wolves live in family units in which two equal partners raise children into maturity.

1

My hands are wide and blistered, swollen with intent: to seek, to clasp, to choke, to burn.

They claw at wet Earth, red palms seeking traction on the side of the riverbank. A precipice above promises life, promises safety. I stretch toward it.

It's out of reach.

Black stripes of soil cake over my nails, fingers clinging to the bank's ice-bitten incline. It's an ugly polish, but perfectly suitable, given the circumstances. Escaping death is woman's work, here in the place where roots burrow deep but branches reach tall, stretched always between two opposing expectations. *She must survive, but she must look good while she does it.*

Beneath me, a chasm of a river splits the Earth in half, calling me toward it like a Siren to a sailor, its white-capped waters offering a beautiful demise. *Beauty is pain.* If I could let myself fall, it wouldn't take long to slide backward off the bank, my hair splayed wide, mouth open in a primal scream, revealing teeth that haven't been brushed in days. The ugliness of it all would be my final act of rebellion. I'd hit the water and sink deep, letting the cold slow my movements, thinking the whole time about the snow, and the forest, and the way it made space for me when no one else did.

But then again, I might think of my enemy. Somewhere in the wilderness, a murderer has kidnapped the man I love, stalking us both down this trail of obsession— threatening us both with death and extinction. As the water fills my lungs, I might— on the verge of death— think of that opponent, faceless, taunting, waiting for me in the shadows of some place I can't reach.

It's too big a risk. I'll have to survive, instead.

My body thrashes, sensing the lure of death. My lungs rattle as they search for air. My eyes narrow, scanning the sheer slope of the bank, blinded by panic. Limbs tangle, scratching on instinct, but then something strange happens:

I laugh.

Even through the terror, the joke is impossible to miss. I've become a fish. A gangly, idiotic fish who swam too close to the river's edge and stranded herself. The thought causes me to stop struggling, and my slide toward the water halts long enough for me to register a new strategy— stillness.

It's in this moment that a mental hole emerges— a vacuum in my world-view. Just as the melting frost fills the gaps in the soil, the cavity in my mind swells with epiphany. The dirt on my nails takes on new meaning, spotlighting some part of myself I've always known, but looked away from. It's an essential piece of my being the world asked me to bury— a piece I betrayed by agreeing.

I've concealed this slice of myself for many years, hiding her behind smiles and pink dresses, lipstick and "so-sorrys." Apologies work best to dull the glint of her teeth. The bars of her cage are built on "after-yous." I've hidden her away deep inside, restrained by padlocks and chains. But now?

I need her.

Suddenly, my hands are not hands, but paws, my nails sharp and ready to slice. My teeth are not teeth but fangs, equipped to rip out the throat of the person who did this to me.

My name is Zoe.

And I am not prey. I'm a predator.

2

———

ne week earlier...

I'M NEW, the world is infinite, and my life will always be made of beginnings.

The words tumble through my brain as our little Subaru zips up a snake of a road, weaving its way toward Yosemite. Pristine, crisp air glides over the silver hood, four new tires bouncing on uneven pavement. Mike wanted to rent a Prius and I wanted an SUV, so we met in the middle. Compromise. A thing I'm learning to live with.

Mike glances at me from the driver's seat.

"It has more get up and go than you thought, right?"

"Maybe," I shoot back, pretending to check the dashboard. "Are you happy with the gas mileage, mister environmentalist? If not I'll pop open the floor hatch and we can Flintstone our way up the mountain."

"Not in these shoes," Mike grins, opening up the

external vents, filling the car with the scent of pine trees and possibility. It makes my head swim, heavy with the promise of an outdoor adventure.

The passenger-side window glides down with ease when I press the automatic button. I un-click my seatbelt, sticking my upper body out the window.

Sheets of green whiz by; dense forest spiraling into forever. I've always loved the wilderness, if only because it's a place where no one expects anything of you.

In my day-to-day life, I'm a hotel manager, and the job requires me to focus on appearances. We're an upscale establishment. Chandeliers trickle from the hotel ceilings like sticky icing on the side of a cake. Walls covered in dense floral wallpaper muffle the secrets of our guests, framed by drapes so soft you could fall into them and never find your way back out again. It's all about decorum, there, and it takes a special kind of person to do the job. Ninety percent of my time is spent addressing grievances with, "We're sincerely sorry for that, ma'am," and "Apologies, sir." The other ten percent involves smiling even though I want to smack someone. But none of that matters out here, in the wild. The forest doesn't care if I'm rude, or dirty, or a beast. She only cares that I show up.

My fingers turn white, gripping the hard edge of the window. My head tosses back, and my lips form a perfect "o" as I howl into the infinite everything.

"Watch out everybody, she's on the prowl," Mike reaches for the back of my jeans and puts a hand on my ass, and I whip around like a dog who doesn't like his tail grabbed.

"You better watch it."

"Or what?"

"Or I'll bite you." I kiss his neck— reckless— not caring that he might take his eyes off the twisting mountain road.

It's been too long since I've had a vacation, and now that I'm in wolf-mode, practical Zoe has left the vehicle.

"Wow," Mike pretends to be surprised. "When I signed up to drive for Uber, I had no *idea* I'd have such friendly passengers…"

This is a game we play sometimes; that we're strangers who are just meeting.

"You're about to get a five star review…"

"Jesus, Zoe, the road—"

"It's your fault for bringing me into the wild," I tease him, still thinking about what it would feel like to be a wolf, with no one to answer to except the forest herself. The wind whips through my open window, and I turn my attention away from Mike's neck and back to the vast landscape outside. This time I lean even further into the openness, sitting on the edge of the window frame like a bird on a perch, one arm extended wide, invincible.

"Careful," Mike lets his foot off the gas a little, always the more cautious half of our partnership. "And I believe *I* requested a tropical setting," he sighs.

It's true. I forced him to come to Yosemite, and promised we'd do something tropical another time. It was a rare moment for me. Usually I let the other person have their way, no questions asked. But years of therapy in carpeted offices littered with chimes and crystals have made me more mindful of my patterns. When I met Mike, I promised I'd break my bad habits. Apparently, I'm a people-pleaser who "struggles to voice her needs, is habitually distrustful of others, and creates distance as a form of self-protection." It's a nice way of saying that I'm an aloof bitch who copes with fear of abandonment by down-playing her own feelings, desires, and investment in a relationship. People never know where they stand with me.

There's a kind of love story— you've heard it before— where the princess is trapped in a castle, and the prince comes to save her. She knows at once he's the one, and they live happily ever after.

Ours is not that kind of love story.

In our story, Mike is the princess. He is kind, and good, and trusting. Flowers spring up on the grass where he walks. His smile makes the sun shine brighter. Animals gravitate toward him because they can sense the purity of his heart.

Meanwhile, I'm the gnarly ogre who guards the castle bridge. I question everyone who dares pass, making them answer three riddles before proceeding. If they don't answer correctly, I cast them into the moat, caustic and brittle in my conclusion that they're not to be trusted.

The hotel I work at is my fortress, surrounding my ugliness with beauty, cloaking the worst of me in wrappings so lush my shortcomings are easily overlooked.

When I told Mike about my metaphor for our relationship, I half-expected him to come to his senses and break up with me.

"Don't you see? You fell in love with the ogre when you should've waited for a prince!"

He laughed. "What can I say? The big ears really do it for me."

That's the thing about Mike. He has his own kind of magic. It enables him to look past the external— the thorns and barbs around the flower of a person— straight into the core of who they are. He only sees the best in me.

An alarm blares, taking me by surprise and making my hand slip from the edge of the window. Suddenly, I'm teetering toward the black asphalt, scraping against the car's smooth paint toward oblivion. I'm sure I'm going to fall, but Mike grabs onto the belt loop in my jeans, pulling me back into the car. We weave into the other lane, but there's no oncoming traffic out here in the wilderness. If we were still in Silverlake, we'd be dead.

"You okay?" He asks, a little shaken.

"Yeah," I answer, trying not to let on how close I was to becoming road kill.

There's a moment of silence in which we're both considering the fragility of what's stable, and the nearness of disaster. Then, a silky sound echoes beside me as Mike uses the driver controls to roll-up the passenger-side window.

We lean in to look at Mike's phone— a text message is the source of the alarm bell— strapped to the dashboard in a holder connected to the vents. It's not beeping anymore, but it shakes as the car hits rough asphalt, as if it dreads the name on its screen as much as Mike does:

Cassandra.

Mike groans, "Not again."

"Do you want to read it?"

"No," he hesitates. "Do you?"

It's a rare invitation. Mike is like a piece of sea-glass, multi-faceted and saturated, hard to look away from but still easy to see through. He doesn't keep secrets, and he's an open book about everything in our relationship, except *her*. He's given me the basics: a disgruntled ex who stalks him, new addresses and phone numbers be damned. He's been fair in sharing details, and revealed that he had a stalker as soon as things between us got serious. He said he wanted me to decide if it was something I could live with, and he'd understand if it wasn't. I stayed, but the ogre in me keeps one eye open, looking not at Cassandra, but at Mike.

Strangely, Cassandra herself doesn't bother me. In fact, I think I might like her. The letters she sends, sprayed with perfume, soft and sweet, not so strong as to be cloying. The way she leaves the mail by the door, stacked in order from important to junk. She might lack boundaries, but even in her trespasses, Cassandra tries to be unobtrusive. I've never met her in-person, but her actions describe her character. There's a permanent question in everything she does, like she's walking through life with her hand patiently raised, waiting to be called on by a teacher who's no longer there. It's a side-effect of some deeper phenomenon all women experience, one I can relate to but can't quite put into words. The closest I've come to describing it is that it's like being told you're a brunette, but looking in the mirror and seeing a blonde. It's some fundamental mismatch between who you are, and how others see you, and I know if I met Cassandra — if I mentioned it, even just the start— she'd understand immediately. If she weren't stalking my boyfriend, I'm pretty sure we'd be friends.

No, it's not Cassandra who makes my inner ogre raise the drawbridge. It's Mike, and his refusal to disclose the details of their break up. My ogre doesn't like his answers to my riddles.

"She's sick," is his favorite refrain, his dark eyes webbed with sympathy. "She's not right in the head. One day she'll get help."

He claims he's trying to shield me from something that's "his problem," but his vagueness makes me sure there's more to it. But then I remember that I have eyes coated in doubt, and that I'm always looking for the worst in people, even in the very best of moments. In the comfortable darkness of night, wrapped in sheets we spent too much money on, the TV humming with the evening news— in the seconds before sleep, when any other woman would roll over and tell the man she loves how glad she is to have him, I curl into Mike's arms and ask a wordless question. It's one I can't utter aloud, but can still reach out and touch, passing it between my fingers like a lucky coin I won't get rid of.

Is there a monster in you?

He's done nothing to deserve the question, and I know enough about myself that I'm sure I'd be asking it anyway, even if Cassandra didn't exist. It's occurred to me that I could, one day, stop asking it, but that will be the moment Mike reveals the worst in him. Call me superstitious, but Murphy's Law applies. The night you don't check for monsters under the bed is the night one eats you.

Temporarily invited into Mike and Cassandra's secret world, I pull the phone from its holster. It's a weapon in my hands, explosive and unstable. I type in Mike's lock code. He gave it to me once to check an email and never changed it. Like I said, he's sea-glass. Other guys won't let you see inside a sock drawer, but on date number one, Mike will give you his banking information and mother's telephone number.

"Drove past your office," I read aloud, wondering what Cassandra's voice sounds like and if it's anything like mine. "Didn't see you through the window. Where are you?" The words are followed by a few kissy face emojis. Predictable and a little tacky, but lacking in pretense. That's another thing I like about Cassandra. She's too screwed up to pretend to be anyone other than exactly who she is. I search for Mike's reaction, but for a moment he's an enigma, unreadable. "At least she doesn't know where we are," I prompt.

"That's true," he answers, but the slant in his voice says it doesn't make him feel any better.

He looks like a person who's just run through his high-school hallways naked, only to realize it wasn't a dream after all. I understand why.

Dating in adulthood— when you're past your college

freshness, and your stories have grown longer with more cryptic endings— means coming into a relationship with a certain amount of baggage. We all have it. Dusty luggage with too many stickers, corners shredded by conveyor belts, locks that don't work and zippers that get stuck.

At twenty-eight, I've spent well over a decade unpacking some of the worst suitcases you've ever seen, only to repack them again and send their owners to the nearest bus depot.

First there was Dave, who forgot to mention that he'd folded up a wife inside his carry-on. Then there was Aaron, who bundled up a debilitating fear of commitment and placed it in the front pocket of his sensible duffle-bag, to be removed only when two years of energy had been spent "working on the relationship." He got married six months later, unpacking another surprise: he wasn't afraid of commitment. He just didn't love me enough. Last but not least was Jerome, whose baggage was basically just that he was an asshole.

Each of these relationships left its mark on me, until one day I opened up my own suitcase (a wheel-along weekender with very comfortable handles), and found an inability to trust anyone, at all, ever. It was probably always there, hiding under crumbs and receipts, but it doubled in size, and I fed it daily like a beloved pet. It kept me safely alienated from the perils of love for awhile.

Then, I met Mike, and the world rearranged itself.

Falling for him happened entirely by accident. He makes furniture— hand-crafted, beautiful things, built from rare types of woods— the sort of stuff ritzy establishments like my hotel invest in.

The day he walked in to try and sell us on a carved wooden table for the sitting area of the lobby, he brought the piece with him, loaded into the back of a busted old van.

It was so beautiful it made me want to cry. Something about it moved; spiraling legs curved into a textured top, every notch built with care. It was so alive it practically breathed.

On our first date, Mike showed me his workshop. His fingers were stained brown with varnish, and he smelled like oak and sawdust. First, we were casual— my choice, not his. Then, we were something else. My ogre let down the bridge and helped him cross the moat, but my defensive walls remained in place, ready to eject him should he prove to be anyone other than the man he presents. When we moved in together, I insisted that the lease be in my name. Dolly Parton once said the key to a happy relationship is always having a suitcase packed. I go one step further and keep my car keys in the ignition. I'm always searching for fangs in the the mouth of the man I'm with.

That's why when Mike, "needed to tell me something" a few months into our too-good-to-be-true relationship, I wasn't surprised. I waited for him to admit to being a serial killer, or an ex-con, but instead he confessed to having a stalker. He'd met Cassandra in college, and they'd had a five-year relationship before she lost her mind and things went South. It wasn't the worst baggage I'd unpacked. And I could relate to the feeling of discovering the person you thought you knew was a Russian stacking doll all along, hiding multiple versions of himself deep under skin and bone.

Prior to Mike, I'd endured the hell of dating apps, taking a last, half-hearted stab at love by creating a generic bio, throwing up a few pictures of myself at the beach, at work, as a butterfly on Halloween.

Even there— in that digital, surface-level environment consisting of impressions and guesses— I encountered the phenomenon of a human within a human— a social turducken. I chatted for weeks with a guy who seemed completely harmless. His name was "Josh Q.," and his interests included video games, baseball, and hiking. We played a game where we wrote to each other in rhyming stanzas, always increasing the difficulty.

> "How was your day? What happened at work?"
> "It was great, how 'bout yours? Just asking to lurk."
> "I didn't do much. Did you watch Game of Thrones?"
> "Why yes, yes I did, And my mind was so blown!"

It was a stupid way to trade messages, but the novelty of it caught my attention. We even made plans to meet, but I cancelled when Mike walked into my life, bringing his toffee-colored skin and reassuring smile. No one could compare, and I deleted the app a few days later— but Josh Q. still found me. He added me on Facebook, and followed me on Instagram. When I messaged him to tell him I was seeing someone, his reaction made me wish I hadn't written him at all.

"Would've been nice to know that before I wasted my time. You bitches are all the same." I resisted the temptation to write back in rhyme: "Us bitches are all the same... we think you're really *lame*."

The experience was a warning, a reminder that people can surprise you, no matter how benign they seem on the outside. It was a small drop in a bucket I've been filling since third grade, when my Dad found a family he liked better, and left me and Mom with nothing but one of his old sweat-shirts, which we donated to Goodwill. It's the sticky feeling you get when you meet someone new, and you wonder if they're even worth the trouble. It's the hand of an older mentor on your back, placed just low enough to introduce a question. It's the humming undertone during dinner at a friend's house, when you notice your friend's husband gripping his wine glass a little too tightly. People hide the worst of themselves. It's a truth I've accepted— one that Mike will never believe, even as Cassandra hovers in the background of his life, never near enough to see, but always close enough to feel. That's the difference between Mike and me. I've learned that all people are either a predator, or prey. It just takes time to know which one you're dealing with.

Mike pulls the phone from my hands and shoves it in the glove compartment, jolting me back to the present moment.

"Let's not talk about her this week," he mutters as he closes the glove compartment too hard. He rarely gets angry, and the emotion hangs from his shoulders like a suit that's too big. "I just want to be..."

He doesn't finish the thought, but he doesn't have to.

"Free," I add. He nods, pressing on the accelerator so that the pine trees whip past my window, turning the world into a green blur that won't slow down for me, no matter hard I try to blink it into focus.

A couple of hours later and we pull up to a worn cabin nestled behind a parking lot. It's missing shutters in all the wrong places, leaving the windows naked and the rooms within exposed to the world. The pine trees that circle it curve inward instead of reaching for the sky, closing in on the cabin as if they know it was built from the bones of brutalized brothers and sacrificed sisters. The parking lot in front of the building is an even greater injustice, covering wildflowers that never got the chance to grow, shrubs that were smothered in their infancy. On the edges of the black asphalt, scattered picnic tables are arranged in a row, serving as bait for haggard parents and their kids. Right on cue, a mini-van pulls into the dirt drive-way, and a weary Mom tumbles out, accompanied by three kids— two boys and one girl, all younger than eleven. She sits at a table and begins laying out a picnic, shouting over her shoulder, "Peanut butter and Jelly time, let's go gang!" I mentally send a gold star her way. Moms do so much work that no one sees.

My boots crunch over fallen pine needles as we

approach the cabin. A battered sign outside reads, "*Circle Bar Horse Tours,*" the words aggressively burned into the wood like a brand on a cow. The letters are in all caps, their width so bold it makes me want to look away.

"I'll check our reservation," Mike says, shifting his backpack to his other shoulder. It's a hideous lime-green thing, with useless, silver reflectors sewn in rectangles across the front pockets.

"Why you insisted on bringing that thing—" I shake my head at the bag.

"Only because you hate it," he grins, opening the front door to the cabin. Bells hung to its frame jingle as it shuts behind him. The effect should be jolly, but the bells are contrasting tones ringing in a minor key. The sound makes my ears burn.

I don't follow, but busy myself with a dusty, plastic display case outside. Pamphlets crowd its face, all of them boasting of horse-tours through different parts of the valley. The pamphlets are a reminder that I'm sitting on a secret— one I haven't shared with Mike, and one that I won't. Their presence is the beating heart beneath the floor boards, the one that makes me want to confess, to admit to the thing I should have told Mike when we booked this tour:

I'm afraid of horses.

Gnawing teeth. An innocent, wide-eyed exterior that hides a thousand pounds of pure muscle just waiting for the chance to trample me into sawdust. Pristine, luscious manes distracting from the danger underneath. Beauty on the outside hiding a monster within. A horse is the external manifestation of my internal fears, and the last thing I want to do is spend my vacation on top of one.

I should've just told him. Mike would have understood. Mike *always* understands. But it was me who wanted to go camping, and he never looked excited about it until he stumbled across the advertisement for a horse tour. It never occurred to him I'd harbor a secret fear of horses, because he sees me as an invincible lover of the outdoors, a regular Annie Oakley. I like when people see me as invincible, but for all the wrong reasons. If no one is aware of my weaknesses, they'll never offer to help me, and I'll never have to accept and find myself disappointed when they let me down. Maybe it's the result of not having a Dad in my life, but I don't run to other people to fix my problems. When I was a kid, my Mom called me "Zoe the Zipper," because it would take me weeks to ask for help with something. No matter how much trouble I'd gotten myself into, my lips stayed zipped.

In adulthood, people label me as "an introvert," or "not a talker," but that's a misdiagnosis. The truth is that a seed was planted inside me long ago— one that I can't dig up. Its roots are deep in my belly, and I've watered it with bad relationships. By now, it's grown into a tree, its branches weaving through my veins, spelling out the words "I'm fine." It's one of the reasons selfish partners love me: I don't ask for much. But there's a dark side to my self-reliance. Mike has entered into a Faustian deal with me, without even knowing it. I'm the innocent girl seeking a lovely trip to the woods, and he's the devil making me face my biggest fear. I've cast us in roles, and Mike didn't even audition for the play.

The wooden porch around the cabin creaks under my feet as I step upward, heading for the front door, ready to find Mike and tell him the truth. I'm about to make those little bells ring again, but it's too late. Mike's already walking toward me, coming around the side of the building, beaming, accompanied by the thing I fear most in this world.

Dust kicks up as the animal's hooves hit the Earth. It's a

palomino, and as it tosses its giant head, I'm struck by the way its mane looks so much like hair. *She's blonde,* I think, almost laughing at how much this horse reminds me of the ditzy receptionist at my dentist's office, who once asked me what "defer" meant and if it was a country. If I'm going to put my life into a giant's hands, she might as well be an idiot.

"Her name is Molly," Mike smiles, motioning for me to move closer. The porch creaks again as I descend, almost as if it's issuing a warning. Mike holds out the reins and I take them in my hands, buttery leather feeling soft and rough between my fingers. I almost drop them when a man steps out from behind Molly's left flank, making me inhale.

He isn't especially tall— maybe 5'6"— but he's shockingly broad, built like the side of a barn, as if God decided to steal a little height from his vertical body and reallocate it to his shoulders. Even through his flannel shirt, it's clear he's pure muscle. Frown lines between his eyes make me guess he's in his forties, but his skin is so sun-damaged it's hard to say how old he is. His mouth contorts into a smile, his front two teeth tilting at an unusual angle, framed by pock-marked skin that hints at teenage acne, the kind that leaves a mark even once it fades away. His hair is thinning, but he's hanging on hard to the few wisps he has left. Good for him. They flip over the side of his head in wavy patches.

"Glad to have you," he shakes my hand. My throat tightens. Something about him makes me uncomfortable, but I can't put my finger on what it is.

"This is Brock. He owns the place," Mike says. When I don't respond, he explains too slowly, as if I'm a forgetful Grandad, "You know, the guy we talked to over the phone?"

"Right," I answer, not mentioning that I don't remember any specifics of our reservation call because I was too busy having a secret panic attack. "Brock. Nice to put a face to the name."

"I'll be leading the tour. Mike says you've never been on a horse before, but don't worry. You're in great hands."

He coughs as he walks away, his gait familiar and strange all at the same time, his breath quivering as it catches in his throat. Suddenly, I know why I'm afraid of Brock:

He reminds me of a horse.

AFTER A BRIEF RUN-DOWN on the basics of horseback riding, Brock is grabbing my leg and hoisting me over Molly's back while I try to remember what the front of the saddle is called. Povel? Pronel? The information seems essential. What if I'm in a life-threatening situation and Brock tells me to grab the front of the saddle in order to save myself, but I don't follow his instructions properly because I can't remember what it's called?

"Put one hand on the reins and one on the pommel," Brock whinnies, frustrated at my lack of expertise.

"*Pommel,*" I whisper, repeating the word like my life depends on it.

Behind me, Mike waves as he pulls himself onto a massive black stallion that might be the biggest animal I've ever seen. The horse is regal in posture, its mane a midnight black so dark it's almost blue, hooves so large that the prints they leave behind look like dinosaur tracks. If Dwayne the Rock Johnson needed a horse, this would be the poor beast they'd give him. I'm not sure *why* Dwayne would need a horse— maybe his muscles are so big he can't fit in Ubers.

"Isn't this awesome, babe?!" Mike shouts over his shoulder, having the time of his life.

"So fun!" I call back, hands shaking.

I lean down to Molly and whisper in her ear, "Okay, you beautiful idiot. Now's your chance to prove to everyone you're more than just a pretty face. Let's do this. You with me?"

Molly shakes her mane— an action I interpret as a hair flip. Molly is fabulous, and she knows it. Brock slaps Molly's flank— a little presumptuous of him, but she doesn't seem to mind— and suddenly I'm swaying side-to-side as she walks toward the trail like a self-driving car, completely oblivious to my attempts to pull on the reins and redirect her.

"Just let her do her thing," Brock calls out, as if Molly were a house-cat scratching the couch and not a thousand pound animal with my life in her hands. "She likes to snack along the way."

"Snack" is an understatement. Tall grass grows upward at the start of the trail, thriving in the shade and taking advantage of the space the clearing provides. Molly meanders through the knee-high streaks of green and brown, pulling out pieces like a prom queen who just found out her quarterback boyfriend has been screwing her best friend. It's the horse equivalent of microwaving ice-cream and drinking it straight out of the carton. She has some major feelings she's working out, and while I support her self-actualization, I hope she's watching the road. If she wanders off the trail and no-one notices our disappearance, my survival plan is to cling to her back like a baby koala, occasionally leaning down to grab my own chunk of grass, which I'll eat to stay alive until she sorts out her feelings and takes us back to the ranch.

Brock expertly mounts his own horse, then leads the rest of our group toward the trail. We're a small party, and there's only three other riders besides Mike and me. With Brock included, that makes six of us venturing into the unknown.

First in line is a retired couple celebrating their forty-year anniversary, who introduced themselves as "Ken-and-Sue-Hardinger," saying both their names like one word.

Sue has bright, curious eyes, silver hair, and a certain way of noticing things— like she's taking a mental picture to retrieve later. Ken is a little thick around the middle, with a red-faced smile and hands that gesture when he talks. There's a carefree aura around the two of them, as if they're children just starting out in life, imagining futures as firefighters or movie stars. I like them immediately, and wonder if they look alike because they've been married so long that they've grown together, or if they've always had the same curved noses.

In the middle of the line-up is Logan, a lone rider braving the trail without a traveling companion. His introduction was brief because he was late to the orientation, but he looks to be in his early twenties, around college-age. He fidgets with anything he can get his hands on— the edge of his glasses, the rim of his baseball cap— making me wonder if he was late on purpose, to avoid interacting too much with the group. His pants are too big, and his shirt features some kind of a computer joke written in that language that's all zeros and ones. It's a surprise, considering his build, which doesn't scream "computer nerd." Just like Brock, he isn't tall, but his biceps bulge and he's wearing a Raiders baseball cap, making me think he might play football. He rarely makes eye contact with any of us, but when he does there's something defiant in his face, like he's out here to make a point. I spin a background story for him. He bought these tickets for his girlfriend, but they broke up right before the trip. Now, he's traveling alone for the first time, far from the security of his college dorm and his video games, but prepared to post plenty of pictures of how much fun he had, just because he'll-show-her.

Mike pulls up next to me, swaying on top of Dwayne the Rock Johnson's horse.

"You ready?"

I'm about to tell him I can't do this, but then he smiles that stupid smile. Am I really prepared to risk my life for this person? What he would do, if Molly bucked me off and trampled me under her hooves? Try and save me? Shrug and find another girlfriend?

"Ready," I answer, and our fingertips touch before his horse pulls in front of Molly, who follows right behind him, bending down to eat her feelings as we go.

The trail vanishes into the forest, and the sunshine fades as we leave the ranch behind. The woods surround us, the trees consume us, and I'm committed now. I'm climbing this mountain on horseback whether I like it or not, following Mike to increasingly treacherous trails, all while perched on top of Molly, who's basically equestrian Barbie.

Somewhere in there hides a metaphor for our relationship, but I'm too busy trying to stay upright to coax it out.

4

———

I'm meeting a stranger.

Her round eyes look up at me from a puddle as Molly trudges along the trail. She's my reflection, and she's not afraid of anything. She's a woman completely at ease up on her horse, and even though it's only been a few hours, some natural instinct tells me I might leave the forest a different person than I was when I entered.

Molly's hoof lands in the puddle, and the stranger disappears.

It really is true, what they say about love being the most powerful force in the world. My love of nature has outweighed my terror, bludgeoning it into submission through distractions, like the snow-capped mountain-tops that prowl the horizon, or the tiny purple flowers that dot the trail, or the intermittent cry of a red-tailed hawk as it streaks across the sky, its tail-feathers disappearing into the watery sun.

Nature is the kind of place where you can meet yourself, all over again. It's a chance to shake your own hand and ask not just what kind of person you are, but what kind of person you want to be.

For the first time in hours, I take my hands off the saddle and open my arms wide. My chest rises as I breathe in the cold mountain air, my lungs tingling with the infusion. Maybe I'll leave here as a new version of myself. A Zoe who doesn't say "yes" when she really means "no." A Zoe who doesn't hide her needs. A Zoe who is definitely *not* afraid of horses, not even a little bit afraid of—

A dip in the trail gets caught in Molly's hoof, and she stumbles like a drunken sorority pledge in five inch heels. A yelp escapes my lips as my numb fingers clutch the saddle again. At the front of the line, Brock snickers, "Got 'ya there, did she?"

Mike turns around, brow furled, silently mouthing the words, "You okay?" I shoot him a thumbs up, waiting for him to turn back around before I whisper in Molly's ear, "Lay off the sauce, alright? It's a long trip." Her mane shakes from left to right; the horse-version of a shoulder-shrug.

Our caravan winds its way through the lower segment of the mountain, enjoying the beauty all around us. Sequoia trees soar toward the heavens like sky-scrapers, their roots deep, their trunks wide. Shafts of light slip through their branches, reminding us that the sun is still up there, hidden behind a blanket of green. Birds hum a song in rounds, each picking up where the other left off. Brock turns around every now and then, piping up with various bits of information, both about Yosemite, and our itinerary. His voice is grating. I tune in and out. The forest is more interesting.

"Right now we're still in the tourist areas," Brock says, swaying in time with his horse. "The valley gets, oh, say about five million visitors a year or so. But by tonight we'll have reached backcountry, and boy, are you folks in for a treat. The backcountry is reserved for serious campers, and the park only gives out so many permits per season. Only a few people at a time allowed out there. Probably one of the last places in the world you can really be alone for miles."

"You obviously haven't been to Barstow," Logan jokes, but Brock doesn't hear him. When Logan speaks, his voice is deeper than I expected. His face says "college student," but he could be older than he looks.

"You've chosen a great time of year to visit. Park services only gives out a handful of permits in the winter, and this group right here represents 'em all. We're expecting some snow later in the week, so I hope you all packed accordingly and brought your cameras. You've never seen anything more beautiful than backcountry in snowfall," Brock looks up at the horizon, wistful. "Now, there's not a whole lotta cell reception once we get to backcountry, so if you have an important call to make, I recommend you do it within the next couple of hours," he adds. Ken Hardinger frantically takes his cell phone out of his pocket, but Sue rides up beside him and grabs it away before he can check his email. She's good on a horse.

"You folks will get the chance to see Yosemite Valley in a way tourists hardly ever do. We got a few stops planned, and most of 'em are off the beaten trail, with the exception of Tenaya Lake. You all have got yourselves a very exclusive itinerary."

"Guess that explains the price-tag," Ken mutters, still upset about his phone being taken away.

"We'll visit a waterfall, clean enough to drink right out of," Brock rambles on. "And we'll take a look at the fissures on the back of Taft Point, the side folks people don't see as often."

"What are the fissures?" Mike asks, genuinely interested.

Mike always looks at the world like he's seeing it for the first time. It's one of the most lovable things about him. He searches for ways the world can show him beauty, and I search for ways it can hurt me. He is a princess. I am an ogre.

"The Fissures are a topographical feature— very rare. It's a bunch of deep crevices in the earth. Some of 'em even go down as far as three hundred feet," Brock answers. "We won't get there for a few days though. 'Gonna spend the first part of the trip riding trails at the base of the mountain, giving all of you who come from the lowlands a chance to adjust to the elevation."

Sue Hardinger clears her throat.

"Sue?"

"How do the horses handle the increase in altitude?" she asks, petting her horse on the neck.

"Just fine," Brock answers, with a tone that says he doesn't really give a shit. "Might get tired a bit quicker, but we're not asking too much of them. Most of the trails we're taking need a gentle gait anyway. Wouldn't ask them to gallop up the mountain."

Ken reaches out and touches Sue's hand, offering a reassuring nod. She sticks her tongue out at him, and pockets his phone as if to say "nice try, but you're not getting it back." Ken laughs, his eyes lighting up like he's just met the woman he wants to spend the rest of his life with. They've spent decades together, but the Hardingers are still madly, totally, completely in love. Mike catches my eye, and it makes me smile, because we're both thinking the same thing.

"We'll make camp by a smaller lake tonight, head onward in the morning," Brock continues. "Over the course of our trip we'll climb to about 3,300 ft."

"Will we get to climb Half Dome?" Logan asks, his voice dripping with anticipation. Maybe I had him pegged wrong. Maybe he's a dare-devil.

"On day five, we'll reach the base of Half Dome," Brock answers. "It's the highest elevation of our trip. You all are welcome to stay there and explore the campsite; check out the natural hot spring if you like. But under no circumstances are you to attempt the cable walk. Rangers shut it down this time of year, because the trail's too dangerous, what with the ice and snow."

"They shut it down completely?" Sue pipes up, curious.

"The trail up there, 'Mist Trail,' stays open all year," Brock answers. "You're welcome to climb it at your own risk. But the cable walk is a non-starter."

"What's the difference between the trail and the cable walk?" Ken asks, suddenly looking like he might want to give the hike a go. Sue rolls her eyes, her face betraying her thoughts: my husband can barely handle the walk from his car to the dinner table, and now he wants to scale a vertical cliff face.

"Mist trail is an average climb that takes you up the base of the dome," Brock answers. "But it can only take you so far before the incline changes, and you need rock-climbing equipment to get up the rest of the mountain. To make the dome more accessible, Yosemite Park Rangers installed a cable walk. It's a trail with two steel cables on either side to hold onto, hopefully with gloves, if you don't want to shred your fingers. It's a steep grade. So steep you gotta tie your bags tight so they don't come loose. One misstep and you could find yourself tumbling down the curve of the dome. But going up is the easy part..."

"It is?" Mike asks, and I silently pray he has no intention of making the trek. I've finally found a great guy, and I'd have an existential crisis if he fell off the side of Half Dome and ended up a human pancake.

Brock nods. "Coming down the grade is the *really* challenging part, especially if there's rain or snow. The cable becomes too wet to hold onto, and the rocks freeze over. Makes it real easy to slip. We had ten deaths last year alone, and that was in *good* weather. The views at the top are somethin' else, and I'm sure it's a sight to be seen in the snow. But there's just no attempting it this time of year. You folks can try Mist Trail if you really have a hard on for it, but my recommendation is to stick to the itinerary."

Mike looks at me and shakes his head.

"I love you," he says. "But there's no way I'm climbing up that mountain."

At the front of the line, Logan watches us, and I'm certain now that he's a lonely college kid with nothing better to do over spring break. His face has the pained expression of someone who just got dumped, and I imagine him holding two tickets to the horse-tour, alone in his dorm room.

"Fine," I sigh, pretending to be disappointed. "I won't make you."

The trail stretches onward, taking us deeper into a dark patch of forest where the trees grow closer together, blanketing the earth in complete shadow. Brock takes a hard right, asking us all to follow, leaving the familiar trail behind and heading straight into the forest, deeper and deeper into the Wild. The Sequoia branches weave around one another so tightly that they form a wall, shielding the rest of the forest from view, closing us in like sardines in a can. Molly shudders, her gait quickening, and it makes my hair stand on end, as if Molly knows something she can't tell me.

Our progress slows, and we proceed one step at a time,

Brock assuring us all the while that it's perfectly safe to leave the trail behind— necessary, even, to experience something special.

I'm at the end of our party, so I'm the only one who hears it when it happens: a twig snapping, somewhere in the distance, close enough to hear but far enough away to be hidden from view. Leaning into the darkness doesn't help me spot the source of the sound, but then something moves, shapeless in the shadows, its form impossible to discern between layers of sequoia branches. It's too large to be a bird, or a rodent. It could be a bear, or a human, but by the time I look again, it's disappeared, an optical illusion or some trick of the light.

I'm about to say something, but Brock raises a hand before I can, pointing ahead of us toward a spot where the forest separates and a flood of light streaks down from the sky. Trees disperse, making room for us, and suddenly it's as if someone has pulled open a set of curtains, revealing a vast, infinite wild. We're on top of a hill, looking over it all, more beautiful than a painting, so alive and untamed. Rivers weave across the landscape like vines on a fence. Brush grows in half-hearted shades of brown, defiantly ignoring the winter cold, reaching ever-upwards, thirsty for light. Peaks and valleys compete against each other for room, all of it untouched by human hands. It might be the most beautiful thing I've ever seen. Brock smiles at our open mouths, agape at the beauty, stunned and silenced, just as he knew we would be.

"Welcome," Brock says, "To backcountry."

WHEN WE FINALLY REACH OUR campsite, the sun hangs low in the sky, casting a golden haze over the forest. We pick a spot on the edge of a clearing, near enough to the Sequoia trees to feel sheltered, but exposed enough to have full visibility of the surrounding wild.

We unpack our bags; each couple has been given a double-sized tent to share, while Logan and Brock have their own individual versions. With some prompting from Brock, everyone gets to work assembling their tents. Mike sprawls the pieces of our tent out on the grass, looking at them like he's working on a rubix cube, trying to match ends to beginnings.

"This one goes into the piece labeled, 'B," he mutters, reading from a guide featuring so many pictures we might as well be assembling a rocket ship. I grab the paper and flip it over.

"That's an eight. Don't you design furniture for a living?"

"After this, I might fire myself," he laughs.

"That's okay, stick with me," I answer, lashing poles together with the included plastic pieces— round semi-circles that click into place if you squeeze them hard enough. "I'm a survival pro, like Bear Gryllis, only cuter."

"Same amount of facial hair though," Mike jokes, and I swat at him, because we both know he loves my face. "Squeeze this one," I tell him, and he grips one of the semi-circles tight, causing four poles to form the outline of our frame. About fifty feet away, a heavy log rests in front of the remains of a fallen tree, and for some reason, I feel like it was meant to be ours.

"We should take it," I tell Mike, motioning at the log. He rolls it over, happy to be helpful again, and suddenly our little tent has become a palace with its own bench right outside.

We stand back to look at it, and when Mike puts his arm around me, an unfamiliar feeling washes over me. It's a sudden realization, even though it's probably one I've been coming to for awhile. It seems urgent, important that I let him know, but I'm not sure what to say, or how to tell him. I almost blurt out, "I want to spend the rest of my life with you," but then the walls around my heart harden, their vice-like grip knocking the words off my tongue. My shoes dig into the dirt, feet firmly on the ground. I remind myself of the importance of caution; homes that look steady are too often built on glass, and women who thought they knew someone wake to find a stranger sleeping next to them. The worst monsters hide behind the most ordinary of people— only time reveals the beast within. Mike and I have barely been together for more than a year. We just moved in together three months ago. For now, that's enough.

The moment is gone now and I won't get it back. It's alright, though, because when Mike leans over and kisses me like it's the most natural thing in the world, I don't feel the need to say anything at all.

Our entire relationship is reflected in this moment.

Mike is the warm, open-hearted person who feels at home anywhere, and I'm the vigilant conspiracy theorist who keeps canned goods and weaponry in the basement-turned-bomb-shelter. Mike assumes the best; I'm always waiting for the worst.

It's one of my favorite things about him, but sometimes, it highlights a distance between us— some space I can't cross. It's like I'm always on the lookout for shadows he can't see, hasn't had to see, and will never understand, through no fault of his own.

The gap is not just ours; we can't claim it as a unique invention. It belongs to the girl who wants to spring for an

Uber instead of walking home late at night, but ends up with her feet on the pavement because her date insists she's safe with him there.

It's borrowed by the Mother who wants to get a second opinion from another pediatrician, but resists because her husband says it's unnecessary.

The gap rests its edges on "it'll be fine" -s and "don't be a worrier" -s. The gap can't be quantified or explained. Trying to measure its diameter will just make it grow. It's better to ignore it and hope it goes away. It's lonely over here, on my side of the gap, and even though I'd never tell Mike, it's a feeling I think Cassandra would understand.

Across the campsite, Ken and Sue have expertly assembled their tent without an unhappy moment to show for it. They high-five. I wonder if Sue feels the gap, and if so, what she does about it. Maybe they've been together so long that they found a way to sew the gap shut, without ever having to talk about it.

Meanwhile, Logan struggles with his tent, trying to connect the wrong ends of two poles. Brock— who had his tent up the second he stepped off his horse— practically pushes Logan out of the way and assembles the tent for him.

We've arranged our tents in a circle, and in the middle dug a fire-pit, where— if I have anything to say about it— we'll melt marshmallows and tell ghost stories. Like I said, I'm Bear Gryllis, but cuter.

My love of the outdoors comes from years spent at a wilderness sleep-away camp, which was basically the coked up version of Girl Scouts. We'd spend three weeks each year learning how to light fires from scratch, craft weapons from sticks, set traps for fish, and survive if we ever got lost in the woods— a possibility that was, ironically, increased by our mere presence at the camp, which was run by a pair of totally irresponsible proprietors. They let us run wild, and only hired about one counselor for every twenty girls, allowing us to get away with anything and everything. It was Mad-Max, but with preteens. Needless to say, there was a lot of hair-pulling involved.

It was sleep-away camp that made me want to go into hotel management. Something about comforting people when they're away from home makes me think of camp.

Brock unloads the food, which he stores in a separate pack. It's a combination of fresh fare and some powdered instant mixes, like mashed potatoes and scrambled eggs.

Brock approaches the pit, and— even though he's also brought a lighter— gives us a demonstration with a fire-starter, looking pretty shocked when I manage to make it flare up on my first try.

"Summer-camp," I say, and Brock frowns, clearly wondering what kind of fucked up camp my parents sent me to.

The fire tosses sparks across the pit, weaving itself into spirals under a cast-iron pan, as if it resents being contained. We cook up potatoes and frozen chicken breast, dishing them out on thin metal plates. The group consensus is that the food is shockingly good. Brock and I are the only ones who don't offer any commentary, probably because we both know that the best meal is always on the first night. By night seven, everything will be powdered, unless someone catches a fish.

When the meal is finished, Brock offers to take everyone to the other side of the lake, to a place where the trout jump at night. It's a ranger favorite, and everyone agrees to go, except for poor Logan, who isn't looking so good.

"I need to lay down," he whispers to Brock, turning green.

"Might be altitude sickness. Are you dizzy?" Brock asks.

"Yeah," Logan leans against a tree trunk. He's feeling even worse than he's letting on.

Brock reaches into his pocket and pulls out a cylindrical object, about the size of a tube of lipstick. Logan flips it over, reading the label.

"Tums?" he says, confused. "But my stomach's not upset. I'm just lightheaded."

"The calcium content will help with the dizziness. Old trail guide trick. That, and some water, and you'll feel good as new in an hour."

He sends Logan to his tent, adding, "If you perk up and decide you want to join us, just follow the trail down that way, and turn left at the rock formation at the edge of the lake. You'll see us."

He leaves Logan with a flashlight and a radio, and our group trudges into the darkness, our eyes still adjusting to a world without streetlights.

No one ever talks about the ordinary miracles.

I breathe one in as I watch the trout jump. These little beings can't even speak— at least not in the way humans do — and yet somehow they mutually agree to leap from the water, together. Counting the fish is impossible. There's too many blasts of light, jumping out of the blue and twirling in the air like silver fireworks. A thousand scaly wonders come in and out of focus, all of them deciding to do something remarkable at the same time.

How do they know when to jump? Maybe it's when the lake is low and cool, and the night is soft enough so as to be inviting. Maybe it all starts with one fish, itchy and dissatisfied, his impatience so palpable it causes him to jump, creating a contagious reaction in each of his friends. They're impossibly in tune with each other; no great divide to be crossed. Even within themselves, they find unity, becoming for a moment not just fish, but also birds, embodying two opposing forces in a single being. It's an effect that extends beyond their own school, sending ripples across the forest as their fins reflect the moonlight, bridging the gap between earth and sky. It's the kind of ordinary miracle that forces a person to either stop and stare, or commit a crime against the Universe by ignoring the magical mundane.

Respectful silence settles on our party, as if we're in a big, open church, where acoustics turn whispers into echoes, and stain-glassed windows turn light into rainbows. Without saying a word, our group disperses to different rocks to watch— to pray. Mike and I find a boulder that's all our own, and for a moment, we're the only two people in the world.

"They're just fish, but they're—" I search for the word.

"They are." Mike nods. He takes my hand in his. "I'm glad I'm here with you," he says the right thing, like he always does. I like to think of Mike as an anchor. He has a heavy bottom that keeps him grounded; invisible cords that keep him tethered to the Earth in a reliable, oaky kind of way. He's whiskey on the rocks, warm and inviting, the sort of thing you drink when you just need one piece of the world to make sense.

My thumb traces circles over the veins below his knuckles. It's a strange thing to like about someone, but the blue-green veins that stand out on Mike's hands really do it for me.

"We should make a list of magical things to see together

before we die," I say, not really thinking about what it means, or the way it implies permanence.

"There's a lot of magic in the world. Seeing it would probably take years. A lifetime, even. To do that..." Mike chooses his words carefully. "We'd have to stay together for awhile."

A splash from the lake as another fish finds its way back into the water. My head lightens, and I can feel myself rising into the air. If Mike is an anchor, I'm a balloon. If Mike is a fish, I am a bird. We're exactly what the other person needs, and we could be together forever, if we could only find the place where the earth turns into sky. They call it the horizon, but experience has taught me that it always moves away, no matter how fast I run towards it.

Mike's looking at me like I'm supposed to say something, but I don't, because there's no way to tell him that I'm still waiting for some unseen side of him to make itself known. If I explain about the monster, he'll want to know when I'll stop looking for it. That's an answer I don't have.

"Zoe," Mike pauses, looking for the right words. "Anywhere you go... that's where I want to be."

It takes herculean effort not to say too much back. I bite down on my tongue, seeking the safety of my walls. Giving away my feelings— all of them, at least— isn't safe. Not yet.

"Same," I say. It's the best I can do.

Mike seems encouraged by my answer, despite the limited verbiage.

"I've been wanting to talk you about where you see us going. About a bigger commitment."

Bigger commitment? We already live together. What does he want now, a dog?

"You like to move at your own pace, and I don't want to scare you away" he adds, his tone laced with the self-conscious caution of a hostage negotiator. I can't blame him. It took me eight months to call him my boyfriend.

"You don't have to say anything now. This could be way off in the future. But I wanted to bring it up so you don't feel blind-sided if one day I ask for more."

Is he talking about marriage?

"Are you okay," he asks, the pained look in his eyes making me hate myself, "with starting the conversation?"

My heart skips a beat, but it's impossible to tell if it's a good skip or a bad one. I'm thinking about the fish, and birds, and how I'm so aloof that I've made Mike get that look in his eye— the one that says he's expecting to be disappointed. The word "conversation" splits open the sky, and I want to tattoo it on my arm as a reminder that Mike's making room for me, here, and it's not a demand, but a walk through the woods, with both of us deciding which direction to go. The seconds tick by and I'm supposed to say something— any normal person would say something— but my inner ogre wraps his fists around my throat, making me choke down some words that sound like "I love you," and "Forever." I scan Mike's eyes for a monster, and even though I still don't see one, some piece of me is waiting, waiting, waiting for the sharp glint of teeth.

A high-pitched whistle splits through the night, and we turn around to find Brock, fingers in his mouth, motioning for the group to get back together. Mike looks at me again, and I have to do something before the moment is gone, so I squeeze his hand and smile. It's a vague action, but it's there. He seems to take my reaction as a positive, looking relieved as he helps me climb down the slippery rock. But in the back of my mind, I wonder if he isn't tired of being with someone who moves so slowly. Maybe one day he'll start looking for monsters in me, too.

~

OUR FLASHLIGHTS CRISS-CROSS against the black as we head back toward camp. Halfway down the road, we're joined by Logan, who's pushed aside his disappointment at missing the trout to annoy Brock with chit-chat.

"I took two Tums and I felt way better. How does it work?"

"It's the calcium," Brock repeats himself, irritated.

"Yeah, but *how?*" Logan presses. "Calcium isn't related to lightheadedness, unless you have a serious deficiency, and a little change in altitude wouldn't cause that..."

"It's a mystery," Brock shrugs. Evidently Logan hasn't heard of the placebo effect.

When we get back to camp, everyone retreats to their individual tents. Mike and I curl up in a sleeping bag.

We roll over, and his body feels warm and perfect on top of mine. I really could be with him forever. Why didn't I just give him a definitive 'yes?'

He kisses my neck, running his hands over my body, putting so many unspoken words into it. The walls around my heart shake again and, for the first time, I seriously think about taking them down, brick by brick, if only because I can't deny one thing about Mike:

My heart recognizes his.

It's impossible to talk about without sounding like a new-age weirdo, but if past lives are real, Mike and I met in one. I've never been the type to believe in soul-mates, but I can't deny a cosmic, magnetic pull between us. When Mike looks at me, he looks *through* me, straight past my exterior into something hidden. It makes me hope he might fix that ache within— the one that makes me feel like I live in a world of the imagined, a place filled with things no one else can see. Even my careful management of the space between us doesn't bother him. He just waits across the divide, hoping I'll close the distance. If I explain to him that I'm working on it, he'll understand. Mike *always* understands.

I'm about to tell him so, when I notice something over his shoulder. It's a photograph, pinned to the roof of our tent. I freeze, and Mike stops, sensing immediately that something's wrong.

"Are you okay?"

I don't answer, but point wordlessly at the offending object, spoiling the aesthetic of the temporary home we built together. When Mike looks at it, his mouth drops open.

It's a photograph of us at Magic Mountain. We'd only been dating a few weeks when we decided to brave the theme park together. I remember it, because Mike made me feel so comfortable. He never pressured me to try a ride I didn't want to try. He didn't even give me a hard time for skipping the Goliath coaster, even though I made him wait in line for an hour before chickening out. So many guys would have been annoyed at the inconvenience, or gotten a sick enjoyment out of my fear— the kind of person who needs someone else to be small so he can feel big. But Mike just put his arm around my shoulder and said, "There's plenty of things I'm scared of too. You shouldn't hide stuff like that. When one person is weak, the other one is strong. And I hate heights, so when we go on Superman, I'm gonna need you to be *really* strong." Then he led me straight to a food cart and bought me a cotton candy, which I smashed in his face. I'm not sure why I did that, except that maybe his smile was too cute, and the moment had grown too serious. The photo documents the second after I caught him by surprise, his smile wide, beard covered in pink, spun sugar, fingers peeling it from his cheeks to pop into his mouth.

Seconds later, he chased me around the cart with blue-raspberry swirl, which ended up in my hair and took three days to completely remove.

It's the kind of moment I *wish* I had photographed— the type of thing you remember forever which, ironically, renders a photograph unnecessary. So I'm not too bothered by the picture's existence, even though it's taken by a third party without our knowledge, our goofy faces un-posed and oblivious, blurry from excessive zoom.

No, it's the words scrawled at the top of the picture in black sharpie, handwritten in all capital letters, that leave me cold:

Dead.

My voice catches in my throat as I try to say her name. I can't speak, but I don't have to. Mike says it for me, but his voice doesn't betray fear— only white-hot rage.

"Cassandra."

5

———————

A crackling sound fills the forest as Brock fiddles with the channel on his radio.

"Right, that's better..." he says to a ranger on the other end. "It was in their tent. Yeah, just the one picture tacked to the ceiling..."

I shiver, and Mike pulls me closer, rubbing my shoulders even though we both know I'm not shaking because of the cold. My skin prickles, aware of some shift in the electromagnetic field that I can't see. There's a primal, instinctual knowledge rippling through my blood, and I'm certain of its veracity, even though I can't explain why:

Someone is watching us.

"I'll let 'em know," Brock nods, as if he's about to give us the weather forecast for the week. He holsters his radio.

"She's not on the list of permit-approved campers, and no one's seen her," he says. "In fact, they haven't had a single person stop by the station since we left. Not even to ask for directions, which happens more often than you'd think. It's a confusing landscape, what with the roads all looking the same..."

I'm about to tell Brock I don't give a shit about how similar the roads look and that I'm more concerned about the stalker following us up the trail, but Mike beats me to the punch.

"It *had* to be her," Mike says, his cheeks reddening. "Isn't there someone they can send? The police or..." he waves a hand in the air, as if to indicate "or whatever you people do out here."

Brock spits out the husk of the sunflower seeds he's eating, an action that feels a little like seeing a priest piss in the middle of a church. Isn't it part of the Ranger oath that he respect the forest?

"Sheriff's about twenty miles out, but I'm not sure what good it would do. She could be anywhere. We'd need to cover a lotta ground; it'd be tough out here in backcountry, seeing as there's fewer trails..."

"Why is she mad at us all of a sudden?" I whisper, partly to myself and partly to Mike. It's a stupid thing to say, and the words tumble from my mouth like pebbles. Even though I've never met her, and even though I tend to see the worst in people, something about Cassandra has climbed under my skin and built a home there. Over time, her presence has become comforting— a reminder that there are people in the world with brains that are more of a mess than mine. I like her. She's like my invisible friend, even though she makes Mike's life miserable sometimes. Mike groans, like he can hear what I'm thinking.

"Zoe, she's insane—"

I cut him off, trying to sound less like a kid whose best friend banned her from the school lunch-table, and more like an expert in psychological evaluation. "She's never threatened us. Not once. It's not part of her profile. Why now?"

Mike considers the question, and his face floods with horror, like he's just realized he's left the stove on. If he's made some connection, he doesn't share what it is.

"It doesn't matter why now," he swallows hard, turning to Brock. "How'd she follow us on foot, without a horse? We camped overnight, so she'd need to have been watching us the entire trip."

Brock mulls this over, chewing on yet another handful of seeds. "Well, if it were me I'd have brought only what I could carry, probly a sleeping bag and some water. Maybe set up a camp behind that ridge over there, so I'd be able to keep tabs on things while staying out of sight."

Great, I want to say. *Thank you for the class, "Stalking 101."* I want to rip the package of sunflower seeds out of his hands and hit him over the head with it. Instead, I smile and nod.

"Right, that makes sense..." I hear myself say, hating that I'm giving Brock a gold-star just for stating the obvious. Still, the only way to get what we want from Brock is to make him feel useful, even though he isn't.

Brock is proving to be about as helpful as a *rock*. The rhyme momentarily reminds me of my poetic pen-pal from Tinder, but I push the thought away to focus on the more pressing issue of Cassandra, and the wild.

"What about a permit?!" Mike's almost yelling now, his eyes wide, hands balled into fists. "Everyone needs a permit to camp in backcountry, right? Isn't that what we paid you guys for? This super exclusive, backcountry experience? How's she out here without a fucking permit?"

Brocks shrugs. "She's breaking the law, that's for sure. And it's not wise to camp alone this time of year, what with the weather. Hopefully she turned around already, otherwise we could be sending a search and rescue party."

Mike exhales, trying to hold it together. "I'm *so glad*

you're concerned for her safety," he snarls, and I step back from him. I've never heard Mike's voice get so low.

Confusion swims in Mike's eyes, their dilated irises not understanding Brock's refusal to take the situation seriously. I don't know how to tell Mike that Brock's vision of Cassandra is a skewed portrait. He sees her as a teenage girl doodling hearts in a notebook, leaving angry post-its on Mike's locker. To Brock, she's a desperate and harmless little gnat, not a life-altering tornado that casts a shadow over every day of Mike's existence. Brock doesn't take her seriously enough to call for backup, and nothing we say will change his mind.

"We should cancel," Mike turns to me, exasperated. "We'll go home. I'll file for a restraining order. I should've done that a long time ago."

The words sting, if only because they've introduced a question into the narrative of our relationship; one I know I'll obsess over now. It's a question that will nag at me off and on over the years, spontaneously surfacing when I'm doing the dishes, or stuck in traffic, or out of *Real Housewives* reruns.

Why didn't he get a restraining order?

Mike took every life-changing, drastic measure he could to avoid Cassandra, from changing his phone number, to moving. Wasn't a restraining order the obvious first choice, long before resorting to extremes?

I want to pick the mystery apart, to tear at its seams, but something Brock says stops me.

"She won't be able follow us much further. Two days, maybe, and after that she'd need to be towing supplies," Brock states simply, scratching at his chin like he's working out a puzzle. "She'll turn around soon as she runs out of food and water. Don't have to be a Ranger to know that. It's basic survival instinct."

Survival instinct.

The blood rushes to my head.

"Mike?"

He doesn't answer. I move to reach out to him, but he's not next to me anymore. He's crouched on a nearby boulder, his head in his hands. He looks untethered, like an astronaut in space, orbiting far outside my atmosphere in a place where I can't reach him.

"Mike," I whisper, stepping closer to him, trying to close the distance between us. I'm about to ask him if there's something I should know— something he's not telling me— but he waves me away before I can.

A yellow flower pokes out of the ground by Mike's feet, a lone pop of bright color on soil otherwise coated by the burnt shades of leaves in the winter. Mike looks at it, then crushes it under his boot, pulverizing it into pieces. His face is expressionless while he does it, and I almost think I hear the flower cry.

The gesture is so unlike him that it sends a tingling chill down my back.

For a second, I imagine myself as the flower, tiny and alone, pulverized into nothingness beneath Mike's boot. It makes me want to agree with Mike, to call off the trip, to go home and move out of our house. I'll have to make up some excuse as to why I don't want to be with him anymore, because "I saw you crush a flower and it made me think you might do it to me, one day," is not something normal people say.

But then I think about the way Mike always gets up before me to make coffee in the morning, and how he brings me a cup in bed. I remember how he once helped me jumpstart my car when it died on the side of the freeway, and the time he packed my purse for me the night before I had a big meeting with the owner of the hotel I manage. "So you won't have to hunt down your keys tomorrow," he said. Later, I found a note in the zip-pocket that read, "You've got this. Love, M."

It was the first time he'd used the word "love."

If I let it, my fear of the monster within others will ruin the best relationship I've ever had, leaving me alone at night with nothing but "what-ifs." My ogre will chip our partnership into tiny pieces until there's nothing left but jagged edges and thin cuts on the tips of my fingers from trying to hold a broken thing together.

"We're finishing the trip," I say, quiet and certain.

"What?!" Mike comes crashing back to Earth, as if my words are a kind of gravity too strong to evade.

"Why?"

"Because," I take his hand in mine and pull him to his feet. "We're on a vacation," I smile at Mike, and he smiles back. Nothing else needs to be said. We make our way toward camp, a bored Brock plodding and whinnying behind us, presumably polishing his "Most Useless Ranger of the Year" award.

Well, maybe not that useless.

"Survival instinct." Brock was right about that. But Cassandra's not the only one who has it.

6

─────────

We burrow deeper into the Forest as our party rides to the next camp site, and I'm starting to understand her like a sister. Her rage, when the wind blows and the trees shudder. Her warmth, when we step off our horses and the soft, padded moss gives way beneath my boots, as if she's making room for me. Weary bees seeking flowers, slimy fish slipping through liquid air, wayward branches dodged by humming birds— the forest has found a space for all these things within her, simply because she loves them. I'm beginning to feel she loves me, too.

It's a simple act of caring— the act of making room— and women do it all the time. We rearrange our lives and our bodies to create space for someone else. We open the door, invite another in, and change the furniture around, trying to Feng-shui our way into wholeness that's really just shrinking. We make the space, somehow, even when it means becoming smaller ourselves.

I wonder how much room I'm willing to make for Mike. I think about Cassandra and what she rearranged for him, only to be left with a disordered room, couches stacked on top of chairs, pots stored in the dresser, everything so topsy-turvey that she never managed to sort it all out.

It takes bravery and selflessness to rearrange your life for another person. Religions tout selflessness as the highest form of spiritual beauty, but too often leave women out of the architecture of their houses. If they'd only let us in, we'd make room for the neighbors, and the children, and every kind of person.

Women are excellent at finding ways to make room. We're remarkably good at it, but the task is viewed as inci-dental, expected— an every-day errand. It's hard to say why, except that it has something to do with the thing Cassandra and I both understand; that feeling of needing to be seen as you are— whole— when everyone else perceives some kind of lack in you. To be seen as incomplete when you know you are whole makes recognition of sacrifice impossible.

It makes me want to never attach myself to another person as a form of quiet protest. "Here she lies," my tomb-stone will read. "The girl who didn't need anyone."

Our caravan weaves down a steep, rocky trail, and I cling to Molly's back, holding tight to the saddle. Maybe this time will be different. Maybe the rearranging won't be one-sided. My couch, Mike's coffee-table, the towels in the refrigerator and the sweatshirts on the roof. The home we make together will be whimsical, an Alice-in-Wonderland hodge-podge of his things and my things, co-existing in fanciful arrangements. We'll make room for each other in equal measure and, if we can't find balance, Mike's pretty good with his hands. Maybe he'll build us new furniture. Time will fill the holes, and one day I'll realize that I'm complete all on my own— that I always was. I'll know I chose Mike out of love, not fear of lack, and suddenly I won't feel the need to be *seen* anymore, because I've finally decided that my eyes and God's eyes are the only ones that matter.

The blank spaces in Mike's story push against the fabric of the future I've woven, but I ignore them, meditating on fullness, refocusing on the trail.

A fly lands on Molly's neck and she shudders, clearly bothered by an itch she can't scratch. But she doesn't buck, she doesn't kick. Instead, she sticks to the trail, more concerned with getting us to our destination than with her own comfort.

I scratch her neck. She notices.

It's midday when we reach the waterfall, and Brock makes a point of gesturing across the mountain range, indicating a pattern of low-hanging clouds off in the distance.

"Might get some rain tomorrow," he says, but I don't believe him. The afternoon sun beats down with such purpose, it's as if he's heard our conversation and lit himself on fire to make a point. The clouds are miles away; the sun is here to stay.

We hitch our horses to an old tree, then gather at the base of the falls, watching gallons of water tumble over a sheer cliff face just to land abruptly at our feet. Droplets splash into my eyes, and Mike laughs as he puts a hand in front of my face as a makeshift splashguard.

"This waterfall isn't as popular as Vernal or Yosemite falls," Brock motions at the cliff, shouting to be heard over the rushing water. "Too far off the beaten path. Makes it a bit of a ranger secret."

He points to a trail that winds around a steep incline to the West. "We'll make our way up there tomorrow. Have to go 'round the base of the mountain and approach from the other side because of the horses. But you'll get to see the falls from two perspectives."

Sue Hardinger raises a hand, and I notice her other arm is wrapped tightly around Ken's. "How far does the water fall?"

"About 1,200 feet from here to the top," Brock answers.

"Will there be any other tour groups on our way up?" Logan asks, his voice tinged with a sharp edge I can't quite place. I wonder if he's lonely. Maybe he came on this trip solo in the hopes of meeting some outdoorsy, sun-kissed sorority girls. If that's the case, he picked the wrong caravan; all he got was the retired married couple, Mike and I, and Brock, who doesn't appear to be Logan's type.

Brock shakes his head. "Not likely. Like I said, this isn't one of the more popular stops, although I like to think it's the prettiest. We don't give out many permits for the back-country in the winter— weather's too unpredictable. This gang is a lucky crowd."

Logan nods, his face impossible to read.

Something moves behind me, and I spin around, preparing myself to find Cassandra, wielding a knife, ready to make good on her promise: "DEAD."

Instead, I discover an unexpected assailant. He's about two feet tall, covered in fur, and looks like a cross between a squirrel and a capybara. His paws are up— the cutest boxer the world has ever seen.

"What is he?!" Mike shouts over the water. The look in his eyes says he's completely enamored.

"That's a marmot," Brock answers. "They're rodents, mostly live in colonies. That one's probably the look out, but they're usually more afraid of hawks and snakes than humans. They're curious little guys. Won't leave you alone if you feed 'em..."

Mike's already rifling through my bag, looking for the other half of a granola bar I ate earlier.

Brock clears his throat, "... so *don't* feed them. Encourages aggression. And we can't have him following us all the way up to half-dome."

Although he tries to hide it, Mike's disappointment is palpable. Brock points to the Northwest, indicating the direction we'll make camp. The group gets back to the trail, leading their horses toward the space that will soon become our hotel.

I wait until Brock's back is turned, then quietly pass Mike the other half of my granola bar, which I've managed to remove from my pack without being spotted.

Mike's face lights up, and he breaks the bar into pieces, tossing bite-sized bits to his new friend.

"We should name him," Mike says. "What are your thoughts on 'Harold'?"

I shake my head. "We can't keep him," I answer, but I can already tell Harold is memorizing our faces. When the bar is finished we follow the others down the trail, and I swear Harold watches us leave, as if making a mental note of where his new best friends live.

Night falls, and she doesn't pick herself back up. She lands hard, blanketing us in stars, bringing with her a circular, enveloping feeling of forever; as if it's always been dark, here, and always will be.

Brock builds us a fire and our party gathers around it, six

moths seeking light in a heavy, silent night. Embers crackle, the rough scent of smoke burning my eyes when I lean in too far, greedy for warmth. Logan circles the group, handing everyone hot chocolate in metal mugs, made from filtered creek water and a powdered mix. We talk for awhile, chattering about nothing in-between sips, but then the silence surfaces again, and Brock breaks out a guitar, strumming the strings with fingers blistered in all the right places. The melody— one I don't recognize— vibrates across the forest, changing its form as it bumps into trees, clanging into the sky, ricocheting between the stars like a silver orb in a pinball machine.

Without prompting, Sue Hardinger stands, flinging her arms out wide and rising in a sweeping circle, her hips swaying, hair down. She's ageless this way, her silver locks reflecting the moonlight, careless as she owns herself, completely at peace with who she is in this exact moment. It's a side of her I haven't seen yet; a piece I like. We all watch her for a minute, letting her make her own magic until she trips in the darkness, breaking the spell. She laughs as she hits the ground, catching herself like she meant to do it. Mike and Ken jump up at the same time, both of them helping her to her feet. Now, all three of them are dancing together, swaying under the moonlight like drunk hippies at a solstice celebration. Mike motions at me to join, but I shake my head— dancing in public isn't for me.

Logan refills his hot chocolate before taking the empty spot next to me, swirling his mug around to disperse the steam.

"Pretty night, isn't it?" he asks, and I nod, because it is. "You don't want to dance?"

"I'm not a much of a dancer," I tell him.

"Me either," he pauses, watching the way Ken, Sue, and Mike spiral around each other like the steam from his mug, free, unencumbered, weightless in the night. "Maybe if I could see myself. If there were a mirror or something."

"That would make it worse," I say, sure that it would.

"At least then I would know if I were bad at it. I could try and adjust, make myself look more normal."

"Mmm," I agree, my stomach turning. Something about the idea of trying to look normal hits too close to home. "What brought you out here?" I ask him, changing the topic.

"Rejection," Logan says without missing a beat. "And commitment. Once I'm on a course, I have to stay it."

So I was right. He wasn't planning on taking this trip alone.

"It takes awhile," I say, careful with my phrasing— we're close enough in age that it requires effort to avoid sounding preachy. "It takes time to get to know someone, to see if things are going to work out."

"Do you think you ever really know someone?" Logan asks, and the question is so jarring that it makes me look away from the moon circle, straight into Logan's eyes. I don't find anything there, except maybe someone trying to solve a puzzle that's missing a piece. The sudden urge to find it burns in my chest, and I want to turn over sofa cushions, check the closet the box was kept in, just to show Logan that holes can be filled.

I've taken too long to respond, so Logan answers his own question. "I don't," he says. "Not really. At the end of the day, no one really *has* anyone."

"What do you mean?" I ask, my heart beating a little faster, wondering if maybe Logan is an unknowing carrier pigeon, sent to me by the Universe to confirm my fears, the dark things that I keep stored in boxes in my brain.

"Human beings always put themselves first. It's just in

our nature," he says it like it's as obvious as blue skies and orange sunsets.

I don't answer him, but turn instead back to the dance circle, watching Ken wrap his arms around Sue, swaying with her. Mike's left the party, and it takes me a moment to spot him. He's off to the side, standing in a clearing between the trees, looking up at the moon like he's trying to remember it. The look on his face says it's something special, something rare, like it's the only moon he'll ever see. I've only seen him make that expression once before, and it was on the day we met, when he said he brought some furniture and asked me where the hotel manager was, and I told him it was me.

Long after the fire burns down, Mike and I lay in our tent, which we've purposefully placed on the edge of the camp for privacy. We make love, and it's different than anytime before, although it's hard to pinpoint how.

Maybe it's the vastness of the forest, or the depth of the night, or Cassandra's note, but the world feels more unstable all of a sudden, like its axis has changed, and now North is South and South is North.

Mike's lips on mine, soft and careful, become avatars for one version of Mike; the one that absolutely *must* feed the marmot, the one who loves kids and goes to Comi-Con, the one with a smile that conveys a belief in the best of the world.

But when his hands pin mine above my head and I feel the power in his arms, I'm reminded of another side of Mike. I don't fault him for it, because it's a side we all have; the piece of ourselves that thirsts and wants, the instinctive voice that whispers nothing if not, "to have."

Mike gently pulls my hair, and we switch positions. I move on top of him, trying to unfold the mysteries of another person through the veil of my own darkness, my own "to haves."

His fingers trace a pattern up and down my back. Mike's always touched me like I'm something precious, something rare, something like that moon. Sometimes when he looks at me he's a little wide-eyed, like he can't believe he's found me, and he's afraid I might disappear at any moment, might not show up again, night after night, reliable and waiting.

I was so close to taking my walls down. I had already decided to unwrap the barbed wire, letting it cut into my fingers— bloody and torn— because I'd finally found someone who was worth the trouble. But now, questions flood the ramparts of my decision, making me step back. That idea of wanting to be seen— that longing— aches in my bones, but now it's carried by its inverse, the reflection of the question.

Do I really see him?

I remember the way Mike crushed that flower under his boot, like it was nothing.

Have I chosen the same man in a different form? Why *didn't* Mike get a restraining order against Cassandra? I want to take our relationship apart and build it back up, stacking the pieces in a better arrangement. The worries fall like raindrops. But then I put a hand on Mike's chest, and for a moment I feel his heartbeat. I remember the fear in his eyes when I asked, "*Why now?*," the depth of his joy by the waterfall, him pulling me back into the car on the drive up, the way he looked at that moon— all of it the work of a human, not a monster. I wish I could break him open, to pull thoughts from his ribs like harmless pieces of thread.

Why are you lying to me?

We roll over and now Mike is on top. I hold onto him, my fingers digging into his back as if letting go will cause him to crumble, the dust of who he used to be floating into the endless night sky.

Mike tilts my chin up and looks into my eyes, brazen and unapologetic.

A relationship is a question, asked over and over across a lifetime:

Will the animal in you, bite the animal in me?

7

———

The flashlight I'm carrying almost slips out of my hand. I'm sweating, even in the cold. I've left a sleeping Mike alone in the tent, and now I'm making my way through the woods, flashlight in one hand, trowel in the other, searching for a spot to go to the bathroom. No one ever said camping was glamorous.

I should've woken Mike up. It's wise to ask for company when there's a stalker following you through the forest. But I still feel some strange, unexplainable connection with Cassandra that makes me think she'd never hurt me. Besides, it's easier to do what's comfortable than what's smart.

In any event, Cassandra must have turned back by now. One person can't carry enough supplies to make it all the way up the mountain. It's not safe, for a lone traveller to tread so deeply into the wild. We're too far away from a cell phone tower to get reliable service, and even an idiot would think twice before continuing the trek on his own. I'm confident she's turned around by now and, if I'm being honest with myself, it's not Cassandra that frightens me anymore.

Instead, it's the blank spaces in Mike's story, the question marks where there should be periods.

I find a spot close enough to camp that I can shine my flashlight between two trees and see the edges of our tents. Brock would probably tell me that's not *nearly* far enough away to be sanitary, but if I'm very wrong and Cassandra is capable of extreme violence, it's not Brock who's coming to my rescue if she tries to make me into a skin-suit. He'd probably see it as a learning opportunity and teach her how to fashion pine needles into thread.

A surly wind bellows through the trees, making my hair flip into my eyes, causing a cascade of leaves to fall at my feet. I zip up my jacket and hurry to find a spot.

When my business is done I bury it in a hole, patting the soil down with my trowel: evidence destroyed. I'm about to make my way back toward camp when I hear something that makes me pause.

It's a static, overwhelming sound, constant and throbbing. It takes me a moment to place it, but then I realize it's a sound I heard earlier today; the clatter of thousands of gallons of water rushing over the waterfall, crashing into the lake at the foot of the trail.

The music of the falls drowns out my thoughts, and I wish we would've made camp just twenty feet closer to the water. It would've been nice to fall asleep to the sound of something other than my own inner monologue.

I'm about to head for the tents when a blinding pain courses through my entire body. I try to trace its origin— the back of my head, maybe— but before I can make sense of it, I'm on my hands and knees, doubled-over.

PINE NEEDLES... Sneakers— blue...

Someone touching me, rifling through my jacket pockets...

The sound of those relentless falls...

IT ALL FADES TO BLACK.

~

WHEN I COME TO, the world is on fire.

Thick air slides down my throat like poison, but my lungs inhale anyway. Ash covers my skin, claiming me, marking me as a lost cause. It can't be wiped off— it coats my eyes, slips under my tongue, adheres to my hair.

The wind is accomplice to the crime, spreading crackling flames from branch to branch, portending of a bigger monster to come. Fire is here, and there's nothing subtle about him. He kicks his way through the forest, toppling her beauty, mocking her art. Cawing fills the air as birds fly away from the fire's origin point. Two marmots streak past my feet, surging toward safety, making me pray that Harold has escaped the flames.

I steady myself on a trunk, seeking a sense of location, an idea of my bearings. This tree— warped— that tree, straight— the boulder marred by lichens— and the two rod-like pine trees I shined my flashlight toward earlier. The trees that served as a reference point for camp.

My heart stops. The trees are ablaze.

Camp is on fire.

It's the origin point from which the animals are fleeing. Against all instinct, I walk toward the source of the flames, a fish swimming upstream.

Mike. Please be alive.

I'm slow, too slow— disoriented. Still thinking about that waterfall and the sound it made, and how I can't hear it anymore. Pain radiates from the back of my head, spreading down my neck in waves. My ears flood with the sound of screaming— a woman, somewhere— and the roar of Fire, pillaging, defiling.

My fingers touch the back of my head and come away coated in flecks of red; blood, but it's dry. I wonder how much I lost.

When I reach what's left of our tents, my legs stop working. Our campsite has been transformed into something other-worldly. The air sits heavy on my skin, hot and thick, rippling like water. Everything is aflame, but in an orderly way. It's too perfect to be spontaneous. Not a single tent was spared. This was the work of a person, not nature. The faint scent of kerosene seems to prove it.

A scan of the tents shows no sign of Mike, but reveals Ken and Sue Hardinger, clutching each other, their faces frozen in horror. I stumble toward them, and my brain connects the screaming I heard earlier to Sue.

"Mike—" I cough. "Where?"

Sue shakes her head. She can't speak. Ken answers for the both of them, shouting over the crackles of the flames. He grabs my arm, his voice filled with urgency, "He went to find you! He was out of the tent the second the fire started— he's okay, Zoe, he's alright—"

I don't even realize I'm crying until Sue uses her sweater to wipe tears off my face. Ken waves a hand at someone on the other side of the tents. It's Brock and Logan, pouring buckets of water on the trees that border the campground. They're fighting a losing battle. Brock empties another bucket and frantically tries his radio again.

Something isn't working. Brock grabs Logan by the sleeve and they run toward us.

"The batteries—" Brock tries to finish his sentence, but coughs uncontrollably instead. He doesn't have to tell me what I already know; someone took the batteries out of his radio.

Cassandra.

"There's a reserve cache of supplies— rangers bury them all over the park— closest one is at the edge of Tenaya Lake, about a four hour hike that way..." Brock points in the direction the flames are spreading. Logan's eyes widen. He's wondering what we all are: can Brock out-hike the flames?

"There's gotta be more batteries inside, medical supplies..."

Brock motions toward the area I just came from, where the animals are fleeing. "Go toward the falls, stay by the water. I'll get to the ranger cache and radio for help, tell them to pick you up there."

"What about Mike?!" I shout. "He's still out there!"

Brock shakes his head. "We deal with the primary danger. He's out there, and he's alive. We won't be if we stay."

Brock takes off his backpack and hands it to me, and suddenly I feel bad for labeling him useless. "Mike can't have gone far. Call for him on your way to the falls— you'll find him."

Brock runs toward a wide tree, where our horses are tied up. He loosens multiple sets of reins and lets the whole gang free— their hooves slap the ground as they gallop away.

"You can't leave them!" Sue cries, but Brock shakes his head.

"They know the way back," he answers. "They do this trail fifty times a year— they'll be home in three days. Now, go!" He points in the direction of the falls and we all get moving, except for Logan, who turns around and follows Brock toward the flames.

"I'm coming with you! Buddy system..." Logan says. He must see Brock as his best chance of survival, even if staying with him means heading the way the winds are moving. Brock doesn't have time to argue with him. The flames are growing taller, the air hotter. If we stay much longer we'll all die from smoke inhalation.

Our group separates. The Hardingers and I stumble toward the falls. As Brock and Logan disappear from view, I'm struck by the horrible thought that our survival depends on them. If they don't make it to the cache, no one will know we're out here. We're two days into a week-long trip. Can we live for five days on our own?

We call for Mike as we feel our way through the forest, using the compass in Brock's bag to guide us. The flames are milder, here, but they still attach themselves to the trees and forest floor, hinting at the danger further up the mountain.

"Mike—" I shout, my voice too scratchy and sore to carry across the forest.

"Mike!" Ken takes over for me, putting his booming tenor to good use. "We found her! Head toward the waterfall!"

Sue joins him, and the three of us shout ourselves hoarse.

We call for an eternity, our voices forming a choir in an otherwise noiseless forest. Mike's name becomes a kind of chant, a prayer— desperate and unyielding— begging for some answer from the Wild.

She doesn't answer, and it's the loudest silence I've ever heard.

8

I t doesn't take long to reach the waterfall. The sun rises during our trek, casting a golden glow over the wild. I curl up on a rock that's just far enough from the falls to avoid getting drenched and pull my knees into my chest, watching ripples form on the surface of a clear, blue basin. It's a perfect oasis in the middle of the forest. In wilderness terms, it's like checking into a five star hotel. I'm here, and Mike is out there, looking for me.

I have to go find him.

I'm about to tell the Hardinger's that I can't stay here, but Sue takes one look at my face and holds up a hand in the universal gesture for "Stop."

"I know what you're thinking, sweetie, and I won't stop you if you insist on leaving, but at least hear me out first," she says, her voice so coated in practicality that now I'm sure they do have kids.

"Brock said it's a four-hour hike to the ranger cache. As soon as he gets there, he can radio for help."

Ken chimes in, adding to Sue's point. "That means helicopters, rangers, search dogs…"

"If you go look for Mike and get lost yourself, they'll be searching for two people, not one," Sue says, her voice apologetic. "Do you really want to divide their resources that way?"

I don't answer. My hands are still shaking, and the wound in the back of my head throbs.

"I know your instinct is to go find him, and I'd feel the same way if it were Ken," Sue continues. "But the best way for you to help Mike is to stay right here. He really is fine. We both saw him jump out of the tent the second it was on fire, not a mark on him. He asked if anyone had seen you, and when no one had, he went to find you. I'm sure he's still out there, and he's *okay*."

Ken nods, his eyes filled with sympathy.

"This will all be over soon," Sue adds. "Only four hours, maybe five, and then the rescue team will arrive. They'll find Mike. You just have to wait four hours."

She scans my face, trying to see if her words have changed my mind.

"You can do anything for four hours, right?"

No, I think. *I can't.*

But I stay anyway, because the thought of somehow sabotaging Mike's rescue is too much to bear. Sue's logic makes me ignore the animal piece of me that yearns to leave. I quiet the wolf within, who howls in dismay because she knows a member of her pack is missing, coaxing her into submission.

Just a few more hours, I tell my inner wolf, smoothing down her ruffled fur, trying to keep my hands away from her mouth.

∼

We bide time.

The water is cold, but we dip our feet in and out, remembering the caress of the flames and how close they came to skin and bone.

We dig through Brock's bag and find some antibiotic ointments and Band-Aids, which Sue uses to patch up the back of my head. She tells me the wound isn't bad, but her voice rises a little, and I'm not so sure I believe her.

The Hardingers ask me about Cassandra, and I tell them what I know, which isn't much. The shallow extent of my knowledge makes my cheeks flush with self-consciousness, and I skip rocks over the pond of the story, avoiding the parts that don't add up to make myself sound more informed.

Why didn't he get a restraining order?

My tone doesn't invite more questions, and thankfully the Hardingers are too polite to push. I wonder if they blame Mike and I for bringing Cassandra's wrath up the mountain. If they do, they don't say so.

The Hardingers invite me into their world, making small talk as if we're in a coffee-shop and not stranded in the wilderness. Ken is a CPA who owns his own company, and Sue is a highly accomplished botanist. She doesn't gloat about it, but based on Ken's description she's one of the best in the world. They tell me about their daughter, Tracy, who's around my age, and— by the sound of it— far more accomplished than I'll ever be.

"Finishing up her postdoc in Sociology!" Ken beams, paternal pride oozing out of his pores. I wonder if Tracy has a boyfriend, and if she picks good men, and whether she's made as many mistakes as I have.

The sun rises higher in the sky, and my instincts clock its position. The fire began under the rosy glow of the early morning— the sun's angle is still low, but climbing. I estimate a couple hours have passed. Brock and Logan should be halfway to the ranger cache by now.

We take out our cell phones and play a sick game of hot potato, passing them to one another and trying to place calls, hoping the hand of another person might magically conjure a signal. I try to send a text from Sue's cell, attempting to outsmart the universe by utilizing a task that requires a lower data rate. The blue bar fills halfway but never reaches its destination.

No one is surprised. We haven't had service since the end of our first day in the forest, when we reached the back-country.

We empty out the contents of our backpacks, combining our resources into a pile and taking inventory. Socks and t-shirts, eight kinds of granola bars, various packages of powdered meals from Brock's pack, and three empty canteens, which we fill with water from the falls. I turn my bag upside down, searching in zippered pockets, trying to abate the vague sense of loss that comes in waves. I know I'm looking for Mike, and even though I won't find him in my pack, I keep searching, just to be sure.

My hands touch something sticky deep in a pocket: a crinkled package of gummy bears. Mike and I had stopped at a Chevron on our way to the valley, even though we had a full tank. He ran inside the convenience store and came out with two scratch-off lotto tickets, and a package of gummy bears.

"Friendlier than the ones we'll meet in the forest," he said.

I scratched the numbers off my ticket. It wasn't a winner. Neither was his. He shrugged, crumpling the losing tickets into balls before tossing them into the backseat. He kissed me, his touch soft and hard all at the same time. "Still winners," he said, breaking open the package of candy. We ate them all the way up to Yosemite, and he was right. I *did* feel like a winner.

The sun fights its way toward the center of the sky, and the wound in the back of my head throbs, making me think the two things are connected. The stronger the daylight, the worse the pain.

We wait as long as we can, but hunger beckons, and we all agree to split a package of dried scrambled egg mix. "Don't think we have to be worried," Ken says, reassuring. "No reason to ration. We'll be out of here in no time."

My eyes resist the urge to roll— declaring that we'll be out of here in no time is the Murphy's law equivalent of walking up to fate and slapping her in the face. No need to tempt the woman when you've gone out of your way to piss her off.

The day slides by and panic bubbles up in my throat. It's been well over four hours now. If I had to guess, I'd say seven. Sue touches my hand, sensing my distress. "Four hours one way, and four hours back," she says, struggling to keep her voice level. "We have to be patient. Brock knows we're here. They'll come for us."

Sue changes the bandage on the back of my head, and I wonder if it really needed to be changed, or if Sue is just looking for something to occupy her hands.

"Is it getting better?" I ask, daring— for the first time— to let myself think about it.

"Much!" she says, patting my shoulder, but I notice her fingers shake a little, and now I'm sure Sue is lying to me.

And as the day wears on, I convince myself she's not the only one.

The sun sinks, growing heavy, and so, too, does my

mood. A spider in my brain knits a cobweb of conspiracy, connecting vague images and words with feverish intent. I withdraw into myself, and even as we're collecting sticks or playing "I spy," I'm somewhere else, waiting, supposing, indulging the many "what-ifs."

What if Mike was the one who...

No. If Mike is not who I think he is, then I've done it again. I've chosen a person I can't trust and, as a consequence, proven that I can't trust myself, or my judgment, or the little voice within that says "there's safety, here." Mike didn't set the fire. He *couldn't* have.

The spider in my brain churns, changing directions, coming at the same idea from a different angle.

Isn't it strange? He disappeared as soon as the fire started...

"He was looking for me," I answer, determined to believe in something good.

Why didn't he answer when you called his name? If he wanted to find you, he would've done it by now.

I can't answer that one, so the spider keeps weaving, his legs at the loom, building new castles from the bones of the ones he's torn down.

He's lying to you about Cassandra... what else is he capable of?

"I don't know," I answer, and I must have accidentally said the words out loud, because both the Hardingers are looking at me, eyes wide with concern. Their hands are still holding the playing cards we've been using for a game of poker, broken sticks as the chips.

Sue puts a hand to my forehead. She pulls it away as if she's been burned. "Definitely warm," she says, shaking her head at Ken.

She insists on changing the bandage on the back of my head again, applying more antibiotic ointment, fretting about whether it's most effective to use it all in one sitting, or dispense it over time. She disappears for awhile, then returns with some leaves. She mutters something complicated about their antiseptic properties, placing them under the bandage with more ointment, but I'm not listening anymore. Still, I tell her not to worry, that she's doing a great job, and that I appreciate her and Ken very much. I don't mention that I'm being careful to say all the right things, just in case I go into septic shock in the night and can't be saved. I want Sue to know I'm thankful for her; women are always being taken for granted — continuing the pattern won't be one of my last acts.

Ken suggests we go to sleep, and I curl up into a ball, using my jacket as a pillow. Ken and Sue are still in their Patagonia puffers, so it must be cold outside. I wouldn't know, because I'm a raging fire.

Sleep calls, and I let the spider weave his web, watching as it becomes a disjointed narrative, dreamlike in the night, but convincing all the same. It's hard to catalogue my thoughts— feverish, racing— and I'm not sure who's at the wheel. But I know the story is about Mike... and about me... and about the wolf inside me who hasn't stopped howling since we left camp.

I wonder over the nature of the fabric between "me" and "him" that makes an "us;" whether there's always been holes in it, or if we make them, or if I see them even when they aren't there.

I turn the word "trust" inside out, and try to define it without using the word itself, but the seams keep showing and I don't know how to scrub them out. I wear the word anyway, buttoning it up over my bra. Suddenly I'm in high school again, walking locker-lined hallways and worrying other people will notice I'm not sure what my shirt says.

Next I'm a wolf in a pack, running, running— we fly through the woods, free and bound all at once, as if we've found that perfect balance between companionship and independence. But then I'm at the front of the pack, and Mike is beside me, and he says to me, "You're a wolf and so am I. How could we possibly trust each other with such big teeth?"

And the next thing I know, he's biting me, ripping my throat out. He says it's a preventative measure, because he can't be sure I won't do the same to him. I beg him not to do it— to put his fangs away— trying to convince him that if we both agreed to trust each other, neither would have to hurt the other. But it's too late and the rest of the pack runs on and on, leaving me bleeding on the forest floor.

For a moment, I'm afraid that Mike will hurt the rest of the wolves, but then I realize he won't, because they're running behind him— not beside him. It's the animals next to you that you have to worry about.

I cover the bite marks on my neck with a paw, and as the bleeding slows, I realize I'm outside a house made from thousands of playing cards. A distorted family unit stands in front of it, holding hands; a Mom, a Dad, and two children — a boy and a girl. Their faces are blurred, but something in my gut recognizes them anyway. I step closer and their features come into focus, confirming their identities. The man is Mike, the woman is me, and the two children are marmots, covered in fur.

The other Me tries to step forward, but Mike pushes her back— keeping her behind him, always two steps away from an equal footing. The other Me tries, again and again, but each time, Mike pushes her back, never letting her stand next him as an equal. Every time he pushes her back, her rage grows, until she pulls a playing card from the house, running its sharp edge against her hand as the house collapses. She slits Mike's throat with it, and he crumples, but so does she; she cries, clutching him, shaking with rage.

Then her hands turn to dust, breaking into pieces, crumbs on a kitchen floor. Mike crumbles too, and the two of them fade into nothingness together, and the last thing I see is the look in her eyes: it tells me everything without saying a word. She never wanted to play this zero-sum game. Destroying him meant destroying herself, but living two steps behind was a slow death anyway. The marmots gather around the weaponized playing card, and I notice it's the Queen of Hearts.

They eat it.

Then I go back to the moment before it happened— before I was hit in the head, before the flames came— when I was listening to the falls.

The sound of roaring water encompasses me, making me believe in something bigger than myself; something benevolent that situated the falls with intent to give life. I arrive at a realization embodied by divine balance: the water can be reached from every side, because each person matters as much as the other.

A man comes to one side, and a woman to the other. They each bend down and drink, imbibing the exact same amount, both equally worthy, equally cherished by that divine something, and by each other. I'm too far away to see their faces, but I pray that it's Mike and me. I want so badly for that to be us.

My legs carry me towards the couple, but before I can get there, someone hits me in the back of the head.

I feel that blinding pain again...

See those blue sneakers...

And a gentle hand rifling through my jacket pocket...

... followed by a sound I heard at the time but couldn't identify.

But now I know what it is. I'm caught in the spider's web, somewhere between sleep and waking, unsure of everything, except for the origin of that noise. It's a sound I've heard a thousand times before.

It's the sound of papers rustling. Simple, eager, insistent — bursting with news, promising that they have something important to say.

IT'S morning when I wake up. A veil lifts— my fever has passed. The forest is in focus again, all her parts presenting themselves in sharp relief. The leaves are more saturated; oranges and greens abound. The air is lighter, the day clear and bright. It's like I've taken off a pair of glasses, only to discover I've had twenty-twenty vision all along.

Whatever Sue did to treat the wound on the back of my head, it worked. She saved my life. She really is the world's best botanist. Across the falls, Sue is asleep, one hand splayed across a rock, like an off-duty super-hero. A few of the miracle leaves she used on my head are scattered near my feet, and I collect them carefully, slipping them into my pack like prized diamonds in case they come in handy later.

My skin prickles. Now that I'm no longer blanketed by fever, the cold cuts through my limbs life a knife. My jacket crunches as I wrap it around my shoulder, but it feels heavier than normal, and the sensation makes me stop.

Disjointed images from the attack race through my

mind's eye. A hand in my pocket. A rustling sound. In my dream-world I recognized it as something familiar.

When the attack happened, I assumed Cassandra was searching my pockets for valuables. But Cassandra isn't a common thief after a wallet or phone. She's motivated by obsession. If she didn't take something *out* of my pockets, maybe she put something *in*.

Fingers trembling, I unbutton the outside pocket on my army-green utility jacket. It's deep, built with function in mind more than fashion, and at first there's nothing there. But then my fingers brush against a smooth edge, pulling out a folded piece of paper.

I don't open the letter right away, hoping it might crumble if I don't acknowledge it.

Then, slowly, carefully, like I'm handling a bomb, I turn crease over crease and smooth the page on a rock. The words are huge— taped together from magazine clippings — forcing me to stand back.

How unoriginal, I think before reading.

My eyes widen.

I KNOW WHERE MIKE IS.

9

If you want him,
    Find him fast,
    My giving nature,
Will not last.
I've left some clues
To guide you there
Try to find us
Truth or dare?
Thursday is
the day he'll die
Unless you get here—
Please, do try.
And now I'll cut
right to the **point**
(if you're wrong
I'll break his joints)
Your first clue is a
President's name
Thanks for playing,
my death-time Game

Tick. Tock.

"Don't you see? It's a game. A crazy, homicidal game!"

My boots crunch over leaves as I pace back and forth, the Hardingers seated on two rocks in front of me, looking like unwilling students enrolled in summer school.

A collection of items rest on a nearby log, all of which were hiding in the pockets of my utility jacket. In addition to the letter— which I've just read to the Hardingers— a search of my trusty coat revealed a compass and a map, neither of which belong to me.

"She's a predator, laying a trap for her prey. She took him! Cassandra *took* him, and she wants me to find him! She'll kill him unless I get there by Thursday, which means I only have..." I pause to do the math, and my stomach churns when I realize how much time has passed. "... Four days. I have four days."

"Okay..." Sue holds up her hands, her voice tinged with the restrained reason of a therapist walking a patient through a panic attack; nonchalant, hinting at false stakes. "That's one possibility. But it's also possible that—"

"What?" I ask, my heart pounding, hoping Sue isn't alluding to the dark boxes I've stacked in the storage cabinet of my mind, the ones labeled *"Mike's Lies: Extremely flammable, handle with caution."*

"That she tried to take him and failed. Maybe her intention was to move Mike to some other location, but he got away, and he's still out there somewhere..."

Ken nods, agreeing. "A lot of things that don't add up here, kiddo. Mike's not a small guy. What's the likelihood Cassandra managed to overpower him?"

I'm about to object, but Sue stops me, adding to Ken's point, "And even if she *did* manage to knock him out, how could she have moved him? Unless Cassandra's a weight lifter, he's probably twice her size. Have you seen photos of Cassandra? Does she look strong enough to move a 180 pound man over a long distance all on her own?"

I shrug but don't answer, because I *have* seen a picture of Cassandra, and she's a wisp of a woman; about 5'1", maybe 105 pounds if we're being generous.

The photo wasn't one I was meant to see. Mike and I had just moved into our new place together, and it was tucked at the bottom of a box filled with Mike's old memorabilia; a UCSF sweatshirt, a baseball trophy from third grade, and a photo of Cassandra, her arms thrown in the air, the hazy outline of the Golden Gate Bridge visible behind her.

Her stringy hair clung to her cheeks, her frail arms mimicking the bones of a baby bird. She was tiny, with a carved look about her, as if someone had whittled her out of wood. The feature that mastered her was her smile, so big it took up half her face. Effervescent and easy, Cassandra's smile offered a stark contrast to the rest of her harsh, angular shape. Her energy was complicated; bubble-gum soft and razor-sharp all at the same time. It was one of the things I imagined us laughing about, if we'd ever become friends.

"Maybe she used a gun! Maybe—" I pause, trying to think of other scenarios, but none appear.

"If you do what she wants, you could be playing right into her hands," Ken says, passing Sue his canteen. "We aren't even sure she has Mike."

"You're underestimating her!" I tell him, my cheeks flushing. An odd need to stand up for Cassandra, to convince them of her ability, makes me pace again. "Mike's had to change his entire life to get away from her. She's capable of more than you think."

"That may be true," Sue answers. "But that's all the more reason to wait for help. Brock and Logan—"

"— aren't coming," I finish Sue's sentence for her, and the silence that follows says I've pointed out the elephant in the room. He stampedes through the forest with his pants off, trunk held high, spouting purple bubbles into the sky, completely, utterly impossible to ignore.

"They're not," I say, driving the point home. "It's been twenty-four hours, and Brock told us he'd be back within eight. Something bad happened to them, or they'd be here by now. Even if *one* of them got into trouble, wouldn't we have heard from the other?"

The Hardingers don't answer. They've been thinking the same thing.

Something rattles inside my chest. It's my inner wolf, and she's chewing through the leash I use to keep her at bay. She breaks free from her restraints, her jaws wide, her direction certain. Without another word, I start packing up my bag, filling it with one third of our remaining supplies.

"Wha— what are you doing?" Ken stutters, his voice colored with fear at my newfound unpredictability.

I hike the pack onto my back, tying my canteen to the strap.

"First I'm going to the ranger cache, so I can radio for help. We need helicopters, search parties, as many rangers as we can get, all looking for Mike. Maybe I'll run into Brock and Logan on the way, but if I don't, I'm getting to the cache on my own. Then, I'm going to find Mike."

"But— " Sue tries to speak, but I cut her off.

"It's not a debate," I tell her, simply. "I wish you two best of luck, and thank you, again, for helping me with my head."

I turn, heading toward our old camp. Twigs snap in my wake, and I don't have to look behind me to know that the Hardingers have followed me, completely unaware that they're being led by someone who's only moving because she's afraid to stand still.

AT FIRST THE landscape is all rock— boulders and sediment — a futuristic quarry where nothing can grow. My boots struggle to operate on the difficult terrain, but then the rocks are replaced by trees and soil, and the earth is soft again. When we rushed to the waterfall, I was so busy calling for Mike that I barely noticed my surroundings. Even though I've seen it all before, the world looks new.

As we make our way toward camp, we stay on the lookout for signs of smoke, but none appear. With any luck, the fire has run its course and cannibalized itself into nothingness, unable to spread very far due to the way the terrain transitions from forest to rock. Charred branches appear with increasing frequency, their blackened edges lifeless and warped, waiting to be replaced by new growth. The winds have died down, hindering the fire's spread even further, and I expect that when we get to camp we won't find any flames. The thought should give me comfort, but I've only traded one threat for another; and between Cassandra and the fire, I'd take the fire.

Goosebumps freckle my skin, and I pull my jacket tighter around my shoulders. The sky darkens, signaling a turn in weather just as Brock predicted. We need to make it to the ranger cache before a sudden downpour.

Our walk gives us time to re-read Cassandra's letter, trying to piece together her clue. The Hardingers chime in with theories, either too good-natured or too bored to deny me their assistance just because they disagree with my direction.

"'*Truth or dare*?' " Ken asks, scratching his chin. "Think that means anything special?"

"She's making me choose," I answer, confident I understand Cassandra better than either of them. "I either have to dare to find him, or admit the truth…"

"Which is what?" Sue asks.

"That Mike belongs with her."

Sue shudders, overtly creeped out.

"What about this, here?" She motions to the letter, singling out a word. "In the word 'Point' all the letters are red. It's the only one with all the same color letters…"

She's right, and I re-read that section of the poem.

"I guess I'll cut right

    to the **point**

    (if you're wrong I'll break his joints)

    Your next clue is a President's name

    Thanks for playing

    my death-time Game."

"… A President's name," I repeat, pulling out the map Cassandra placed in my pocket.

The map is a comprehensive overview of the park, geared not just toward tourists, but toward the serious mountaineer. Various landmarks are indicated by tiny icons; waterfalls, bridges, scenic overlooks, topographical features, and altitudes are all outlined in impressive detail. I scan the page, looking for anything Presidential, gasping when I find it.

"Here!" I point at the map, where a camera icon indicates an overlook. "Taft Point."

Ken and Sue look over my shoulder, and Ken smiles, forgetting for a moment that this is a puzzle arranged by a homicidal maniac and not a game of Jeopardy.

"You got it!" he claps me on the shoulder. "President William Howard Taft... If that's not it, I don't know what is."

My finger traces a path along the curving yellow lines that designate hiking trails from Taft Point to Tenaya Lake, where Brock said the ranger cache was located. There's no single trail from one point to the other; instead, various yellow lines shoot off in opposite directions, none of them directly connecting the two landmarks in question. To get to Taft Point, I'll have to cut straight through Yosemite backcountry, and the vast, empty wilderness. My chances of running into the casual hiker just decreased dramatically. It's a long, isolated journey. I have a sick feeling that Cassandra planned it that way.

"It's about twenty miles from the lake to Taft Point," I say aloud, trying to calculate the amount of time it might take me to make the trek. Based on my past camping experience, I estimate I can hike about three miles per hour with a heavy pack. That's around six or seven hours to get to Taft Point.

A strong temptation to head straight to Taft Point washes over me, but if we reach the Ranger Cache, one call on a radio could save Mike's life. It might be possible to divide and conquer, but the Hardingers don't have any wilderness experience, and I'm afraid they won't make it to the cache on their own. Best to split the difference.

"When we get there, you two can look for the Ranger

Cache. I'll keep heading south while you search the lake. When you find it, radio for help. Tell them where I'm going. Tell them about Mike, and the letter."

The Hardingers don't argue with me this time.

Sue's eyes widen, and her expression changes to that of someone who's just remembered she left her stove on. "Oh no," she shakes her head. "I've just realized—"

Sue looks around, waiting for someone to jump in and come to the same conclusion she has. No one does.

"Does any one of us know what a ranger cache looks like?" Silence. Sue presses on.

"They must mark it with *something*. A specific rock, or a stump— something *they* would recognize, but not so noticeable that hikers might dig it up to borrow supplies. Does anyone know what that thing is?"

Ken shuffles in place a little, absorbing the problem, growing more uncomfortable as the idea takes root.

Sue takes the map, estimating the circumference of the lake. "Not to mention, it's about two, maybe three miles walk around the lake. Did Brock say *where* they put the cache?"

Ken and I both shake our heads. Sue's right; we're looking for a hide-a-key in a vast, unyielding wilderness.

"It's our best bet," I sigh, shaking off my doubts. "We're in the middle of nowhere right now. Tenaya Lake gets more foot-traffic. Even if we can't find the cache, at least if we head toward the lake we'll be more likely to run into someone who can help us."

Ken and Sue nod, encouraged by a confidence I emit but don't feel. We walk onward, looking up at the sky every so often, checking for signs of rain. I swear the sky sees us, and with each glance, turns her face away.

The temperature drops, shadows darken, and the sky's refusal to speak to me promises one thing only:

Rain.

WHEN WE REACH the remains of our campsite, tiny droplets leak from the clouds above us, plunking onto the bones of our tents. The three of us stand shoulder-to-shoulder in front of the wreckage, taking in the damage.

The soil is covered in ash, the trees burned black, their leaves disappeared like flash paper. Warped metal poles are still standing in some places, melted and strange, held up by plastic pikes buried deep enough to avoid the fire's wrath.

I wonder if the flames grew big enough to attract attention that might lead to a rescue crew, but I'm certain they didn't: the area was too small, the burn time too short. Someone would've had to have flown over backcountry at the perfect moment, and called in to report the flames. Although it felt apocalyptic at the time, the fire probably went unnoticed.

I imagine Cassandra, moving between the tents under the cover of night, a gas can in one hand and a lighter in the other. She could have killed us all, but she didn't care. All that mattered was her hunger, her thirst, her needs, her wants.

What was her endgame? Did she worry about killing Mike in the fire? Did she wait until I had left the tent to light it up, in the hopes that Mike would try to find me and she'd catch him on his own long enough to incapacitate him?

The destruction represents a paradox, an impossible meeting of strategy and emotion. On the one hand, Cassandra is a person impetuous enough to commit arson — an unpredictable crime that doesn't allow the arsonist to choose their victims. As a weapon, fire is unpredictable, independent, and anything but precise. It's a tool based in emotion, in rage. Cassandra's use of fire paints her as unhinged, possessing intent that's chaotic; she's a canon, not a laser, blasting away anyone unlucky enough to cross her path.

On the other hand, Cassandra has proven herself to be nothing if not a strategist. She had the foresight to create a demented scavenger hunt, to place the clue in my jacket, to bring enough supplies to survive the duration of her journey, and to gain geographical knowledge of the area in a way that's enabled her to follow us without being detected. Even her choice of secondary location show tactical thinking; she's sending me across the backcountry, off the designated trails, where I'm unlikely to encounter any rangers or park visitors.

I'm left with two images of the woman who's turned my life upside down, and I can't seem to reconcile the halves into a single person. Despite never meeting her, I've always thought of Cassandra as a friend, another person like me who's not quite right inside but doing her best to function anyway. The rage, the calculated intensity present here, doesn't *feel* like her. When Cassandra leaves a note under Mike's windshield, there's always flowers doodled on the envelope. Her letters are creased into perfect thirds, her handwriting marked by flawless loops and sweeping lines. Cassandra— as I imagine her— is nothing if not thoughtful. She's gentle in her bids for affection, soft in her pursuit. She's the girl in the bar who never speaks to the guy she might like, but sits near him whenever she can, following him from barstool to barstool, hoping he'll notice her with every move.

A scan of the campsite reveals nothing new— just more melted poles and singed tree branches— but I keep looking anyway, trying to bring my mental picture of Cassandra into focus. A groaning sounds echoes behind me, and I'm interrupted by Ken, plopping onto a log, massaging his leg. "Just my knee," he says, clearly underplaying the amount of pain he's in. "Acts up sometimes, especially when it's cold."

Sue rubs his back, her hair frizzy and unruly in the rain, the hint of grey roots starting to show.

For the first time, I'm reminded of the Hardingers' age. Up until now, I've seen them as immortal, parental figures, flush with answers and advice, embodying a kind of invincibility in their reliable magnetism. But now, I'm aware of their weaknesses. They're just as lost and afraid and I am.

The thought unnerves me. It's like watching Superman become Clark Kent.

We rest for awhile, and I try to hide my impatience. Right now the rain is only a drizzle, but if we don't get moving soon, we could get caught in inclement weather that slows us down. The last line of Cassandra's letter reverberates in my ears; "*Tick. Tock.*"

Four days isn't long in the wild, and I can't help but feel that every minute we waste resting brings Mike a minute closer to death.

Finally, Ken stretches. He says his knee has stopped bothering him, but I'm sure it hasn't. We make our way to the trailhead where we last saw Brock disappear behind the flames, surveying the way onward.

It's a steep trail, at a higher grade than any we've climbed so far. Uneven rocks that could've served as useful steps have been made slick and dangerous by the rain. Trees surround the path, and we'll have to hold back their wiry branches to clear the way. I take out my map to locate the trail diagnostics. A red box with an exclamation point gives me bad news: this trail is rated five on a scale of one to five.

For extremely competent hikers only. I look back at Ken, who's absent-mindedly rubbing his knee, and Sue, who's already out of breath from the walk over here. It's not an ideal scenario.

"It's a tough trail," I show them the map and the warning box.

For a moment, no one says anything, but then Ken shakes out his knee and states, simply, "Well... Ladies first."

Sue laughs and takes his hand. I lead the way, digging the rubber of my boots into the dirt, leaning forward and grabbing onto whatever I can to steady myself.

Little by little, we make our way upward, leaving the scorched pieces of our campsite behind us, heading for Tenaya Lake and the promise of safety.

10

———

He's been dead for awhile.

His hand was the first thing I noticed.

We'd been hiking for six hours, our progress slowed by Ken's arthritis and the rain, which turned the trail into a muddy, hazardous slip-and-slide. We weren't even three quarters of the way to the lake when I saw it.

At first I thought it was a stick, but some animal instinct made me look twice, as if a piece of me beyond conscious thought could sense death in the air.

Now I'm sure: it isn't a stick.

It's a finger.

He's been pushed to the side of the trail, leaves and branches piled over his face, only his limbs visible through the foliage.

Someone screams. It might be me.

Mud fills my boots and suddenly I'm on my knees, saying Mike's name over and over, sure it's him on the edge of the trail, discarded and forgotten. Somehow, I connect Mike's death to my own inability to tear down my walls, to commit to a lifetime together, to give him some answer other than a smile when he hinted at getting married.

I should have said 'yes,' right then and there. Why didn't I just say 'yes?'

It's like I've killed him myself.

But then Sue clears the leaves away, and the face isn't Mike's. It's someone else's, horse-like and pockmarked.

Brock.

His eyes are still open, and blood clumps in his hair. His jaw is set at an odd angle, stiff and cartoon-like.

Sue gasps. Blood rushes from Ken's cheeks, his face pale. Sue starts crying and gagging at the same time, and when she disappears behind a bush, the sounds of her retching echo across the landscape.

I want to throw up too, but not because of Brock's body. I'm disgusted with myself. When Sue cleared the leaves away, the wolf within me howled, and I only felt one thing: relief.

What's wrong with me?

"WE SHOULD BURY HIM," Ken says, his voice firm.

I shake my head.

"We don't even have a shovel."

Finally, we settle on collecting wildflowers from the forest floor. The three of us weave them into strands, scattering them around Brock's body. Ken waits until Sue isn't looking, then closes Brock's eyes and moves his jaw into a more ordinary position. He thinks I don't see him, but I do.

We gather around the bed we've made, listening to the rain, helpless to stop it from washing away our work.

"Someone should say something," Sue whispers.

I think for a long time. The sounds of the forest surround me— a hooting, hollow symphony— and the first thing that strikes me is that I've miscalculated. The picture of Cassandra— the one I've built up in my mind— says more about me than her. Out of anyone in this world, I know the horrors that lurk within a person, hiding under skin and bone. When Mike and I asked Brock to call for help tracking Cassandra down, I accused Brock of underestimating her, when I was guilty of the same crime. I wonder if that irony occurred to Brock, too, when she broke his jaw.

I don't take any pleasure in the thought. Even though Brock wasn't my favorite ranger, and I didn't always agree with him, an animal knowingness tells me we're connected. We're both built from the dust of stars that exploded billions of years ago, making him part of me, and me part of him. I know it the way birds know to fly south for winter— it's in my nature to acknowledge our connectedness. We're entangled, all of us, the good and bad pieces of ourselves orbiting around each other, their patterns causing solar flares in another person's universe.

Brock tried to help us all sense that connectedness by leading us into the Wild, and now, he's rejoining the Great Everything. I imagine roots weaving around his body, hugging him close, whispering the secrets of the Earth in his ear. Those same roots grow into a tree, and the tree drops a piece of fruit, which becomes another tree, and another, and another.

The last flower leaves my fingers as I place it into Brock's hand, and say, simply;

"You mattered."

WE GO FORWARD, but not because we want to; only because there's no other option.

The path fades, and now we're pushing our way through dense forest, leaves crunching under our boots, a long walk ahead of us. The trees casts shadows over our party, making the hour feel like twilight, an uncomfortable gap between day and night. We walk in silence, still thinking of Brock, and the angle of his jaw, wondering whether he can still see us in some unknowable way.

It's Sue who speaks first, whispering to me at the back of the group, letting Ken forge ahead until he's out of earshot.

"Do you think she got Logan, too?" Sue asks me, her voice shaking a little.

"No," I say, pushing the thought away. "His body would've been there, wouldn't it? Maybe Brock sent him ahead. For all we know, Logan could have already found the ranger cache."

Hours pass by as we hike, and the landscape seems to fold in on itself, repeating shades of green and brown that once were beautiful wilting in a world without Brock. Ken insists we use extra caution, as Cassandra could be in the area. He's vigilant in his work, peeking around trees, wielding a stick for defense. For someone who originally doubted her capabilities, he's certainly come around, debating whether he should stay up front or take up the rear in case she attacks us from behind. I point out that Ken and I have switched sides: he's convinced Cassandra is our biggest danger, and I'm fending off a nagging skepticism. Seeing Brock's body made me question the profile I'd built for her, but now, I'm reversing my position.

"You were right," I tell him. "Something doesn't add up. She didn't use a gun. Brock hadn't been shot— he'd been hit in the jaw."

Sue cringes, remembering the injury.

"I *have* seen pictures of Cassandra and she's smaller than I am. What person her size plans this entire situation so strategically but doesn't think to bring a gun? Why would Cassandra risk physically attacking someone twice as big as she is, when she could just shoot him?"

"I don't know," Ken says, waving a hand at me as if details no longer matter. "Maybe she's working with some-one." He pauses a beat. "Zoe, have you..."

Ken's about to ask me something, but Sue catches his eye and he stops himself.

"What?"

"Have you got any idea what her capabilities are? Martial arts training? Past history of violent behavior?" I shake my head, and he trudges on. "Well, whatever the case, she's here and out for blood. We need to be on the lookout."

Ken surveys the forest like a sniper. It's a ridiculous sight, and it takes extreme restraint not to roll my eyes. For some reason, seeing violence first-hand has made me less afraid. With any luck, the feeling will last.

The rain stops when we reach Tenaya Lake. It's a vast expanse of blue, a cool and quiet oasis in the middle of the desert, the surface of the lake a smooth piece of glass lain over the deep. The lake is wide, its edges pulling in opposite directions like a deflated balloon pulled taut, the rubber stretched to capacity. Various trails weave along the circum-ference of the lake, each a different scenic route. Any one of them could be hiding the cache.

We're tempted to split up in order to locate the ranger cache more quickly, but Ken— our self-appointed security officer with all the gravitas of a mall-cop— vetoes the idea. Instead, we mark our position on the map and slowly, painstakingly begin circling the water, looking for anything that might indicate a hidden stash. After much debate, we pick the biggest of the trails. It's the most accessible and sticks close to the edge of the water. We reason it's a likely bet that the rangers would put the cache on the easiest trail — one that doesn't involve an incline— if only to make it more reachable in an emergency.

We've been searching for about an hour when a sound cuts through the trees. It's far off in the distance, and at first I can't tell if it's human or animal; but whatever it is, it's definitely in distress. Sue hears it too, and as we get closer to our target, the noise becomes clearer, sharper, more distinct.

It's a man, calling for help.

Our party veers off from the trail, heading instead into unmarked wilderness. After pushing through branches and foliage growing in tangled nets over the Earth, we stumble onto another trail, one of the more difficult ones. It cuts deeper into the forest, wildflowers dotting its edges. Fifteen minutes later and a human form emerges, hunched in a ball, hidden by shrubs at the edge of the trail.

It's Logan, sitting on the ground, tied up with bungee cords. They're wrapped around his torso, pinning his arms to his body, immobilizing his legs. A piece of fabric loops around his mouth as a gag, but he's managed to pull it free. Bite marks mar the gag, and I wonder if he tried to chew his way out before finally loosening it enough to shout for help.

When he sees us, Logan starts crying, reminding me of a homesick college student. Ken and Sue untie him, and he averts his eyes away from me, embarrassed to be found this way.

When his hands are free, he turns his baseball cap around so it covers his face, and points to a hole in the ground a few yards away.

"I have so much to tell you guys," he says, nodding at our salvation:

The Ranger Cache.

11

The ranger cache is empty, but I stick my hand in anyway, just to be sure.

"She got it all. The radio, the food packets..." Logan says, his mouth watering when he mentions the food. Ken immediately opens up his pack and starts mixing some scrambled egg powder with water, rehydrating it into something like food.

I examine the cache, which was cleverly hidden under a rock with a gold plaque on it. The plaque reminds me of the little markers used to indicate different species in botanical gardens. It's discreet enough that anyone passing by would think it was labeling the point as a landmark, or describing different types of plants— not indicating a stash of supplies.

"Brock was behind me when he saw someone coming up the trail," Logan says. "He had already described the ranger cache to me, and he told me to run and find it while he dealt with Cassandra."

"Sounds like Brock," Ken nods, passing Logan the sad excuse for eggs. Logan pours the rehydrated eggs into his mouth, chewing like it's the best meal he's ever had.

"I looked around for a long time and finally found the cache. I had to dig it up with my hands, but before I could finish, someone hit me on the back of my head, and I blacked out. When I woke up, the cache was empty, and I was tied up."

He looks at the ground again, refusing to make eye contact with anyone but Sue, who's bandaging the back of his head— she's an expert at it by now.

"I tried to crawl to get help," Logan continues, "but I couldn't get very far with the bungee cords. I found a rock on the way and tried to saw them off, but it didn't work." His cheeks flush, as if he's embarrassed to have been so badly beaten by a girl. It's a reaction that irritates me, and I'm about to vouch for Cassandra's abilities before remembering that she's a murderer, and not my best friend.

"Did you see her?" I ask, my heart pounding.

Logan shakes his head. "No. I was so focused on digging up the cache that I wasn't looking around. I was awake one second, and out the next."

"What did she attack you with?" I press. "Did she have a gun?" Now's my chance to unravel the mystery of Cassandra with a person who's experienced her first hand.

"I don't know" Logan says, still chewing. "She could have hit me with back of a gun I guess, but it felt more like a rock. It happened so fast..."

"But she didn't kill you?" I say, and I must sound disappointed about it, because the Hardingers are looking at me, mildly horrified. It's like I've danced naked at a funeral.

"Gee, thanks Zoe," Logan says, less offended than the Hardingers.

"No!" I exclaim, backtracking. "I mean, I'm glad you're okay, it's just— I keep trying to paint this mental picture of Cassandra. To get inside her head— to really *know* her—

and I can't piece her together. On the one hand she's a crazy murderer, and on the other hand she's so strategic about everything."

Ken nods, agreeing with me. "You're right. Why kill Brock and not Logan?"

"Wait... Brock's... he's *dead?*" Logan asks, and I realize we haven't told him yet. I nod, and we're all quiet for a moment, remembering Brock and everything he did for us.

Eventually, Sue breaks the silence. "She killed Brock because he knows the valley inside and out," she says, stating the obvious. "If we'd reunited with Brock, he could've helped us get out of here. He's useful. Logan's not."

"Still here!" says Logan, waving a hand in the air as if we've forgotten him.

"Sorry, sweetie," Sue says, patting his leg. "You're useful in other ways. I'm only saying it's clear Cassandra is trying to remove anything that would enable Zoe to leave the forest. The ranger cache... Brock..."

"... Mike," I finish the list, imagining Mike on his back, leaves covering his body, in the same position as Brock, except that his jaw has been rearranged not by blunt trauma, but by a bullet. I fold the image in on itself, crumpling it in a ball and shoving it in one of the brain-boxes I never open.

"Did you find him?" Logan asks. When I don't say anything, he elaborates on the question. "Mike. He went off into the forest after the fire, right? Did you find him?"

I exchange a glance with Ken and Sue, too tired to talk about the letter, or Taft point, or whatever twisted scavenger hunt Cassandra has planned for me.

I shake my head, and we leave it at that.

The sun hangs low in the sky, and we decide to make camp near the edge of the lake on the surface of a smooth boulder that rests just a couple feet above the water line. Ken and I help Logan limp his way to the site, and when we get there, Sue gets to work arranging sleeping bags while Ken and Logan hunch over a fire starter. Everyone is pre-occupied with a task, and I take the opportunity to slip away.

"I'm 'gonna fill my canteen," I announce. I disappear into the forest just in time to hear Ken shout back, "Don't go out of earshot!"

I yell that I won't, and then I do exactly that, because I don't remember voting for Ken as head of camp security.

It's a fifteen minute walk along the edge of the lake until I'm far enough away that I'm out of earshot.

The solitude begs me to inhale, and even though it burns my nose, it's all I want. My nails dig into my skin as my eyes try to forget what they've seen— the way a face looks when the heart it belongs to has stopped beating.

Suddenly, my jacket is too tight. It cuts into my armpits and lays heavy on my chest, restricting the blood flow to my upper body. If I don't get it off soon, my face will look like Brock's.

The zipper screams as I rip off the coat, shedding it like a second skin before sitting cross-legged at the edge of the lake. The air is cold and my flesh prickles, but I don't care.

I make a rattling sound that's somewhere between crying, screaming, and the letter "e." It's a strange sound— one I'd never make in front of another human, but it doesn't matter.

I'm alone.

The pine trees lean in, their branches spread wide with concern; they recognize the sound of animal suffering. I'm still feeling trapped, so I pull my shirt over my head, balling it up on top of my jacket. Next I unbutton my jeans before realizing I'll never get them over my boots. My shoes land in a pile, and then I'm vaguely aware of unclasping my bra, and before I know it I'm totally naked, crouched in front of the lake, wondering where the Earth ends and I begin.

I take Silence by the hand, and even though I know she's stolen, I'm sure that she'll be mine forever. We ease into the water together, and I'm careful not to splash, in case Silence changes her mind. We push outward to greater depths, until the water's at my chin. It rolls into my mouth, hungry and soft all at the same time.

It would be so easy, to sink into the Great Everything.

Instead, I back float over it, letting my arms move over my head, feeling like I'm a part of something even if I don't entirely understand what it is.

The water directs me, sending me wherever the Great Everything wants me to go, and I imagine that my path has something to do with the way the Earth spins, or how close the moon is to the Sun. I picture the sun and the moon, orbiting around each other in circles, and for some reason the sun's face is my face, and the moon's is Cassandra's, and we're each reflecting the light of the other in prismatic patterns. The need to know her burns in my stomach, but not because of Mike. We're connected by something else. She would be able to put a feeling into words for me— to describe the desperate ache of wanting to be *seen* by a man, like you'd turn yourself inside out if it would help him really know you. It makes what she's done to us all the more horrible.

I thought you were my friend.

A red glow coats my arms. It's the lake reflecting the sunset off her glassy eyes. I'm sure I don't belong to myself, and the water whispers a confirmation in my ear, telling me that it's true; but I don't belong to anyone else either.

I belong to the Great Everything.

I ask the water to wash away the new parts of me, the ones I learned, the pieces that weren't present in the sketch of my original design, the ones that obscure the me who wants to be seen. She hears me, and I think she does it.

The sun dips below the mountains. It's night, now, and I'm staring up at million tiny stars, like holes in a blanket.

I wonder how long I've been out here, but then I remember that time is just an idea, and that forever has no end.

My fingers are blue. They touch something sharp— my numb hands are wrapped around a branch. I've been pushed ashore because that's where the forest wants me, even though I'd rather be at the bottom of the lake.

Round rocks scatter as I stumble back onto land. The moon is bright tonight, turning my reflection silver on the water. My hair is tangled and matted, my eyes wide. My arms are too skinny, bony compared to the width of my shoulders. My waist is wide, and one of my breasts is a little bigger than the other. I'm defiant in my failure to be beautiful; and in this moment, I think it might be the best I've ever looked. If I'm really honest, I always feel beautiful when I'm alone. It's when other people are around that the feeling changes.

Why didn't I push Mike for answers when we were in a better place? My stomach knew he wasn't telling me everything, but I accepted his story about Cassandra with no questions asked.

My reflection looks up at me from the surface of the lake — so fierce and unapologetic. She would *never* make the mistakes I've made.

I ate the fruit the world fed me. I didn't push Mike for answers because I believed it was my job to make other people comfortable, even before myself. Fear of asking a question that might put Mike on the spot superseded my own basic, animal need for security. And instead of daring myself to step outside my comfort zone by learning to voice my own needs, I closed myself off. Better to hide than to change. Putting up walls didn't solve the problem, either. I protected myself, when I should have *restored* myself.

I should have stripped off the world's input like the clothes I left at the edge of the lake, and lived in my natural state— the way I was meant to be— true to myself and the way the Great Everything made me.

I should've said what I was thinking and voiced my concerns like a raw, animal thing, devoid of human censorship.

I should've asked Mike why his story about Cassandra made my hair stand on end.

What aren't you telling me?

I should've told Mike that I hate horses.

I should've been the truest, purest version of myself— and dared him not to like me.

Take it or leave it, this is me.

The woman in the water reaches out to me, and I make her a promise as our hands meet.

From this moment on, I'm the most animal me.

I'll never ignore another gut instinct.

Another need.

Another howl.

WHEN I GET BACK to camp, everyone is sitting around a fire, talking about my absence and what it means.

"Maybe we should be looking for her," Sue suggests, her breath transformed to fog in the cold, night air.

"I don't know," Logan answers, swirling what's probably the last of our instant coffee in a tin mug. "She was acting weird. Maybe she just needed a walk?"

"Or she's gone to think. She might be sorting out the same thing I am..." Ken says, not noticing my figure crouched behind a tree, hidden in the blackness of the forest.

"Which is what?" Logan leans in, like a middle-school kid waiting for gossip at the lunch table.

"Well, it's strange isn't it," Ken continues. "Mike disappeared right when Cassandra set the fire, and no-one's heard from him since. Meanwhile, Brock is dead, and it appears we're part of a very strategic, well-orchestrated plan..."

"Which *could* have been put in place by Cassandra," Sue reminds him, her tone suggesting they've had this conversation before.

"Or?" Logan prompts.

"I didn't want to say anything in front of Zoe," Ken continues, "... but maybe Mike's not such an unwilling hostage."

"Ken!" Sue shushes him.

Logan sips his coffee, as if discussing my boyfriend as a murderer is the most natural thing in the world. "You said there was a letter though, right? Why would Mike stage his own kidnapping?

Ken shrugs. "I don't know. But I think the odds of Cassandra covering this much ground alone in the wilderness are slim. She has *someone* helping her, and there's only one person missing..."

Their mouths shut when they spot me, dripping and

shivering, a ghastly figure under the moonlight. Ken starts to say something, but Sue puts a hand on his arm.

The circle closes when I take a seat. Now all four of us are gathered around the flames. Sue offers me a granola bar, and I take it.

The sound of my chewing colors the night. Nobody says anything until I'm finished.

"We need to talk about next steps," I say as I crumple up the wrapper, pulling Cassandra's letter from my pocket and rereading it in case if I've missed something.

Logan's eyes widen and I can tell he wants to ask me if he can read the letter, but Ken shakes his head.

"There's a resort," Sue says, treading carefully, like she's talking to a feral animal who might snap at any moment. "It's on the other side of the lake. Brock told Logan about it as they were hiking up here."

The fire clouds my vision, its heat stroking my eyelids each time I blink.

"It's supposed to be really nice!" Logan adds, as if a vacation is just what we all need. "It's settled between the lake and Perception point— Brock said it's beautiful when it snows."

I don't give a fuck what it looks like.

"Do they have radios?"

Sue nods. "Brock told Logan he should go there if he couldn't find the cache."

"How far is it?" I ask, even though I can guess at the answer.

"Well, that's the thing..." Sue sighs.

"How far?"

Sue doesn't answer. Logan takes over.

"Three days," he says, looking around at the others like he doesn't understand why this is such a big deal. "Wouldn't be so bad except that it's not a flat hike. Brock thought the mountains might slow us down."

My nails dig into my jeans.

"We have enough food, and once we're there we can radio for help," Logan continues, ignoring the unaddressed tension.

We sit in the silence for a minute, letting everything we're not talking about fill the air until it becomes too thick and sticky to inhale. A three day hike means we won't arrive until Thursday— the day Cassandra expects me to find Mike. Moving on could be Mike's death sentence. But Ken isn't worried about that, because he's not even convinced Mike's been kidnapped.

"Zoe—" Ken starts to say something.

"It's fine," I tell him, holding up a hand. I don't need to hear anymore. I already know what he's going to say.

"We have to think about our kids, about getting back to them." Sue adds, her voice rising an octave, dripping with a pleading tone that makes it impossible to look at her. "And Ken's knee is—"

"You're just taking care of your own. I get it."

Sue's eyes water and she looks like I've slapped her, but I've only said what we all know.

Ken and Sue already have their pack: the people who are their first priority, the people they would kill for, the people they would die for, the people they never doubt. And that doesn't include Mike and I.

It doesn't mean the Hardingers are bad people— they're actually quite lovely.

They just know where they belong.

∼

Everyone else goes to sleep before me.

When I finally shut my eyes, I tell my body not to succumb completely. Two hours, tops.

We have places to be.

My body obliges and keeps me up with memories. I replay them, again and again, half awake and half asleep, treating them like dreams even though I know they really happened.

The one I replay the most is of Mike and me. We'd only been dating a couple months, and Christmas-time was fast approaching. Every piece of tinsel caused anxiety, every red bow made me itch. Our relationship was new, and expectations weren't clear— would we spent Christmas together, or apart? We were volunteering at an animal shelter where Mike's friend worked— one of the guys he hired to help him build furniture, someone who knew his way around a table-saw— when it happened.

Metal cages and concrete floors were decorated for the holiday, row upon row of homeless dogs hiding behind red and green candy-canes and festive signs, hoping to be taken home by Christmas morning. We stopped at each one, taking one dog after another out for a walk. Big dogs. Small dogs. Ones with long fur. Ones with short tails. But with each new dog, Mike got more upset, his smile flattening as if someone had smashed it with a mallet. He excused himself, then stepped outside, and didn't come back.

I waited ten minutes. Fifteen. Finally, I went after him, and found him leaning against the back of the building, smoking a cigarette like it was a thing he did every day.

"Zoe, I can explain—" Mike said as soon as he saw the look on my face.

"So you smoke now?" I asked him, my heart running in circles, trying to find a way to evacuate my chest. Two weeks after we started dating, I'd found a packet of cigarettes in Mike's apartment, and he claimed they belonged to his ex. I told him I couldn't date a smoker. He swore he wasn't one. "Is there anything else I should know? Anything else you're lying about?" To me, it was evidence of the monster within, some piece of himself he was hiding.

"I smoke when I'm nervous. I quit when we started dating." My face must show that this isn't quitting, because he added, "Mostly quit. I tried. It's—" he paused, running a hand through his hair. "Seeing the dogs. It just gets to me."

I turned to leave, but Mike called after me, "Zoe, stop! I didn't tell you because I know how you can get about these things!"

"How do I get?" I asked, even though I knew exactly what he meant. I'm always looking for a reason to leave, and even though it's unspoken, it's no secret between us.

"Seeing these dogs without a home gets to me because, I'm—" Mike tossed the cigarette aside, scraping it against the concrete with his shoe. "I'm on my own most holidays."

"What do you mean? You said you go with your Dad to your Uncle's house on Christmas."

"I go, but I'm not a part of it, not really. My Dad couldn't take care of me when I was a kid because he got remarried and his new wife didn't like children. I was fourteen, so I went to live with my aunt and uncle, but they already had kids. They had their family, and I was always just this additional person hanging around. I'm not an orphan, but I'm —" he pauses, trying to find the right word, "— extra."

My brain lurched, trying to process this new information, struggling to switch gears. I expected to see the monster within Mike, but instead I found another part of him, something hidden, but not dangerous.

"When I look at those dogs," Mike continued, "I know

how they feel. People put up with them, but no one really wants them."

For a moment, I stood under the eaves of the animal shelter, not knowing what to say in a place so marked by abandonment, so filled with creatures wanting homes. Then, I reached into Mike's pocket and pulled out the pack of Marlboros and the lighter. It took me two flicks to get a flame. I kissed him, then passed him a lit cigarette.

"I really want you," I said, holding up the pack of cigarettes. "Even if you come with these."

That year, Mike spent Christmas with me, at my Mom's house. We all made cranberry sauce, and my Mom made sure there were three stockings on the fireplace mantle. In the morning, we opened presents, leaving wrapping paper scattered on the floor, none of us caring if it stayed messy for awhile.

Nobody felt like they were extra.

IT'S STILL DARK when I make my move. My eyes adjust as I survey our camp. It's hard to tell who's who in the blackness, but I count three bodies, their chests rising and falling. Someone is snoring; it might be Ken. There's no way to know what time it is without a watch, but the heavy feeling in my eyes makes me guess it's two, maybe three o'clock in the morning.

My legs stretch long of their own volition— they can sense the hard walk ahead.

My sleeping bag barely squeezes into my pack, and as I push it down, I vaguely take note of how much dried food I have left. Whatever it is, it'll have to be enough to get me to Taft Point.

I climb backwards down the edge of our boulder, on the side that faces the forest, not the lake. My foot slips a little, causing a cascade of smaller rocks to tumble into the shrubbery. The noise is loud enough to wake up our camp, but only one person stirs. By the body shape, it looks like Sue, moving in her sleep. She doesn't get up. I've escaped an uncomfortable goodbye.

My feet hit the ground, and the second that they do, I'm a wolf on the move, laser-focused on one thing only— Mike.

Maybe he's hiding something. Maybe he hasn't told me the whole truth about Cassandra. Maybe I'm just imagining red flags that aren't even there. But whatever the explanation is— whether Mike is good, bad, or a little bit of both— he's still mine. He's a member of my pack, and I won't stop until I find him.

A rustling sound echoes from the trees behind me. My fists fly to my face as I look over my shoulder, ready to fight. A woman steps forward, and I'm sure it's Cassandra. She's happy that her plan worked— she's found me, alone— and she's going to accomplish what she came here for.

But then the moonlight falls on her face, revealing that she's not Cassandra at all.

"Sue," I drop my arms.

"I didn't want you to think—" Sue pauses, trying to find the right words. "I didn't want you think no one cared."

We stand across from each other, two women suddenly connected by the very thing that divides us. A long chasm stretches between us, as wide as it is deep. We build a bridge.

Sue crosses it, handing me something. I hold it up to the moonlight. It's a Ziploc bag, filled with five packages of powdered eggs, and a fire starter.

"I can't take these," I start to say, but Sue doesn't let me refuse.

"Take them."

"You guys might need them..."

"We'll manage," Sue says. Then, she holds out a hand, and I take it in mine. We shake on it.

What "it" is I can't exactly verbalize, except that it's a silent agreement as old as humanity itself. It's the one that led to cities, and to storytelling, and to families, and to me, and to you. It's a contract woven into our DNA. We break it as often as we abide by it, but it's never rendered invalid. It never expires.

It's tempting to talk about it out loud— to address the magic of it— but Sue's eyes connect with mine, and I think better of it. Being party to an unspoken agreement is like making a wish on your birthday; if you talk about it, it might not come true. Instead, I settle for something simple.

"Thank you," I say, and Sue nods, because she knows what I mean.

"When we get to the resort, we'll radio help to Taft Point, right away," she promises.

My lips feign a smile. I'm trying to be encouraging, even though I know help won't find me. By the time Sue reaches the resort, I'll already have left Taft Point. If Cassandra's letter is to be believed, I'll find another clue on the mountain, which will lead to another clue in a *different* location, and another, and another, until so much time passes that Mike and I belong to the forest, just like Brock.

Sue releases my hand and I turn to leave, but a loud noise stops me. It's a scream— a man's scream— and it's coming from the direction of our camp. It's such a primal sound that it's felt more than heard. The entire forest sits up and pays attention. Sue's face floods with fear.

I start to run back toward camp, but Sue grips my arm.

"Go! You've waited long enough," she says, nodding toward the direction I was heading.

"What if it's her?! You guys might need—"

Sue cuts me off. "We don't need anything," she says, and the words sting a little, even though she's saying it for all the right reasons.

"But—"

Sue shakes her head. "You get yours, I'll get mine. Now, go!"

She pulls me into her arms and hugs me tight, and the embrace is so quick I barely have time to capture the memory. Then, Sue's running back toward camp, shouting over her shoulder, "Go, Zoe! Run!"

There's no time to think about it. My legs take over, and before I know it I'm speeding away from the camp, from the lake, and from my friends, the Hardingers. Branches hit my face and my feet ache in my boots, yet I push onward, driven by the primal desire to put as much space as possible between myself and Cassandra.

I'm not sure if I've done the right thing. But I keep running anyway, my breath catching in my throat, eyes watering as I think about Sue's promises to Ken, and Mike's promises to me, and what we all owe each other.

12

———

I stay close to the edge of the lake for as long as possible, but eventually I'm forced to break off and wade deeper into the forest. Tenaya Lake disappears from view, growing smaller with each glance over my shoulder.

The Lake served as an easy indicator of location. Now, as I push deeper into the trees, I'll have to stop more often to track my direction. A compass is not a GPS, and if I get off course, I won't be able to call on a satellite for help with pinpointing my exact coordinates. I'm like an ancient maritime sailor, using the stars and a sextant to locate my position in a vast, empty ocean. The sun won't rise for hours, and the forest knows it; the wild is so quiet and devoid of human life that it might as well be the Atlantic.

My flashlight doesn't offer much illumination, its rays weaving through the trees, struggling to make the world clear again without the benefit of moonlight bouncing off the lake. The forest is dense here, and the pine trees grow so close together that their needles crisscross over each other like stitches. My progress slows as my feet stumble over pinecones and fallen logs. The trail is gone.

Anyone else would stop and make camp until daylight, but I'm afraid to lose my head-start. If the scream Sue and I heard means that Cassandra found our camp, then she's behind me, not ahead of me. Mike is safe— most likely restrained and incapacitated— but safe, for now. She can't kill him if she's not near him. Maybe I can beat her to the end destination, wherever that is.

The forest leans over me, blanketing me in shadow as I try not to think about what might have happened to Sue, and Ken, and Logan. Images flood the night: their bodies laid side-by-side, just like Brock's, their jaws shattered, eyes wide open. Instead of looking at them, I distract myself by counting steps, or how many times an owl hoots. Better to focus on the mundane. Dwelling on worst-case scenarios might make me curl up in a ball and never get up again.

My feet tangle up in some brush. A branch scratches into my arm, leaving a thick, searing line. I try not to look at it, pressing deeper into the emptiness, feeling more alone with every step. Minutes pass by, turning into hours, my heart speeding up with every step, because it knows that I'm approaching something awful.

I saw it on the map when I first developed a strategy to reach Taft Point, and immediately felt my stomach turn over. Avoiding it with another route would have taken days. And Mike might not have days.

Moonlight shines through branches and the trees scatter, fading into a less dense arrangement— a sign that I'm close. My pace slows. If I approach too fast, I might make a fatal misstep. My flashlight turns in my hand as I clutch it closer, waiting for the world to open up.

It does, and my relief at heading in the right direction is tainted by bone-chilling dread of what comes next.

My feet are at the edge of a tall ravine, a deep valley carved between two mountains. I'm positioned on the shorter side, and while it's not a completely vertical drop, the incline is extreme enough that scaling it qualifies as rock climbing more than hiking. My mouth goes dry and my fists clench. Vertigo makes the world spin.

It's difficult to estimate the slope of the ravine without teetering over the edge. My hands wrap around the straps of my backpack to keep it from slipping off as I bend over. Rocks scatter, free-falling in mid-air, taking eons to hit the bottom. This side of the mountain isn't a perfect right angle, but it's pretty close— maybe a ninety-five degree spread. Just short of a vertical cliff face. Walking down is not an option. I'll have to descend with my back to the ravine in order to find footholds in the mountain.

My flashlight tosses light at the side of the ravine, but it can't illuminate the bottom because the distance is too far. Tree roots stick out of the soil, and layered geology has created uneven patches of metamorphic rock. There's plenty of places to hold onto, and if I'm smart, I'll probably make it down alive.

At first glance, the bottom of the ravine is just a gulley of rocks hidden in shadow, their outlines difficult to make out through the darkness— harmless, until I think about where they came from, and the possibility of rock slides.

You don't know for sure that they came from the mountains. Maybe they were already there, I lie to myself.

It's too late to find another route. I'm committed to this.

I hang my flashlight around my neck, letting it dangle freely as I get on my hands and knees and back myself toward the edge of the mountain, grasping onto a tree root in order to ease myself over the side.

This is the hardest part. Beginning is always the hardest part.

My feet flail against the soil for a moment, but then they find traction, slowly, carefully guiding me over the edge of the mountain.

One hand at a time.

Anything is possible if you break the process down into tiny, manageable pieces. The thought makes me stop to take in the width of the ravine, and suddenly I'm thinking of Mike, and the day that I met him, and the feeling that there's always been a distance between us that I can't seem to close.

My climb becomes a pattern, which I rinse and repeat. First, my right hand— the dominant one— grabs the flashlight from around my neck and searches for a new hold. Once my right hand is safely gripping a tree branch, or clutching around a rock, I work on the left. When both hands have found safety, it's time for the feet. Sometimes I'm lucky and my boots are able to rest on a protrusion. Other times, they're flat against the mountain, creating an almost unbearable tension in my biceps. I'm nearly blind in the dark, relying on pale moonlight for most steps in my pattern.

Relying on patterns— on the things that I know, the things I can trust— is the key to my survival. This is something Mike's never understood.

My hand closes on a round rock, and for a second its smooth exterior becomes the handle to the front door of my last apartment, the one I lived in before Mike and I moved in together. The building was a historical landmark, a fancy label that only served as an excuse for the land-lord to avoid renovations. Hallways lined with paisley carpets, rife with the wet, clinging scent of mold. Lead paint peeling from the lobby walls. Gold mailboxes with curling leaf accents and keys bent from too many years of use. The building needed work, but for every hazardous piece of it, there was also something beautiful, something rare. Stained glass windows on the entire first floor. Original mahogany molding on edges of doorways. French doors, fire places, and built-in cabinets in the luckiest of apartments, including mine. Sure, it was falling apart, but it was *my* falling apart.

The first time I brought Mike over to my apartment, the round, dated door-knob on the front entrance to my unit came right off in my hand.

"Does that happen a lot?" he asked, staring at the gold orb cradled in my palm.

"Depends on how you define a lot," I answered, popping it back into place with the motion of a practiced expert.

Mike offered to fix it for me, right up until the day we moved in together.

"It's not safe," he would argue. "Anyone could waltz right in!"

"But 'anyone' doesn't *know* about the doorknob, so who cares? If someone wants to break into my place, let them try. I've been wanting an excuse to buy a new TV."

For once, Mike didn't laugh.

Logically, Mike was right. I needed a new doorknob.

But I loved the way my apartment was just a little broken, and the fact that I knew how to fix it. I loved peering into the inner workings of the door, glimpsing exposed bolts and metal, a clock-work mystery revealing itself to me.

There was no way to explain to Mike— without hurting his feelings— that letting him help me felt like a greater threat than hypothetical robbers. If we didn't work out, every time I came home— every time the door knob didn't pop out in my hand but rested quietly in place— it would be a reminder of something lost.

My patterns weren't perfect, but they were mine, and they kept me from getting hurt. It was an impossible thing to convey to him, and the fact that he couldn't understand it made me feel far away from him, like we were standing on opposite sides of a ravine as wide as this one.

My arm trembles in place, and my right hand misses the branch it was grabbing by a fraction of an inch. The misstep takes me by surprise, jogging me back into the present moment, but not quickly enough. My left hand relaxes, and for a second my body churns with the sensation of falling, certain that I'm tumbling down the ravine, heading for the jagged rocks at the bottom that lie in wait. My left hand manages to find another hold, and I'm back in position, shaken, but spared from death.

My stomach settles. I've learned my lesson. Focus.

I'm not sure how long it takes me to finish the descent, but the journey feels infinite. At some point I decide it's never going to end, and resign myself to a future like Sisyphus, rolling a stone up a hill for all of eternity. Hand over hand, foot by foot, I rinse and repeat.

This is my punishment for being closed-hearted, for not letting Mike fix my front door. An eternity climbing down a mountain with no end.

My butt hits the bottom of the ravine before my feet. I'm not expecting it, and in response, my hands release their vice-like grips. Suddenly I'm lying on my back over a pile of rocks, staring up at star-speckled night sky, laughing like a drunk hyena.

I've never felt so alive. If I did this, I can do anything.

Watch out, Cassandra. I'm coming for you.

THE BOTTOM of the ravine is a world all its own. The air sits heavy on my shoulders, like I've reached the deepest piece of a dark ocean crevice. It's silent, here, with no sign of animal or plant life— just a rocky, desert trail that cuts through the forest, a thread that weaves back in on itself with no beginning or end.

The muscles in my arms are useless, exhausted from the descent. Climbing the other half will be harder, and if I can sleep in this endless, desert wasteland, I should try.

Rocks scatter as I kick them away, clearing a flat space on the dirt using just my feet in an attempt to let my arms recover.

I unzip my sleeping bag, trying to calculate how much sleep I've had in the past two days. A couple hours on the boulder by Tenaya Lake. Restless fevers the night before. An exact amount can't be calculated, but whatever it is, it's not enough. They sky is lighter than it was when I started my descent, but maybe I can doze off before the sun rises and trick my body into sleeping longer.

The sleeping bag wraps me in soft, gentle fabric, but my body won't relax. It's on high alert, waiting for some predator to find me. Every breeze that streaks through the ravine is Cassandra. Every twig that snaps is a warning.

For some reason, I feel the need to light a fire, as if the flames will keep my enemy at bay. I reach for the fire starter and collect some brittle, dry branches from the bottom of the ravine, pieces that fell from the trees up above. They snap as I arrange them in a small pyre. It's cold, but the air isn't too moist— perfect conditions. Metal strikes metal, and a spark jumps onto the sticks, creating a blaze. I've done it on my first try.

Flames warm my knees— my legs are curled up at the edge of the pyre, my sleeping bag repurposed as a pillow.

My eyes are closed, but dreams won't come. I'm coated in awareness of being on my own, and it's a feeling that's too big for me. I want to shrug it off like a dress I bought at Goodwill and later came to regret. The adrenaline rush I experienced earlier evaporates, and I'm left clutching some endorphins who hang around like the last guests at a party, wondering why everyone else went home so early.

Mike would understand. It's true, he couldn't grasp my need to leave a broken doorknob as it was, but the ravine between us isn't as wide as I sometimes imagine it is. Mike is an expert at understanding strange feelings, even the most insignificant ones. Sometimes he even comes up with words to describe them.

On one dreary Saturday in Silverlake, when the sky was dark and clouds hung heavy over the hilly streets beside our house, Mike and I decided to break up the day with comfort from our favorite deli. It's an unimpressive place. Laminate countertops and a white tile floor. A glass display case with pastries inside that always look the same. But for some reason, being there makes us feel like we're a part of something. Maybe it's the fact that the menu labels the place as a "local establishment," or just that the cashier remembers our names and agrees that the coffee is no good.

On this particular day, I stepped outside my comfort zone and ordered something different than my usual, specifically requesting extra pickles and no dressing. The second the sandwich slid over the counter I regretted my decision— the bread was too oaty, the pickles too salty, the cheese too mild. It was waste of a sandwich, but I couldn't morally justify getting a new one, because this one was exactly what I ordered

"What do you call this feeling?" I asked Mike.

He thought about it, chewing on his perfectly-made turkey-cheddar combo.

"Breadshamefraude," he said. "From the Latin root for 'Shame,' meaning 'to cover,' the German 'freude' meaning 'joy,' and the English 'bread' meaning— bread."

"Joy?" I said, picking at the crust of my terrible sandwich. "Why joy?"

He grabbed a plastic knife and cut his sandwich in half, passing it to me across the table.

"Joy at having a boyfriend who's willing to share."

It wasn't just that Mike shared, but that he didn't belittle a ridiculous feeling. He named it for me. He's always naming things for me. It's a small characteristic in a person, but it's the kind that grows on you over time. It's the kind that makes you forgive him after a fight, the sort of thing that keeps you coming back to a person again and again, always wanting more, even when the road is rough.

Ken was wrong. He has to be wrong.

The thought makes me roll over, trying to find a way to out-maneuver the ache in my chest. My eyes blink open against my will. A hazy red glow spills over the edge of the ravine. The sun is up, and I'll never fall asleep now. My body clock is off, my REM cycles destroyed from too many nights out of sync with the Earth. A quick stretch, a yawn, and I'm scanning my surroundings; everything is as I left it, except that my fire has burned down.

It's morning, and I'm alone.

The powdered scrambled eggs Sue gave me make a swooshing sound as I mix them with water, swigging from my canteen as I go. A choking, nagging feeling bubbles up in my chest— it's the feeling that I've forgotten something, even though I'm not sure what it is. Finally, I realize it's that

I'm used to talking to someone else every morning. Since Mike and I moved in together, I've lost the ability to wake up alone and feel okay about it.

Loneliness isn't a new feeling for me. Not being able to cope with it— that's something novel, something unsettling.

When I'm done with breakfast, I wash my face with water from my canteen, then roll up my sleeping bag. The ravine is beautiful in the morning, but I'm so distracted by an omnipresent feeling of lack that I barely pause to take note. I feel the need to search through my pack and make sure I haven't misplaced anything. It's like I've lost a limb but I'm not sure which one.

Someone once tried to explain the difference between solitude and loneliness to me, but it didn't seem relevant to me at the time, so I didn't listen.

I think it was my High School English teacher, Mr. Sandoval. He was well-intentioned in a painful way. His idealism coated him in a kind of invincibility that allowed him to completely ignore the kids who talked about him behind his back, making fun of him for his badly-groomed goatee, imitating his lisp in the hallways after class. None of it ever affected Mr. Sandoval, who was the personification of Teflon. He let every unkind word roll off his back, and continued to teach with the same enthusiasm, the same verve, he'd always had. He never mentioned a family, or indicated that he had people who cared about him, waiting up for him at night. Yet, somehow, he always seemed perfectly happy.

I used to feel sorry for Mr. Sandoval. Now I wish I were more like him.

Solitude. Loneliness.

What was it he said?

One is a choice, and the other is an unmet need.

This is the second one.

AN HOUR LATER, and I'm crouching in front of a seam where two pieces of Earth have been sewn together by years of seismic activity. My arm bends at a perfect right angle, trying to estimate the incline, confirming what I suspected but didn't want to believe:

This side of the ravine goes straight up.

There's no slope. No slight grade to help me make my ascent. Just a completely vertical cliff face.

Three checks of my bag confirm that it's zipped. Cassandra's letter crackles as I fold it, then unfold it, then fold it again. The compass won't fit neatly in any pocket, so I move it from spot to spot, trying to find the ideal place to store it. Somewhere it won't escape from. The plastic bag Sue gave me whines as I rip it into shreds, fashioning a pair of hand-wraps to protect my palms from sharp edges. My shoelaces don't look right, so I tie them more neatly, then try for a double-knot before changing my mind and tying them again, just once, in a bow.

I'm procrastinating.

Finally, my hand reaches out for the mountain, and as my feet lift off the ground I imagine I'm bouldering back home in a gym, but with a very unreliable climbing partner. He's the guy who half-heartedly yells "On belay!" while holding his phone and checking his Instagram account. I name him Frank, and promise myself I won't die because of him.

Fuck you, Frank. Pay attention.

My arms have— for the most part— recovered from my earlier climb, but I still try to use my legs as much as possible. My pattern for the ascent is the reverse of the one I used to climb *into* the ravine. My feet take the lead, finding nooks and crannies to shove the toe of my hiking boot into. I'm forceful each time, ensuring that both shoes are deeply wedged within the mountain before I dare to move a hand.

This side of the ravine presents fewer tree roots than the last, making it difficult to find good holds. Options to move myself upward are limited, presenting themselves as holes in the rocks, or boulders that jut out at strange angles. Each time my hand finds a cutout, I swallow, praying that it won't meet a snake or a lizard hiding in the dark recesses of the mountain.

Dozens of holds later, and my aching muscles make me zero in on a ledge that sticks out from the rest of the cliff—an opportunity for rest that's too good to ignore. Gingerly, my left arm reaches toward the dirt-covered shelf, testing it with my weight before allowing my right arm to join it. I pull myself over the edge and sit with my legs dangling over, giving my arms a break. Then, in the middle of safety, I make a huge mistake.

I look down.

My stomach turns; the powdered eggs threaten to come back up. I choke them back and look away. The climb didn't take long, but I'm already about three quarters of the way up the side of the mountain. The ravine stretches out beneath me, and while I'm not sure how far down it is, the change in perspective tells me it's far. Rocks that were the size of my head when I started my climb are now as big as my fist. The world spins.

I shouldn't have looked. My eyes close, resisting, trying to get back in the frame of mind that enabled me to make it this far.

I'm in a gym. I'm rock climbing in a gym. Frank is an

unreliable idiot. If I fall, there's a mat. But I should try not to fall.

"Okay, Frank!" I shout into the void, knowing no one hears me. "If I end up a human pancake because you're not paying attention, I'm coming back to haunt you."

Frank doesn't answer. Probably still on Instagram.

"Belay on?"

Somewhere, a creature hoots, and even though it's definitely a bird and not Frank, I decide it was "On belay!" and take it as my sign to continue.

Shaking, my fingers reach for a crevice about ten inches above my head. It's a reliable hold; now, a spot for my opposite leg. The toe of my boot discovers a home and pushes me upward, allowing me to grab onto another miniature rock formation with my left hand. The climb continues, the procedure repeated again and again. Leg, hand, other leg, boot...

It's tempting to look down and see if I'm still above the ledge, but I'm too afraid to risk it. Instead, my boot finds another foothold. It's a little narrow, but it's a necessary stop, so I force the hold anyway, jamming my boot in with all the strength I can muster. It's a secure enough hold that my hands can release in search of the next move. My palm closes around an orb, and a peek upwards reveals that my fingers are wrapped around a tiny rock. It's not great, but it'll do. That glance down was costly. It ruined my concentration, instilling a sense of urgency, making me want to finish my climb as soon as possible. Without testing it first, I put my entire body weight onto the small stone, letting go of my other grip.

The tiny rock pulls away from the side of the mountain, slipping out of my fingers so that I'm left holding onto nothing but thin, unhelpful air. It's nearly a complete disaster— one that's about to send me tumbling down to the bottom of the ravine— but I manage to avoid a fall by jabbing my left hand into a cutout, a tiny sliver in the Earth that's the difference between life and death. For a moment, I've avoided danger, but then, something terrible happens.

The tiny, meaningless little rock cascades down the side of the mountain, causing a chain reaction like nothing I've ever seen before. Two medium-sized rocks about the size of my head break free, tumbling after the little rock that supported them, causing five more to follow suit. It's apocalyptic, and I swear I see a hole open up at the top of the cliff. It looks like the mouth of a dragon, breathing jagged, rocky fire in my face.

Huge rocks tumble toward me, hundreds of them, dislodged and angry, seeking to enact revenge on the person who disturbed the littlest among them. The entire mountain is coming down.

The ledge juts out beneath me— my only hope, maybe ten or fifteen feet directly under my shoes. If I can jump down in time, I might be able to avoid being knocked off the side of the mountain like a rogue pinball that's escaped its machine.

I try to pull my boot from the crevice it's in, but it's lodged too tightly. The rocks are coming, and they're going to shatter my bones and fracture my skull, leaving me broken and bleeding at the bottom of the ravine. There's only one thing to do.

I let go of my handhold, falling backward, and suddenly I'm hanging upside down, blood rushing to my head, hands covering my face as dirt and debris cloud my eyes. My boot is still stuck, preventing me from dropping toward the ledge like I'd hoped.

Something hits my leg and I scream, feeling a burning

sensation in my shin. The pain brings with it a hyper-aware-
ness, wiping all conscious thought from my brain and acti-
vating my instincts. My body acts on its own, like a runaway
train who's ejected her incompetent conductor. Without my
consent, my fingers reach upward, my abs engage, and in
one desperate motion, I crunch up and pull at my shoelace.

It comes loose and my foot slips out of my boot, and now
I'm falling, falling, praying I land on the ledge and not at the
bottom of the ravine.

My body slams into the Earth.

I've landed somewhere, but before I can figure out
where it is, everything goes dark.

MY EYES FEEL OPEN, but everything is black, so they must be
closed. Maybe I've blacked out. Maybe, this is what darkness
feels like— a coma, a living death.

My right arm tries to move, but it's trapped above my
head. I'm curled in the fetal position, my arms covering my
face, shielding me from impact. I blink. The world stays
dark.

I shift my head back and a space opens up. A vague
shape comes into focus. It's beige with uneven edges— a
boulder that landed millimeters away from my face,
obscuring the light.

Moving away isn't an option. My arm is still trapped
above me, and something else is pushing into my back. I'm
buried alive, rocks covering my body, trapping me in a
coffin, waiting for me to die so they can consume me, make
me one of them. I thrash— panicking— but finally manage
to flip over onto my back, freeing my arm so I can slip out of
my stone cage.

Dirt and dust scatter. Tiny pebbles shake out of my hair and off my shoulders as I step back, trying to find perspective in the new, bright light.

The space I've escaped is a pile of rocks, and most of them are small, except for two, massive boulders laying side by side. One of the boulders— the one that trapped my arm — is carved into a crook-like shape, with a cutout in the middle like the letter "C." The longer ridge trapped my elbow over my head, but the groove in the middle kept the boulder from crushing me completely.

Something about it makes me want to cry, and suddenly I'm thinking about that doorknob at my old apartment, and all the plans I've made in my life, and how none of them— not one— ever stopped me from getting hurt. This boulder was cut to perfection, pre-destined with me in mind, carved to create space so that I would survive. No amount of planning, no adherence to a pattern, could have saved me from its wrath. Only the Great Everything could do that.

"Thank you," I whisper into the forest— into the Great Everything— because she saved my life.

When I stand, it feels less like an act and more like a resurrection. All my weight moves to my right leg, because something is wrong with the left one, but I won't look at it. If I do, I might decide to quit and let myself die on this ledge, and that would be a poor way to repay the Great Everything. A dark, cranberry stain marks my jeans around the calf area, and even though it's blood, I'm not about to roll the leg of my pants up and investigate the damage.

After making my way back to the line where the ledge meets the mountain, I look up, taking in the distance.

Twenty-five, maybe thirty feet to the top. Climbing down is the more difficult option— I'd have more distance to cover, and would be stranded at the bottom of the ravine, dying a slower, more painful death than a fall. There's no choice but to finish what I've started.

An object juts out from a crevice in the mountain: it's my hiking boot, still stuck in the hole, a sad acknowledgement of my near demise. A rush of gratitude fills my lungs that I didn't double-knot my laces.

At this point, three competing strategies outline the way forward, and none of them is particularly appealing.

In one scenario, I climb up, retrieve my boot, put it on, then continue to the top. This carries with it the risk that my arms give out, the muscles fatigued to exhaustion, leaving me stranded on the ledge or crushed at the bottom of the ravine.

In scenario two, I forget the shoe completely. It stays wedged in the hole while I climb straight to the top, and carry on with my journey as best I can without it. This is problematic, though, seeing as walking through the forest shoeless comes with multiple risks. The least of these is damage to my foot that leads to an infection. The worst is frostbite and loss of toes. It's not snowing— for now— but the bitter, cold rain we had earlier was a warning sign. What if the weather gets worse, and I really, *really* need my shoe? Sure, I have a sock on, but that won't help me if the ground is covered in slush, or if my feet get wet.

Then there's scenario three, where I combine both strategies and head straight for the top, but try to grab my shoe on the way, holding it as I continue the rest of the climb bootless.

Scenario three it is. My hands shake as I approach the mountain, and with every step I instinctively look up, expecting a shower of rocks to fall across my face.

You've already caused one rockslide, I lie to myself. How many more loose boulders could there possibly be?

My body wants to rest, to wait before trying another climb, but my panicked brain associates resting with death. I've gotten myself into a bad situation, and I can't stop until I'm out of it.

The climb begins.

My progress is slower this time, partly because my left leg hangs uselessly at my side, unable to take much weight. I'm sure the damage is bad, but I'll have to deal with it when I get to the top. For now, I focus on using my right leg and my arms. My arms are taking more pressure than I'd hoped, but as long as my body stays close to the mountain, it's not unbearable.

After what feels like a lifetime, I reach the boot. Ignoring it and continuing with my climb is an option, but I can't bring myself to move on without trying, at least once, to get it back.

My body's full weight balances on my good leg and my right hand. When I'm confident in my hold, my left hand to punches at the boot's heel. It wiggles, and if I pull in the right direction, it might just—

Pop!

Freedom. The boot is in my hand, but I can't climb while carrying it. Tying the laces in a knot and stringing the boot over my shoulder might work, expect that I can't do it with just one hand, and my right arm is growing tired, slipping, slipping, with every second that goes by.

Inaction is a choice, too, and if I don't do something soon, I'll fall. Left without any other options, I open up my mouth and bite down on the tongue of the boot. My left hand returns to the mountain and my muscles sigh with relief. The climb continues, the boot in my mouth, which is arranged in a permanent snarl.

Hand over hand, one move at a time, with slow and

steady progress, my fingers reach up and finally touch soil; horizontal Earth.

I've made it.

I pull myself over the edge of the mountain, rolling onto my back, heart pounding as my jaw relaxes, dropping the shoe onto the ground beside me like a dog letting go of a bone.

I've never appreciated a shoe so much.

There's something romantic about this, but I can't quite put my finger on what it is. Then, it comes to me.

I am the world's most pathetic Cinderella.

13

I t's a long time before I work up the courage to look at my leg.

I prepare myself for the worst-case scenario, visualizing every possible horror. Bone that pokes through skin. Flesh rippling over pink meat, flush and ripe in its exposure. An intricate network of stretchy tendons and veins, recoiling from the harsh bite of air. By the time I roll up the bottom of my jeans, I know that whatever I find there won't be worse than the carnage I've imagined.

The jeans get stuck above my ankle— I'll have to take them off to investigate the wound. I know better than to wear skinny jeans on a camping trip, but it was my first vacation with Mike, and skinny jeans are the only things that make my boyish butt look curvy.

Before this trip went off the rails, I envisioned a picture-worthy, idyllic romp in the woods— hence the logic behind wearing my ass-lifting skinny jeans. I even thought we'd recreate that much blogged-about photo series where the girl with impossibly perfect hair leads her boyfriend around the world by the hand.

Now— as I strip off my pants and try not to cry out at the way the denim peels off the meaty, searing wound on my leg — that vision seems like something from another lifetime. I'm not a perfectly coifed catalog model leading Mike through the forest in pristine, romantic bliss. No, I'm a raging lunatic chasing him down the side of a mountain, screaming in terror, my hair matted with soil, my face streaked with dirt. Appearances are last on my list of concerns, and the fact that I ever worried about what I looked like strikes me as the kind of random factoid you'd find in a trivia book.

Did you know that elephants are the only animals that can't jump?! Also, Zoe used to worry about what she looked like!

My breath crystallizes in the air. Today is the coldest I've experienced in the valley, and my skin can't be exposed to the elements for too long.

My jeans land in a crumpled pile as I toss them aside to look at my leg. The wound isn't deep— there's no bone visible— but the length of the injury takes me by surprise. Most of the pain up until this point has been focused on my shin area, but the cut wraps straight down my leg and around the left side of my calf. The rock must have slammed into my shin first, then scraped its way toward my heel. My shin is black and blue, but my calf looks worse— the skin has been stripped away, revealing the pink, bloody flesh underneath. It's begging for an infection, but Sue has taught me well. I open my pack and remove a few of the leaves she salvaged, laying them on top of the wound like garnish on a steak. The rest, I place gently back in my pack, saving them for future injuries that now seem inevitable.

Thinking of Sue makes my heart hurt, but I can't do anything but focus on the task at hand.

Please let them be okay.

Focus allows images to come, thoughts of Sue, Ken, and Logan safely at the resort, all three of them sharing a meal, telling rangers where to find me.

"She went South at Tenaya Lake," I picture Sue saying in her exact, scientific way, "Send a helicopter, and search dogs. Bring her a cheeseburger too."

My hands shake as they rummage through my pack, looking for anything to bandage my calf. The map, the compass, the letter, granola bars, my canteen— nothing helpful materializes, until I find two extra pairs of socks. I'd forgotten I'd packed them. They're fraying at the edges and the toes are stained, but they tie perfectly in a knot, creating a bandage around my injury. When I put my jeans back on, the fact that they're tighter than any other pair I own turns out to be a blessing in disguise— the pressure alleviates some pain.

Stopping to clean the injury would've been smart, but the idea of pouring icy water over an open wound makes me want to pass out. Instead, I search for a walking stick, settling on a fallen branch that ends in a pitchfork-inspired split. It looks like a trident— when it's flipped upside down, the forked end digs into the earth as I move.

No one would believe it by looking at the visible damage, but my shin hurts so much more than my calf that I wonder if I've fractured the bone. Nothing but an x-ray will tell me, and there's no clinic to visit out here in the wild.

A quick consultation of the map, a glance at my compass, and the journey begins again. As I push my way through the forest, running on nothing but fumes and refusal to fail, the forest leans in like I'm something worth watching. Taft point is only hours away, and the wind carries the scent of answers on its wings, promising me this will be worth it.

My staff hits the ground and I'm making good time even though my gait is uneven. As I walk, I picture myself as a curmudgeonly recluse with secret powers who's leaving her cabin in the forest to save the planet from some unnamed forces of darkness. I'm like a cross between Gandalf and La Femme Nikita.

I think again about that photo series of the girl leading her boyfriend around the world, and even though my version isn't as pretty, or as photo-shopped, I can't help but smile.

This is so much more badass than that.

HOURS OF HOBBLING LATER, and I'm standing on the edge of a precipice at Taft Point, which overlooks the entirety of Yosemite backcountry.

My arms stretch out to the side— fingers open wide— taking in the boundless beauty in front of me. Sometimes big things have a way of making a person feel small, but I'm so high up that size is just a concept. All things are small, even the largest ones. Under the shadow of the mountain, the valley carves into the earth like a thumbprint, leaving pine trees and rock formations as forensic evidence. A river weaves through the trees; a single thread holding together the fabric of the forest. A pair of red-tailed hawks spirals in the air, the sun glinting off the edges of their wings. It must affect them, seeing the world from on high, making them wiser than us.

I try to guess how far it is to the bottom of the valley, but I settle for "thousands"— thousands of what, I'm not sure. Feet? Meters? Years? I'm staring into the eye of the Great Everything, and in her irises I see certainty, and trees painted like matchsticks in a box, and the glint of sunlight off the edge of a miniature lake. Her pupils are the wide open sun, and she tells me to find the light that always was and will always be. She promises it's in this moment, and I want to catch it like a butterfly, but it only lands on me when I stay still.

The sun dips below the mountains, bouncing pinks and purples off a sky coated in clouds, and in this place— this infinite, cascading, achingly indescribable piece of nature— I'm not sure how a person doesn't believe in God. I understand the mechanisms, but crediting the means with the result seems like blaming the paintbrush for the painting. I'm an astronaut seeing the Earth from outer space for the first time, and it's as if I've learned to speak a new language. What used to be gibberish, is now poetry, made clear. The words are different, but the message is consistent: you are a part of the Great Everything, and the Great Everything is a part of you.

This is what they call an overview.

It grounds me in the core of myself, the center of my being. I won't return home the same.

I hope Mike likes his new girlfriend when he meets her.

A step forward and the ground beneath my feet disappears, making me feel like I'm floating on thin air. A cold wind whips past my ears, and I swear I smell Mike on its edges. I'm close to him. I can detect his presence like a bloodhound following a trail.

I move away from the ledge and start searching the mountain for Cassandra's purported clue. I have no idea what I'm looking for, but it's here. It has to be. Whatever it is, I need to find it before the sun sets and the light disappears, making my search all but impossible until morning.

I stumble around for awhile, checking trees, bushes, and

cracks in the rocks for any sign of another clue. At first, nothing— but then, the landscape changes into alien territory, and I know exactly where Cassandra has hidden the clue.

The Fissures. Brock described the unusual geological feature on the first day of our tour, but his words didn't do the Fissures justice.

A flat piece of land extends in front of me, its surface wrinkled and broken like the top of an over-baked cake. Cracks in the Earth zig-zag into the distance, as if someone slammed a mallet into the ground. The crevices vary in size — some are as thin as my ring finger, others are wide enough to swallow me whole. Slivers of reliable Earth weave between the cracks, but one misstep could mean death.

It's a maze. The perfect place for Cassandra to hide a clue.

I approach with caution, stopping at the first fissure and peering over the maze. I try to count the fissures, but stop when I get to fifty. They fall into three distinct types; the first is narrow, so thin as to be harmless. The second is enormous, big enough that I could tumble to my death if I slipped and fell inside. The third is combination of the first two— narrow in some spots and wide in others.

Standing on my tippy-toes gives me a better view, and I can almost see the entirety of the labyrinth, crevices of varying size weaving over each other like tangled vines. It's a game of eye-spy, and I'm looking for anything to designate the center of the maze, some flag telling me where I'm supposed to go. At first, nothing registers, but then I notice a familiar object poking out from a fissure deep in the center of the maze. It's blue, and warm, and cost seventy-nine dollars; I know, because I bought it.

It's the sleeve of Mike's windbreaker.

For one terrible moment, I think he might be down there, dying or already dead. But the fear fades when I remember that Cassandra is a predator; a cat who likes to play with her food before she eats it. An ending this abrupt would hardly satiate her. She'll want to watch the mouse run the maze before she eats its.

The fissure I need to reach is smack-dab in the center of the jagged labyrinth, and reaching it will require me to find the least hazardous route. The crevices look like lightning bolts carved into the Earth. It's as if someone has turned my brain inside out and spread it across the mountain, tangled and broken, neural pathways tripping over each other to try and make sense of the world.

There's no option but to step over the fissures. I pick the path of least resistance and pray I can make it there and back again before the sun dips below the horizon.

Using my good leg and the walking stick, I step from space to space, holding my breath as I hop over each fissure. Some are deeper than others, but they generally go so far into the Earth as to fade into nothing but darkness. A few of the gaps are big enough that I could fall inside and never be heard from again. I take my time with those. It's hard to gain perspective in the middle of the labyrinth, because the ground changes its elevation depending on the location. When the higher elevations emerge, I seize the chance to track my progress, standing again on the edges of my feet, keeping my eye on Mike's jacket.

Finally, I reach the fissure in question and kneel down beside it, stretching out to touch Mike's windbreaker. It emerges from the crevice like an artifact being stripped from a tomb. The jacket feels strange in my hands, a relic from a time and place I can't go back to.

I hold it close to me and sit with it for a minute, like it's a life preserver in the middle of the ocean.

The day I bought it was a Tuesday— I remember, because Mike's birthday was just a week away. My gift to him was a replacement for his old college jacket, faded and unraveling, dying a little bit each day, but difficult to find a substitute for.

Every kind of store was visited in the quest for a replacement. Trendy coat shops in the weaving streets of West Hollywood. The bland, sterile men's section of every department store in the Westfield mall. Finally, I found it, at an unassuming outlet in the valley, owned by a proprietor with a mustache who followed customers around in case he could "answer any questions."

The jacket was a robin's-egg blue, and nothing special at first glance, but then the store's owner showed me how the hood detached, and the pockets were made for particular items; one for sunglasses, one for a water bottle, one with a leash for keys.

There was something joyful about the way the jacket fully prepared its owner for any situation, and the spirit of it all reminded me of Mike, maybe because he leaps so willingly into everything life has to offer.

When he unwrapped the packaging— newspapers tied with a rafia bow, because I'm not the best at gift-wrapping— Mike loved it immediately. He wore it every day for weeks, and his old college jacket fell by the wayside, retired to a box at the bottom of our closet.

It was a gift with thought put into it, something I worried about and searched for, because I was trying to use an action to say everything I couldn't with words. The fact that Mike liked it made me feel like I knew him, like maybe I was reading him right, and there was no hidden part of him hiding in shadows, lying in wait for the chance to bite me. He loved it so much he didn't even want to take it to Yosemite, because he was worried about it getting ruined. A cog turns in my brain.

He didn't pack it.

Mike didn't bring this jacket with him. Cassandra was in our house. There's no other explanation.

Something flips in my stomach, and suddenly I'm angry. Angry at Mike, for leaving the jacket at home. Angry at Cassandra, for violating us. Angry at myself, for suggesting this trip in the first place.

I turn the jacket over in my hands and pull at the fabric, wanting to rip it to shreds. It represents a life I can't go back to; one that's been stolen from me. The longer I'm surrounded by the wilderness, the more it consumes me, erasing the avatar of who I used to be, returning me to my most pristine, unaltered self. Being in the wild has made me a wild thing, and I wonder if the world at large will make room for my new temperament. I'm not the same woman I was when I started this trip, and I'd venture to guess that Mike feels different, too.

A possibility enters my mind, as dark and foreboding as the bottom of a fissure. What if Mike and I somehow survive this, only to find that we don't want to be together anymore?

It's a very human concern.

I push it away, because I'm not a normal human anymore. I'm part of the Earth, and the Great Everything. My mind shuts down— driven to inactivity by loneliness— so I listen instead to my inner wolf, who focuses only on the present moment. She's overcome by a howling, scratching desire to be reunited with her pack, and I know that even in the most animal parts of me, I recognize Mike as someone I'm meant to be with.

A clapping, roaring sound echoes across the valley. At first I think it might have come from inside my chest, but then I realize it's something external. I look up, and a flash of light streaks across the bloody sky. Droplets fall on my cheeks like tears, as if the Earth feels the same way I do.

First comes thunder, then lightning, then: Rain.

The water will turn the edges of the fissures into slippery blades, smooth in the moonlight, treacherous and deadly. My return trip through the labyrinth will require me to navigate a sea of gaping holes, always one step away from death. Leaving now— while there's still enough light out to illuminate my path— is my only shot at making it out alive.

The jacket shakes in my hands as I turn it upside down, searching for the next clue. Something falls out of a side pocket— the one meant for sunglasses— bouncing off the ground and almost tumbling into a fissure, where it would be lost forever. I manage to grab it before it disappears over the edge. It's cold and familiar against my fingertips. My heart skips a beat.

I'm holding Mike's cell phone.

It's turned off— most likely to preserve the battery life— but when it's turned it on, I'll find Cassandra's next clue, waiting.

I'm about to power it up, but then the sun disappears behind the horizon, plunging the world into darkness, heavy and final, like a period at the end of a sentence.

I'm suspended in the blackness— frozen in the absence of light. The beauty I experienced earlier is replaced by primal fear.

Lightning burns across the sky, briefly illuminating the

treacherous route back, carved with fissures that I won't be able to see in the night. I'm surrounded, trapped in a death-labyrinth with no way out.

The flash of light disappears. Darkness swallows me whole.

14

———

There are no stars tonight. There is no moon.

All that exists is the darkness, and a gunmetal grey expanse of clouds that blankets the valley with caution. Every creature lies in wait. Birds confine themselves to their trees. Gophers hide in their holes. Where there once was movement, now, all beasts are still.

Except for one.

I scratch my way across the first fissure, holding my flashlight in my mouth, crawling on my hands and knees through the labyrinth. The rocks are soaked with water, and rain beats down upon the Earth in a relentless surge.

The other animals watch me from their hiding spots, wondering why I don't stay still, why I won't wait out the storm.

I want to tell them it's because I'm afraid. My claws are new, and not as sharp as theirs. My ears are large, but freshly grown. If the rain overtakes me and I fall into a fissure, I may never climb my way out. My only hope is to escape the maze, to find my way back to the start.

I progress on four legs, returning to my origins in more

ways than one, traveling in the way I first learned to— as a child.

I crawl sideways, and the process takes so long that being on four legs begins to feel normal, as if I was made to walk this way. Navigating my way around fissure after fissure, I work backwards, remembering my path to the maze's center and reversing it.

My movements are timed by the lightning. My eyes scan the fissures when it strikes, seizing the opportunity to make a mental map of the landscape. I'm not human anymore, but a beast, focused only on the present moment and nothing else, nothing abstract, just the tangible world and my place within it.

I'm almost in the clear when it happens. My hand moves to make contact with solid ground, but finds nothing except open air. The sensation of falling fills my lungs, and for a terrible moment I think I've stumbled into the second kind of fissure— the kind that can swallow me whole— but then my downward motion stops. I'm not dead. At least, not yet.

I'm positioned partially inside a gaping crevice, my upper body trapped in a vacuum that's sucking me downward, a black hole attempting to swallow me. I try to pull my arm back, but the fissure is like quicksand. My shoulder won't budge. Another bolt of lightning illuminates the Earth, revealing that I'm trapped in the third type of fissure; uneven and varied in size. It widens in certain areas, but the portion I'm stuck in is surprisingly narrow. In the rain, the fissure is an animal trap— easy to slip into and hard to escape. My arm is buried up to the shoulder, and no amount of pulling sets it free. Thrashing upward makes no difference— my arm won't budge. Chewing it off seems like the only option.

I lean into the Great Everything, asking her to help me, and she whispers the word *"move"* in my ear.

But I can't move. I'm trapped, not just in this fissure, but in a way of being. I've walked through the world in a cage built by others, forgoing the most basic, primal pieces of myself to gain the approval of others. I don't want to die before I've found the real me. I won't be ready to go until I shake her hand and look her in the eyes. That day will come, but that day is not today.

Move, the Great Everything says again.

Another upward pull, but my arm won't budge. A second bolt of lightning flashes across the sky, illuminating the length of the fissure, which cuts against the mountain in a jagged, uneven line.

An uneven line.

Suddenly, I know what the Great Everything wants me to do. My breathing slows. My heart rate lowers. I'm not afraid anymore, because the Great Everything wants to help me. My mind works in conjunction with my instincts, and suddenly I'm both beast and woman, all pieces of myself orchestrating the next steps, together.

The Great Everything's instructions are followed: I move. Not upward this time, but horizontally along the length of the fissure.

First, I pull my arm backward, but the fissure is too narrow for me to make any progress. Pushing in the opposite direction works better, even though the space is tighter than where I am now.

It's counter-intuitive, but the wolf within me senses it's the way out, even if my mind resists. My opposite hand searches, feeling across the gap in the Earth; it gets narrower before it gets wider, but if I can squeeze my arm through the thinnest piece, I'll find my way to freedom.

My mind is satisfied. This is the way out. With much squeezing and scratching, I'm able to push my arm deeper into the narrow line. The jagged edge of the fissure scrapes against my arm, but I don't cry out, because emotion can't exist here, in this calm, quiet, well of necessity.

I push again, focusing on what I stand to gain; it's a birth, a new start, a chance to do everything all over again, as my new, cohesive self, part animal and part human, integrated pieces joining together to make a whole.

Just when I don't think I can move any further, my arm pops into the wider segment and out from the fissure. I sit back, soaked, wiping rain from my face, cradling my scraped arm.

The climb across the fissures continues, carefully, as I feel my way through the rest of the maze. Fissure after fissure lands behind me: the exit must be close. I'm nearly there. Soon, the Earth is smooth, devoid of cracks, absent of flaws. I think I might have made it, but I'm afraid to stand in case I'm wrong. It's best to wait for light. Minutes pass, and another flash of light illuminates the mountain— the labyrinth is gone, and the ground in front of me is nothing but solid rock.

I've reached the end of the maze. A smart mouse.

Cradling my scraped arm, I run toward hazy trees in the distance, hoping to find shelter.

A cluster of branches appears, and I crouch underneath them, shivering in my wet clothes. The trees grow close enough together to offer decent protection from the rain. A new home for the mouse. After wringing out my wet jacket, I create a makeshift umbrella by hanging it between two boughs. Then, Mike's windbreaker wraps around my shoulders, fitting loose and warm like the day I tried it on in that store.

A deep craving for warmth makes me consider lighting a fire, but the sticks around me are too wet. There's no choice but to wait out the rain, trusting that the Great Everything will lead me onward when the time is right. She's saved my life twice now— she must have plans for me.

A disjointed bible verse plays in my head, but I can't get the words quite right, or remember who said it. It doesn't matter though, because the feeling is the same, and I know what the Great Everything is trying to tell me.

You matter.

There's a puddle next to me, and for a second I think I see Brock's face in it. I whip around, expecting to find him standing right behind me, but there's no one there— just a vast expanse of forest. The figure in the puddle was my own reflection, gaunt and hungry, a woman on a mission.

The phone.

I pull it from the pocket of Mike's windbreaker. It's a little wet from the rain, but Mike has one of those military-style, unbreakable phone cases from the commercials geared toward men. *"Run it over with a truck! Flush it down the toilet! Light it on fire! The phone you're going to replace in a year anyway will be just fine."*

Holding down a button on the side makes an Apple logo appear. I'm an Android user who refuses to convert to an iPhone, if only because it's what everyone else has. Mike, in contrast, has never had a problem liking what everyone else likes.

Mike's lock-screen is a picture of two cups of coffee, both with impressive foam art on top. The day he took it, we'd stopped at a café in Silverlake— one of many. You can't walk a block in Silverlake without finding yet another funky coffee shop, usually featuring books on the walls, or light fixtures made from broken beer bottles. This particular cafe set itself apart with succulents; cacti of every kind dripping from the ceiling, in the center of each table, perched on the cash register. The barista who made our coffees was monastic in his focus, painting matching foam swans on both coffees like he was working on the Sistine Chapel.

"Do you care that we're going to destroy these?" I asked him, pointing to the intricate loops of white on top of my drink.

"That's the best part about it," the Barista answered, stroking his goatee, "Just because something's temporary, doesn't mean it wasn't important. It made you smile, right?"

I nodded. It did.

"You guys make a cute couple," the Barista added, taking for granted that Mike and I were together. I was about to correct him, to tell him we hadn't had the big "talk" yet and that we were just dating, but Mike jumped in before I had the chance.

"Thanks," he said, "She's the better-looking half."

It was so simple for Mike to define us that way; with no anxiety, no fear. Mike entered our relationship naturally and with ease, as if he'd never been hurt before.

At least, that's how I saw it at the time. The picture of our matching cups of coffee— so preciously saved, so intentionally taken— hints at a need for reassurance, a cataloging of moments. "They both had swans on their coffee," the photo seems to say, "... so they belong together. They're the same." Maybe Mike feels the gap between us sometimes, too.

I type in Mike's code and his phone unlocks.

My breath catches in my throat. There's a blinking icon in the upper left-hand corner where the signal strength usually is. Mike has a different carrier than me, and maybe — just, maybe— their satellites can find me at this higher altitude. Cassandra is probably too strategic not to have thought about the potential for a signal, but still, it's worth a try.

The screen blinks. Two words appear:

No signal.

The revelation makes my heart sink, but there's no time to indulge disappointment: I need to find the next clue.

Where would Cassandra hide it?

I debate between opening notes or text messages first, then settle on starting with text messages. Cassandra would want my discovery of the clue to feel personal, and might have typed it as a draft in her conversation with Mike.

A tap on the blue speech bubble and Mike's text messages open. Cassandra is the most recent person to have written him. Their conversation fills the screen. Mike has put two bright, red "X" emojis at the start and end of Cassandra's name, as if to say "proceed with caution."

My breath hangs in the air, frozen and heavy. Rain pounds against my makeshift umbrella, and a buzzing noise fills my ears.

This can't be right.

My makeshift umbrella-jacket sinks a little, causing rain to drizzle over the side. I don't move to fix it, though, because I'm too busy staring at the screen.

I don't know who kidnapped Mike. But it isn't Cassandra.

 **W**EDNESDAY, November 5th

5:45PM Xx **CASSANDRA** xx: Hey jellybean. How are you?

THURSDAY, November 6th

10:13AM Xx **CASSANDRA** xx: Sorry to bug you. Had the craziest dream last night & it made me think of u.

7:28PM Xx **CASSANDRA**xx: Drove by your place on the way home from work. Did you see me?

. . .

7:35ᴘᴍ Xx **CASSANDRA**xx: No car outside but the lights are on. Zoe must be home. I bet she misses you when you're gone.

8:02ᴘᴍ **XXCASSANDRA**xx: I know I always did. :)

THURSDAY, November 7th

12:30ᴀ.ᴍ. **XXCASSANDRA**xx: Did you tell Zoe about me?

1:37ᴀᴍ **XXCASSANDRA**xx: Did you tell her what happened?

2:32ᴀᴍ **MIKE:** Cass— Next time you drive by our place I'm calling the cops. I don't want to, but I will.

2:33ᴀᴍ **XXCASSANDRA**xx: I like the flowers you planted.

2:45ᴀᴍ **XXCASSANDRA**xx: That's it?

3:15ᴀᴍ **XXCASSANDRA**xx: Are you there?

. . .

4:23AM **XXCASSANDRA**xx: Do you ever wonder if we would still be together? If things hadn't gone the way they did that day?

6:55AM **XXCASSANDRA**xx: Fine. Don't answer me.

7:00AM **XXCASSANDRA**xx: Remember when I said it wasn't your fault?

7:01AM **XXCASSANDRA**xx: It WAS your fault.

7:02AM **XXCASSANDRA**xx: Everything.

7:24AM **XXCASSANDRA**xx: You ruined my life.

11:08PM **XXCASSANDRA**xx: I'm sorry.

11:09PM **XXCASSANDRA**xx: I didn't mean it.

11:45PM **XXCASSANDRA**xx: Please answer me.

. . .

<u>FRIDAY, November 8th</u>

9:30PM **XXCASSANDRA**xx: Drove by your house twice today. Couldn't tell if you were home.

11:05PM **XXCASSANDRA**xx: Parked outside across the street.

11:35PM **XXCASSANDRA**xx: Mike?

12:53PM **XXCASSANDRA**xx: Still here.

12:54PM **XXCASSANDRA**xx: Where are you guys?

<u>SATURDAY, November 9th</u>

1:02 AM **XXCASSANDRA**xx: Fell asleep in my car.

1:05 AM **XXCASSANDRA**xx: I'll stay the night.

1:07 **XXCASSANDRA**xx: I miss you.

. . .

3 A.M. **XXCASSANDRA**xx: Could you look out the window, please? So I know you see me.

3:23AM **XXCASSANDRA**xx: Do you see me?

4:30AM **XXCASSANDRA**xx: Do you see me?

5:38AM **XXCASSANDRA**xx: Do you?

AIR ENTERS MY LUNGS, but the oxygen isn't getting to my brain. It congeals in my throat, making the forest spin and my fingers tingle. My makeshift umbrella-jacket is completely overflowing now, but I'm only vaguely aware of the water streaming down my face.

It couldn't have been her.

Forgetting where I am, I move to stand and head into the kitchen to make myself a cup of tea — my habit in anxious times, although I never really drink the tea. It's more about the process of making it. But there is no kitchen, no tea, no honey, no milk. Just dark trees, dripping branches, and a bitter taste on my tongue that I can't wash away.

Everything is upside down.

I turn my umbrella-jacket over to empty out the water that's collected, then crawl back underneath it and pick up Mike's phone, scrolling through the messages a second time, looking for anything I might have missed. Some pivotal piece of information that will turn my world right-side up again. Nothing new appears. The facts stay the same, confirming what I always knew deep in my gut.

Cassandra didn't do it.

She was outside our house at 3 a.m. on Saturday morning. Our first night in Yosemite— the night someone pinned a photo to our tent with the word "DEAD" scrawled across its surface— was Friday evening.

While Mike and I were trying to convince Brock to search the forest for Cassandra, she was sleeping in her car, outside our house in Silverlake— a seven-hour drive from the valley.

It couldn't have been her.

But I *want* it to be her, because Cassandra is a known entity; one I've always felt strangely comfortable with. The notes she leaves in the mailbox, the perfume she sprays on their envelopes— all of it's familiar, from a friend. If she's not the one doing this to us, then this is the work of some darker, chaotic, random evil, some wickedness I can't understand, can't decode.

I need it to be her.

My brain runs wild, trying to close the gap between what I want to believe and what's true. It's cognitive dissonance, and it allows us to believe things that aren't real, but I don't care— right now, it's a survival technique. The pieces are in front of me, and if I can solve the puzzle, I'll explain how Cassandra might have achieved the impossible and been in two places at once.

Maybe she's working with someone.

It's a theory that might answer some logistical problems, but it's not realistic. Even though I've never met her, I feel like I know Cassandra. I imagine her quirks, the way she might wring her hands while she talks, the loose, sad way her hair hangs by her face. Cassandra would never reach out to a stranger and trust them with a task that involves Mike. She loves him too much, and she would consider the risk involved. If it went South, she would never forgive herself. Not to mention that hiring a professional killer requires a job, and money— two things Cassandra can't seem to hold onto.

Leaves crunch under my boots. Without realizing it, I've stood up to pace. I'm out in the rain again and my injured leg feels like it's on fire, but I ignore it, because right now I need to move, need to think, need to breathe.

Maybe she wasn't really outside our house.

A scroll to the last text message reveals a selfie, taken by Cassandra, her close-mouthed smile highlighted by the jaunty tilt of her head. It's not a sexy selfie— there's no attempt at duck-lips, no blouse opened to reveal just the right amount of cleavage. It's the kind of picture you'd send to a friend to let her know you're outside, waiting to pick her up. Harmless, hardly the work of a cold-blooded killer. She's behind the wheel of her car, and the house behind her by is marked by ugly, canary-yellow paint on the front door. It's our neighbor, Mr. Henderson's house, and if he knew Cassandra was parked there, he'd be furious. Mr. Henderson is the self-appointed watchdog of all street parking in our neighborhood. The color of his door stands out in my mind, if only because it matches the sickly, jaundiced tinge to the whites of his eyes.

The picture's not staged: she's definitely outside our house.

She could have taken the picture before she got here, and waited to send it as an alibi.

A more in-depth scroll of their text conversation reveals Cassandra's love of selfies.

Normally excessive selfies would make me dislike a

person, but Cassandra's are so well-intentioned it's hard to hold it against her.

Picture after picture appears; Cassandra eating lunch, holding a glass of wine with the caption, "my new favorite red!"

Cassandra outside the window of a pet store, pointing to a puppy with her free hand, wearing a look on her face that seems to say, *"Remember?,"* which makes me wonder if they ever owned a dog together.

Cassandra curled up by a fireplace in flannel pajamas, reading a book, her hands up in a shrug that suggests she's not sure if she likes it yet. None of the pictures were taken out of vanity, but from some desire to share her life with a person. Her desperation to be noticed is so tangible that it burns through the phone, jagged and smokey, a blaze of desire.

The picture from Friday night isn't an excuse, or an alibi. It's right in line with Cassandra's typical modus operandi. It would be more suspicious if she *hadn't* sent a selfie.

Not to mention, if she'd waited until she reached the valley, the picture might not have gone through at all. My reception disappeared the moment we got into backcountry, just as Brock said it would. Mike faired a little better, but he still lost all service by Saturday morning, when he couldn't look up the weather.

"Look at the sky, there's your weather!" Brock had said to him, rolling his eyes as if he was one more city-boy away from quitting his job entirely and moving off the grid, presumably to a cabin where he'd grow his own food, compost his waste into fertilizer, and never have to speak to another person again. It's jarring to think that Brock isn't alive anymore, and I imagine that he's still out there somewhere, wandering through the forest and muttering about useless city-folk.

The time on the selfie reads: 3:08 a.m., Saturday morning. My phone had already stopped working at that point. Obviously Mike still had service, because he was able to get the messages, but there's no guarantee Cassandra's phone would have been so operational out here in the forest.

Mike still had service.

Something about that last point strikes me as sticky and warm, like taffy in the sun. What if Mike sent himself the messages, from a second number?

Ken's words echo in my ears, but I can't allow myself to indulge them.

Mike would never do this to me. It can't be him.

I'm feverish again, but this time, there's no flush to my skin. The rising heat is simply a sign that the spider has returned to knit cobwebs over boxes and scrapbooks— the things in my brain I don't open.

I look at the selfie one more time— noting the hope in her face, the openness in her eyes— and suddenly I feel guilty for blaming her for all of this. My initial instinct was right: Cassandra is harmless. I re-read her messages, going back to the section I didn't understand.

XXCASSANDRAxx: It was your fault.

XXCASSANDRAxx: You ruined my life.

What was his fault?

My legs curl up underneath me as I pull Mike's windbreaker tighter around my shoulders, wondering if my journey across the wilderness has been a quest for a liar. The cold makes me shake, and even though it kills me to do it, I pile leaves over my body to try and insulate myself, thinking of Brock's corpse the entire time.

My body grows heavy. Sleep calls, but I don't answer because my heart is beating too hard, making me wish I didn't have one. Then I'm thinking about the cowardly lion, and I picture myself as a strange kind of Dorothy, talking to the wicked witch of the west, who tells me I have it all wrong — she's been good this whole time. Her face is Cassandra's face, and she's holding my hands. She tells me not to go see the wizard, because he turned her skin green, and he'll do the same thing to me, if I let him. She says people can survive almost any yellow-brick-road, no matter how arduous or painful, if they know *why* they're doing it, if they know what reward is waiting for them when they get to Oz.

She asks me what I think is waiting for me, and I tell her I don't know, but my leg hurts, and I'm sad, and I wish she would stop looking at me that way— like she's keeping a secret under her witch's hat, and I won't know what it is until it jumps out and bites me.

"What are you hiding under there?" I ask her, pointing at her hat. But she just smiles and says, "You'll never know, if you don't ask."

"I *did* ask—" I start to say, but then Cassandra-Witch waves a hand and suddenly my tongue ties itself in a knot.

"Go ahead, *ask!*" she says, laughing because she knows I can't.

I'm about to run away, and I've already turned— my legs preparing to take me anywhere else— but then I stop, because I realize I've forgotten what I am. I'm a wolf, and wolves don't let others bind their tongues.

My four legs pound the Earth, and instead of running away, I charge at Cassandra-Witch. My haunches contract as I launch myself into the air— jaws open wide— and in one smooth motion, I rip the hat off her head.

She screams, and for a moment her face turns into Mike's face, but then I look closer and realize the face was mine, all along. I'm looking into myself, seeing my own image reversed, not as it looks in a mirror, but the way other people see it. My nose is misshapen, my eyes uneven. I want to ask myself why I did this to us, but I can't because wolves don't speak.

I grab the witch's hat— my hat— with my teeth and flip it over to see what's inside, but all I find is a dark crevice, deep like the fissures, sucking me inward to a bottomless darkness with no end.

16

———

The sun wakes me up, placing her warm hand on my cheek, causing me to turn over and sigh. It's stopped raining, and the forest drips with potential for new life, soon-to-be-flowers shivering under the soil, waiting for their chance to emerge into being.

The leaves I used to insulate myself fall off my body as I rise, making me into a tree, shaking herself clean from fall into winter. The taste of a new day clings to the air. I bend down and examine the wound on my shin. It's turned a strange color— a cranberry charcoal shade— but it hurts less, and I can walk on it without support, so I have to assume nothing's broken.

Last night, I'd considered turning back and heading for the resort at Tenaya Lake, where I'd be met with a hot meal and a radio. Everything I'm fighting for has been inverted and tarnished: Cassandra isn't the villain, Mike ruined her life, and he's definitely, without a doubt, been lying to me.

But now, in the warm glow of the morning sun, it's clear: I'm not doing this just for Mike. I'm doing it for *me.*

I've spent so much time looking for the monster in

others, that I've lost touch with pieces of myself. I want to dig them up, to unearth them, and try again. There are bits of me— shredded, ripped bits— that operate independently from the parts I can control. They sneak through the shadows and whisper thoughts in my ear. They make me love broken door-knobs, and put leases in my name. They're the worst pieces of who I am, and when I try to track them down— scanning my veins, unspooling my insides— I can't find them anywhere.

I don't know how to dig them up, except to continue heading deeper into the wild, in the hope that the Great Everything might turn me into the original version of myself, untarnished by darkness.

Already, the wild has seeped into my skin, leaving new shades of being behind, creating an unbridled immediacy to all of my needs.

It's made me a person who *takes* what she needs, and right now, that's answers. I think of all the times in my life I've been called selfish, and I smile and nod. Yes, selfish. That's me.

The witch's hat must be turned over.

I'm a wild thing now, and I need to find the person who did this to us. It doesn't matter who it is.

My hands move so quickly that my bag practically repacks itself. Water soaks the ground as I wring out my wet jacket, its fibers stretching when I tie it to my pack to dry throughout the day.

Ahead of me, light peaks through the trees, along with a chance to find warmth. I leave the shade of the forest behind and push toward rockier landscape. A cluster of boulders is perched further up the mountain, their edges already absorbing the morning light. I pick the biggest rock, and stretch out across it like a lizard in the sun.

After soaking up the stillness, I unlock Mike's phone again— but this time I go straight to "Notes."

The next clue is the only note saved on Mike's phone.

It's there, waiting for me, so I reach out and take it, my nose in the air, teeth-barred, every piece of me hungry for the way forward.

~

CONGRATULATIONS, dirty thing
You've made it to
The second ring!
Grab ahold
And hang on tight;
The way gets harder
When you fight.
Set the cycle,
Break the plate—
Clean away
The mess you ate.
This place lies
Between two cliffs;
Detergent is
its hieroglyph.
So wash those dishes,
Wash them well,
and look out for
A hefty swell.
Hold your breath
and search for red!
Find it quick,
Or else he's dead.

IT TAKES me a second to connect to the poem's theme. It's referencing something distant; an activity from my previous life.

Break the plate... set the cycle...

Washing dishes. Out here in the wilderness, there's no such thing as a dish. The kidnapper— whoever it is— must have written this in advance, if only because being immersed in nature to this extent changes a person's mind-set. When presented with infinite natural beauty as inspiration, even the worst poet in the world wouldn't resort to talking about dishes.

Detergent is its hieroglyph.

The word "Hieroglyph"is out of place in the context of the rest of the poem, which adds importance to its presence. It wouldn't be there if it didn't *have* to be there. The word evokes images of Egyptians and pyramids. Maybe I'm supposed to look for a pictograph somewhere, carved into a tree or painted on a rock. But then I remember what a Hieroglyph actually *is:* it's a symbol conferring meaning, with one thing standing in the place of another.

My legs criss-cross. I sit up and dig through my pack, pulling out my map of the valley and searching through the various landmarks, looking for anything related to the word "detergent." Hundreds of points of interest are marked by minute font and tiny icons. I'm afraid to miss something important, so I break my search into tiny sections, starting at the upper left hand corner. With every landmark eliminated, my pulse quickens.

What if I can't solve this clue, and I never get to stand face-to-face across from the person who did this to us?

For some reason, leaving the backcountry without

answers seems like the worst possible outcome now—
worse, even, then falling to my death in the ravine, or starv-
ing, or catching hypothermia in the night and allowing
sweet oblivion to take over as my organs shut down . The
opportunity to face my attacker— to show him that I'm
more than what he bargained for— is an essential survival
ingredient, on par with water, or air. This wild, new person
I've become, this most animal me, won't endure beyond the
borders of the valley unless I seal my transformation with a
poisonous kiss. If I don't find resolution, the new me will
melt away, leaving behind the familiar husk of who I used to
be. I want to take my enemy by the throat and make him
understand that he's pissed off a lion dressed as a lamb, not
because I need to convince *him* of the permanence of my
transformation, but because I need to prove it to myself.

My finger stops at a landmark represented by three wavy
lines— but it's not the icon that has my attention. It's the
words underneath it, the name of the spot: "Bunnel
Cascade."

I don't know what 'Bunnel' means. It could be the name
of a person— like the first man to mark the place on a map.
I imagine him as a self-righteous explorer in colonial wig,
claiming his discovery without regard to the people who
knew of its existence generations before his arrival. Or,
maybe, 'Bunnel' is the name of some famous person way
back in history, and the falls were christened in his honor
without his knowledge, the way streets are named after
Lincoln and Washington. Whatever the case, the word 'Bunnel' isn't what intrigues me. It's the second word, 'Cascade,'
that makes me pause.

Detergent is its hieroglyph.

An object enters my mind, so sharp and clear I can
almost reach out and touch it. It's a green bucket, filled with

squishy gel-packs, each one smelling generically clean. The label on the front reads, "Cascade Complete."

Dishwashing detergent.

Matching the number on the landmark to a box in the information panel gives me a description of the place, written in tiny font: *"Bunnel Cascade is at its peak volume in mid-winter. Situated on the Northwest side of Bunnel Point with a forty-five degree incline, the cascade serves as a cross between a river and a waterfall. Visitors should not attempt to enter the cascade, due to rocky terrain and strong currents."*

A search of the map for other cascades results in two more possibilities, but neither one meets the other requirement established by the poem:

This place lies between two cliffs.

Bunnel is the only cascade bordered by two mountain ranges, predictably labeled "The Cliffs of Bunnel."

Whoever Bunnel was, he must be thrilled to be remembered so well.

I outline the fastest path to the cascade, then fold up my map and slip it into my pack. As I walk, the forest beckons me onwards, and I obey, trusting the way she takes me by the hand, promising a chance to put my fangs to the test.

It starts with a single snowflake.

She settles on my eyelash, and in the seconds between her crash landing and my labeling her as "snow," I've already blinked her away. Her twin drops onto my cheek, followed by another, and another. My legs work harder against the slippery forest floor, pushing me on to my desti-nation, determined to get there before everything disappears under a blanket of white. I will myself into the distance, but the snow carries on with her plan, indifferent.

Blue mountains soar over the horizon, their caps dyed white against the sky. The pine trees drip with ice, their branches coated in cream-colored dust. Piles of slush adorn the forest floor. Before, my steps were crunchy, marked by the snapping of twigs, the bristling of leaves. Now, my feet sink into the earth like anchors in the ocean. I enter into a negotiation with the forest, asking her not to take away *all* the green, but to settle for a smattering of powder rather than a blizzard.

Keep the snow on the mountain caps. Not here. Don't send it here.

Still, more snowflakes fall, looking like dots of ice rather than the complex, individual miracles they really are. Focusing on the patches of land that aren't yet covered doesn't help; they grow fewer and far between until suddenly the forest is still, and the silence is so wide it makes me stop in my tracks just to take in the infinite blank-slate that is the world. In just a few hours, the forest has been completely coated in snow.

My negotiations have failed, and I don't like it.

The landscape's stubbornness reminds me that everything, absolutely everything, is out of my control. The only thing I exercise dominion over is myself, and the choices I make— to stay, to go, to start, to stop, to love, to leave. These are the things I am in charge of. The snow, the wind, the rain, Mike's honesty (or lack thereof), are all out of my hands, and nothing I do will make them bend to my will.

So, I keep walking.

The process is heavy and slow, but I can't be sure if it's due to the snow, or some weight inside me, a kind of gravity sucking me under: I can't control the world, so why bother moving?

The landscape changes. Mountains flatten and what used to be a dense wall of trees is replaced by a thin smattering of branches, all of it covered in powder. It's a beautiful monotony, and the longer I'm in the middle of it all, the less I feel the cold. I tell myself it's because I'm moving, getting my heart rate up, but my skin is numb, and the insides of my boots are wet, and the temperature has dropped so low that my systems are shutting down. I haven't eaten in hours, but I'm not hungry— just tired. Resting isn't an option, because resting is death.

You have to keep walking.

My focus shifts to steps— only steps— even though I'm not even sure where I'm going anymore. My entire world is walking, and if I stop, I'll cease to exist. Step by step, my legs move forward, feeling stranger with every move. I've lost awareness of my body, even though it's clear I have one— I know, because I looked down a few paces ago, just to make sure my arms were still there. Still, the visual proof isn't enough. My limbs are gone, because I can't feel them. I'm a specter, a ghost, a bodiless soul wandering through the forest, haunting the woods with steps that leave no footprints.

Hours pass, or maybe minutes, I can't tell anymore—

And then I see the wolf.

She's hiding behind a tree, and I might have missed her, if it weren't for the snow. Her gray coat stands out against the clean, white backdrop, looking almost metallic by comparison.

I stop. The wolf stares.

Her eyes are almonds, their blue irises cutting through me like a knife turned on its side. She doesn't mask her distrust. She makes no apologies for the way she scans my figure, a hostile smirk itching at the corners of mouth. Her incisors peek out from her lips, and she doesn't bother to hide them. Her muscles ripple underneath her skin as she turns her nose upward, sniffing the air for truth, asking me every question and taking the answers from my mouth before I have a chance to speak. She's a woman fully engrossed in her own power, so sure of herself, exactly the way the forest made her.

And yet... for all her power, she can't control the weather either. Maybe she was as disappointed as I was, to see the snow. We have the same limitations, except that she's maintained full dominion over the most primal gift of her own divine being. You can see it in the way she moves. Every cell in her body belongs to her, and her alone. No being except the Great Everything tells her what to be, or how to be it.

The wolf steps forward, her paws sinking into the snow. I can't explain how I know she's a woman, except that I can see it in her eyes. Her ears tilt toward me, pointed and soft, offset by the length of her narrow nose. She walks toward me, and I sit down, kneeling, holding my arms out. I don't know why I do it, except that maybe I'm asking her a question, and I'm willing to die for the answer.

She snarls, her mouth pulling back, tail bristling. I'm surprised by how white her teeth are.

"It's okay," I say, my voice sounding like it belongs to a drunken stranger. "We're made from the same stars... it's— you and I are the same. Everything is inside of us, and *we're* everything— not all of it, just a piece. You and I..."

I'm not making sense, but I can't stop rattling on. I try to put my words into sentences, but they tumble out in pieces, scattering across the snow. The cold is getting to me. I've lost the ability to speak, which means I won't be able to tell this wolf how I feel, and I've never, *ever* wanted anything more than that.

The anguish of it all rips me apart, and suddenly I'm crying, which is impossible because I don't have a body anymore, just a spectral self, which this wolf is going to tear into shreds. I want so badly to be like the wolf that dying by her hand seems less terrible than it should. I'm alright with dying this way. It's not the prospect of death that makes me cry. It's that it's happening before I've had the chance to tell the wolf how *right* she is. She doesn't need to hear it, of course, but I still want to say it, for myself, to make it real.

She's beside me now, her nose sniffing my face, her incisors twice as big up close. My eyes try to close, but I hold them open, because if I'm going to die, I want this wolf— this free, untamed, perfect, wild being— to be the last thing I see.

She circles me three full times before she makes up her mind. The conclusion lodges itself in her brain like a law, final and immutable.

You're one of us, she says to me, not with words, but with her eyes— bottomless, haunting.

I want to be, I answer. The wolf nods her head, assuring me that although there's much to learn, the hardest part is over, because that was the part where I had to find myself buried deep in the Earth and dig her up, piece by piece.

The wolf steps away and howls. The sound makes my bones shatter, echoing through every empty space inside me. A soft padding sound echoes over my shoulder, and three more wolves appear: two pups, and their father.

She has a family.

The pack surrounds me, sniffing me, pulling gently at my jacket with their teeth, like they're wondering why I've shaved off all my fur and covered myself in fabric. The two wolf pups go through my bag, pulling out my last granola bar. They struggle with the wrapper, and I open it for them, splitting it in two exactly equal halves.

The female wolf waits, watching, her mate behind her, looking so similar to her except for his darker coat. They'd be almost impossible to tell apart, if it weren't for the coats.

It strikes me that there is no leader in this pack. I'd always heard of alpha males being King in wolfpacks, but now, as I watch the pups' father nudge them away from my bag, it's clear to me that this is a marriage of equals.

The male wolf looks at his partner with a question in his eyes, like he's waiting for her to choose the next steps, and wherever she goes, he'll follow. He buries his nose in her fur, and she leans against him. This moment— insignificant as it may look— is what my entire journey has been leading up to.

The Great Everything wanted me to see this.

I've been called to the wild not just to discover my most primal, individual, self, but to witness what a partnership can be, when it's left alone, untamed, wild, and free. My fears about marriage— about closeness— seep out of my pours, dripping onto the snow like blood. I was afraid to commit to anyone because I'd never seen a model for marriage that I liked— at least not in the human realm, the civilized realm. The wolves lean into each other, entirely free from ego, just doing what needs to be done— together.

You are my model.

They nod at me, acknowledging that this can be mine, too, if I only pick the right person, if I find someone who can live in the wild with me.

I hope that person ends up being Mike. But even if he isn't, I know what I need, now.

The female wolf stands, stretching her legs and yawning

as she looks up at the sky, sniffing the air like she can sense the day passing. It's time to move on.

The male wolf nudges the pups, and moments later they're all standing in the same position, their haunches rippling, preparing for what's to come.

Run, the female wolf says to me, and before I know it we're all bounding through the snow, kicking up slush as we streak through the forest. My right side is flanked by the male wolf and the pups. I look to my left, and there she is— the female wolf— a silver bullet that's just left the mouth of a gun. My heart pounds, not just because I'm running, but because I'm so terrified of not keeping up, of ruining this magical, perfect moment— the time I got to run with a pack of wolves. My fears are unfounded, though, and we run together for what feels like a lifetime. For some reason, I never get tired. Trees zip by, and the forest is a blur.

I'm my truest self— pure, authentic, unobserved— running through the woods with wolves. I think about the phrase "man's best friend," and images weave through the trees; images of women in caves, sharing food with wild dogs, convincing them that yes, these humans *are* to be trusted; images of 1950s, stay-at-home Moms taking the family pet for a walk, the two soldiers keeping each other company in the only sphere they're allowed; images of modern young women crying over the latest heartbreak, the latest disappointment, snuggled into the shoulder of a dog who understands, and loves them exactly as they are.

The female wolf locks eyes with me, and we take something back for ourselves, reclaiming it with a confidence that says it never stopped being ours in the first place.

THE WOLVES STAY with me until I reach Bunnel Cascade. Their strategic presence makes it clear: the Great Everything sent them to me as guides. Without them, I'd be dead, or at least asleep, surrounded by snow and oblivion. The wolves made me run when I needed it most, causing my heart rate to rise, keeping me from giving into the cold. Now, my body is warm, and my brain is functioning again. The wolves saved my life.

When we reach the cascade, a steep riverbank appears, bordered by tall cliffs in the shape of the letter "V." The map was right when it noted that the cascade is neither a waterfall or a true river, but something in-between. It flows down the mountain at a forty-five degree angle, steeper in some places than in others.

I side-step my way down one of the cliffs to get a closer look, but stop when I notice the wolves are gone. For a moment I'm afraid they were an illusion, something I imagined in the cold; but then I spot the pups, playing with a pinecone, their father not far behind. The female wolf looks at me with regret in her eyes. Where I'm going, she won't follow.

It's okay, I tell her. *Thank you.*

She sniffs at the air one more time, like she she's recording my scent. Then, she's off. Her pack follows her, disappearing into the trees.

I'm alone.

I creep toward the riverbank, ignoring every natural instinct that tells me to stay away. When the cascade comes fully into view, it makes me gasp. It's a chaotic, churning, cauldron of chaos, the antithesis of a peaceful creek, the embodiment of unpredictability— a thing I hate.

White-capped waters pound against the rocks, creating rapids that lap against the bank's slush coated sides. Despite the drop in temperature, the cascade has refused to freeze. She winds across the valley, unbridled and untamable; God help anyone caught up in her currents. The cascade cannot — *will* not— be controlled. It's a death trap, especially in hostile weather, and I wonder how many animals have approached it— lured by the promise of a drink— only to find themselves swept away by the strength of the current, trapped and unable to climb up the cascade's steep sides.

I turn away from the churning cascade and open up my pack, taking out Mike's cell phone to re-reading the second clue:

"Hold your breath
and search for red!
Find it quick,
Or else he's dead."

Whatever I'm looking for is red, which should be easy to spot. I decide to walk the length of the cascade— easier said than done. The process is tricky, requiring me to creep along the edge of the icy bank in order to maintain a clear view of the cascade. If my boots lose traction at any point, unpredictable water awaits to break my fall.

I'm halfway along the cascade when the next clue reveals itself.

It's a buoy, bobbing up and down in the cascade, tethered in place by bungee cords to reinforce against the current. Somehow, it's managed to stay in place, despite the cascade's impossible willfulness. A tall pole protrudes out of its top, accented by a bright, red flag. The flag shudders in the current, taunting me, too far for me to grasp without completely submerging myself.

My adversary must have chosen this spot because it's the most hazardous. Here, the cascade's current is at its strongest, the incline steeper than any other spot along the water's path. To make matters worse, the cliffs are practically vertical, preventing an easy exit. It's such difficult terrain that I wonder how my enemy even planted this buoy in the first place.

I stare at the landscape for awhile, trying to form a strategy. I try to create a kind of choreography, a dance my body will remember, but no amount of planning will help me defeat the cascade. She's too strong, too unbridled, and there's only one way for me to capture what I seek:

I'll have to give up control.

It's a thing I hate doing. I walk up the bank, heading upstream from my ultimate destination in order to give myself time to maneuver within the water. I take off my pack and hang it on a warped, strange-looking tree I know I'll be able to identify later. My jeans and jacket land in a pile underneath it. I hate to strip them off, but I can't risk getting them wet.

I keep my boots on, climbing toward the edge of the cascade in nothing but my bra and underwear. Cold air bounces off the snow and my breath freezes. My body shivers, reminding myself that speed is everything. Moving fast is the only way to avoid getting hypothermia.

Pebbles scatter as I stop at the location I've chosen, maybe twenty feet north of the flag. My arms cross over my chest. They rise with a deep inhale.

Half-naked, freezing, and terrified— this is the only way. I need to work *with* the current, not against it, and for once, let go of my need to dictate the terms. For a second I think about Mike, asking me if I saw us planning a future together, and I want to run away again, to stay silent, to say nothing.

Instead, I close my eyes and slip down the bank, plunging feet-first into the unknown. The snow cuts into my back like a thousand tiny daggers, but I barely have time to register the feeling before I'm shoulder-deep in icy water.

A gasp— the sound of my own breathing. This feels so much worse than I thought it would.

Hurry.

The current pushes me downriver, my head dipping underwater no matter how hard I fight to stay afloat. The floor of the cascade is uneven, and my feet don't consistently touch the bottom. My arms shake involuntarily against the cold. I've purposely positioned myself north of the buoy, hoping the distance will give me time to compensate for the currents. I can't control my motion in the water. My best chance at getting the flag means becoming a human pinball, caught inside a watery machine.

Flailing helplessly in the currents, I keep an eye out for a specific cluster of rocks— the next step in my plan. Brown boulders poke out of the water in an uneven formation, and I ready myself, taking a deep breath and preparing for impact.

Smash. My body hits the first boulder at full-speed, knocking the wind right out of me. I try to inhale, but my stomach won't let me. For some reason, the impact knocks me into a different time and space, and suddenly I'm sitting on that rock again, watching the fish jump, a small, checkered bird wondering if building a home with Mike will mean forgetting how to fly.

My hands scramble over the boulder's surface, searching for an edge to hold onto. The surface is too slippery, though, and before I can latch on, I've missed it.

Damnit.

No time to think about it. The boulders are upstream from the flag, and the closest one is just a few feet above the buoy. If the current directs me toward the final boulder, I'll be able to orient my body toward the flag and use the current to my advantage.

A sharp, angular rock pokes out of the water, this one less centered, more off to the side. Not ideal, but it's a second opportunity to control my direction. My arms reach out, and for a moment my feet touch the bottom of the cascade. I try to kick off from the bottom to propel myself toward the rock, but the Earth falls out from underneath me before I get the chance.

The second boulder whizzes by.

No.

Brock's whistle echoes in my ears, and I remember climbing off the boulder, Mike taking my hand in his, leaving the moment behind without an answer. I always assume there will be more moments, but what if I missed ours, because I was afraid? What if he never asks again?

I'm down to my last chance. The flag is in sight now, bobbing up and down in the distance. In front of it sits the biggest boulder yet, an oblong, uneven island in the chaos of the water.

I reach out, praying the Great Everything can stop my forward motion. This isn't up to me anymore, but to the Cascade. The current pushes me onward, and at first it seems like I'm going to miss the boulder, but then another white-capped wave rolls over my head, and the Cascade is pushing me sideways, back to the center of the stream. My hands slam against rock, my fingernails scratching at its surface, determined to find a hold. They do, and then my elbows are on the boulder, and suddenly I'm not moving anymore.

Third time's the charm.

My lungs expand— I'm dizzy from being tossed about in foamy water. As much as I want to stay still, my legs are shaking, and I can't feel my face anymore. Time to end this.

I look over my shoulder, gauging the distance to the flag. I'll need to estimate the perfect trajectory before I launch myself toward the buoy, like a missile heading into space.

When I'm sure I have a strong grip on the rock, I rotate my body toward the flag. My boots push against the boulder, and suddenly I'm thankful for their presence even though they add extra weight. My legs bend, and in one smooth motion I'm pushing off as hard as I can, shooting toward the flag like a cannonball.

I've committed. There is no choice now but forward, and I'm imagining this is what it would have felt like if I'd said yes to Mike by the lake where the fish jumped, if I'd told him I'd build a home with him in the place where Earth and Sky became one.

My body makes it halfway there before I'm back in the water and the currents are moving me away. My arms thrash. My feet kick. I muster the last of my strength and fight— a fish swimming upstream—forcing my way toward the buoy. I think I might miss it, but then my fingers brush up against cold plastic, and even as water fills my mouth, I've never been so glad to be exactly where I am.

I grip the buoy, examining it for any sign of a clue. I think about pulling down the flag, but as I reach for the pole, the top unscrews. It twists in my frozen fingers and the buoy breaks open, causing the pole fall into the water. The blood-red flag floats for a moment, then disappears down-stream, never to be seen again.

My hand searches inside the hollow buoy, landing on something slippery. It's the next clue, laminated in plastic to avoid water damage. Something about the lamination strikes me as important, but I'm too cold to think about it now. I roll it up into a scroll and stick it under my bra strap, readying myself for the third, most important part of my plan: escape.

I pull myself along the bungee cord that tethers the buoy in place, using it to haul my body toward the river bank. It's tied around a rock and only covers half the distance; I'm forced to swim the rest of the way. When I reach the bank, my fingers dig into the earth. The snow along the cascade's edge has melted a little, revealing soil underneath. The soil has been soaked by melted snow, creating mud. My boots dig into the ground, and I push myself upward, bit by bit.

The earth is too slippery and suddenly I'm falling back toward the water. I'm so cold— submerging myself again could be a death sentence. I thrash, trying to stop my descent toward the cascade. Some voice in my head, one of the darkest pieces of me, tells me that yes, it knew this would happen all along. This is what always happens when you give up control, when you jump without looking first. Mud soaks into what little clothing I'm wearing, coating my skin, making me look like a thing of the wild.

A fish, I think, laughing at how stupid I must seem, thrashing about the bank. But then I remember that I'm not a fish: I'm a wolf.

Stillness slows my slide. Neurons form new connections. Something in me breaks. I howl into the forest, a guttural, primal sound, declarative in its essence. A light illuminates those dark pieces inside me, catching them flowing through my arteries, ripping them out through my mouth so they evaporate with my howl, fading into the cold, winter air. I'm back in that moment by the lake, and this time I tell Mike that I love him, and I'm not afraid to plan a life together, because I've found my wolf, and she handled the currents.

Bit by bit, paw over paw, I claw my way up the bank, landing on soft, forgiving snow.

Every piece of me shakes as I pull the clue out from underneath my bra strap. My priority should be getting back to my warm clothes, but the clue can't wait. I unroll it, and begin to read.

17

Congrats! Good luck!
        You're nearly there,
        You've stuck it out,
You've showed you care.
At this place sits
The man you seek—
Its incline isn't
For the meek.
It's not a whole,
It's not so stable,
It's not a third,
Please grip the cables.
Not tough to spot,
Wherever you roam,
You'll always see
Its curved, round dome.
So come get Mike!
At least, you'll try.
I'll be waiting,

butterfly.

HALF-DOME.

He wants me to go to half-dome. A second search of the map for other possibilities comes up dry, confirming it. No other landmark even comes close to meeting the requirements of the clue.

Not a whole, but not a third. Curved round dome. Grip the cables...

Mention of the cables shocks me back into my body, and suddenly I remember that I need to get back into dry clothing. From the time I stripped down to the time I entered the water, less than five minutes have passed. But the cold can kill in ten.

I run up the bank, searching for the warped tree where I left my pack. A spare pair of socks sits inside; they're rough on my arms, but I use them to scrape the frost off my skin. Fabric blankets me, but I don't stop wrapping layer after layer over my shivering limbs— tank top, thermal shirt, my trusty jacket, three pairs of underwear, my jeans, and mittens on my hands. It's everything I packed, but I'm still not warm.

Heading straight for half-dome is an option, but there's a strong chance I won't survive the trek. It's only a few hours walk from here, but my stomach caves in on itself with hunger, and I've been cold so long that "warm" is more of a concept than a feeling worth remembering. I need to start a fire. To eat. To rest.

The ground is still covered in white powder. It's possible to build a fire on snow, but doing so would require dry materials to work with. Every twig at ground-level is coated in slush. In the search for dry tinder, there's nowhere to look but up.

The strange, gnarled tree looms over me, its branches twisting at awkward angles. It might not make for a pretty sight, but it's perfect for my purposes. My arms wrap around the tree, asking it to help me for the second time today. I pull myself upward, grabbing onto the lowest hanging branch. Hand over hand, I climb toward the top, where thick piles of leaves have spared one section of branches from the snow's touch.

Breaking off the dry branches without disturbing the leaves above— which form a miniature umbrella, filled with snow— is a tightrope walk. Slush rests on the higher-up leaves, waiting for the chance to fall. It can't be allowed to soak the dry tinder— for all I know, these are the only branches in the entire forest that were spared from the snow.

Snapping noises fill the forest as I break off the dry branches one by one, slipping them into my sweater so as not to disturb the snow above. When it's done, I exhale, letting myself relax on the climb down. My feet hit the ground, and it's onto the second challenge—

Lighting a fire.

My fingers are numb, so I pull off my mittens to investigate. The tips have changed from pink to beet red; pale white patches of skin glisten next to small sores growing near my knuckles. If my fingers were a picture in a medical textbook, the caption underneath would read, "Early Symptoms of Frostbite." I'll lose them if I can't get a fire going.

My original intention was to find a less exposed place to make camp, but there's no time. This strange, warped tree is my new home. I crouch down underneath it. Hands shaking, I arrange the tinder in a pyramid, leaving enough room for air to pass between the twigs. Too tight and the flames will be smothered, too far apart and they won't spread. When the twigs are the perfect distance apart, I palm the most precious piece of the equation— a woven bit of kindling salvaged from an old bird's nest up above. It's a miracle the nest didn't get wet in the snow. Accidentally dropping it into slush would be a poor way to repay the Great Everything.

Placing the fibers underneath the pyre, I reach for my fire starter.

Images of Mike's face emerge in the dark— the way he always looks at me like he's a little surprised, the scar over his right eyebrow, the side of his face that gets more freckles than the other side (a mystery we haven't had the chance to solve).

One.

I strike, but no spark appears. My hands shake, signaling that I don't have much left in me. My legs used the last of their strength to climb the tree. If I can't light this fire, I'll fall asleep and become one with the forest. My body will be found later, frozen, fingerless, eaten by the snow.

Fingers. Hands. Suddenly I remember Mike's hands, intertwined with mine, on a night months ago when I almost got fired from my job. A guest told the hotel's owner I wasn't "friendly" enough, prompting him to invite comments from the rest of the staff on areas in which I could improve. We spent an hour as a group, workshopping ways to provide "warmer customer service," or more specifi- cally, "ways to make Zoe less of a bitch." No tears were spilled until I got home. Mike held my hand until I fell asleep.

Two.

I strike again. A spark appears this time, but the kindling

doesn't catch. Now my whole body is shaking, and I have to promise myself that I won't give up, no matter how tired I am. If I die and some future hiker stumbles upon my remains, my skeleton will be found holding the fire starter, its arms bent in the middle of trying to strike again. Quitting is not an option. If I'm going to die, I'll die trying.

I crouch over the pyre, hoping a change in angle will shield the spark from the wind. The position reminds me of a morning I spent hunched over the toilet, hungover and vomiting after too many mai-tais while celebrating a friend's birthday. Mike held back my hair. I told him not to come in. "I'm fine," was the reason I gave, but really— I was afraid to let him see me that way. We'd only been dating a few months, and this moment would ruin the illusion, the smokescreen of perfection I'd created. Mike needed to see me as a photoshopped Instagram model, not a real person. I slammed the door in his face. He came in anyway.

I strike again.

Three.

Swoosh! The fire starter makes a spark, which leaps to the kindling. It glows red. Air grates against my chapped lips as I blow on it, fanning gently in the hopes it will grow. It flickers as if it might fade, but then it doubles in size. My hands poke at the kindling— not caring if the flames lick my mittens— prompting it toward the twigs. The fire leaps onto the pyre. Blue-orange flames spread from twig to twig. In just an instant, the whole thing is ablaze, and for the first time in a long time, I remember what "warm" is. I lean back, letting the edges of the fire kiss my neck.

Mike's face swims inside the orange pyre, conjuring memories— the way we met, the feeling of entering unknown territory, guessing at who he might be and what we might become, together.

Lighting a fire is like starting a relationship—hazardous, marked by the feeling that you're only one error away from total failure. But every now and then, a spark ignites, and it makes you remember why you agreed to take on the whole terrible process in the first place.

18

The moment is big, and I am small.

Half-dome towers above me, casting a shadow over the world, stable and imposing. Its scope makes me too aware of the space I take up. Tracing my outline doesn't help— it's impossible to calculate how much room the universe intended me to have. Whatever space I've carved out for myself, it's too much: half-dome needs it.

A smattering of thin trees skirts the base of the beast. Their branches are skinny, devoid of leaves, almost as if they've tried to make themselves smaller so as not to impose. They live in the shadow of the mountain, and it's hard not to wonder what they could've been, if they'd taken root somewhere else.

It makes me want to look at my own roots— to make sure nothing's impeding my growth— but there's no time. My ascent begins.

The trailhead to the cable walk is marked by a tilted wooden sign. It's easy to miss in the snow, but dusting it off reveals an arrow pointing me in the right direction, toward "Mist Trail." I've officially left the backcountry, and I can't help but hope I'll run into another park visitor— someone brave enough to face the cables in the snow. It's unlikely, given the weather, but it makes me smile to think about an accidental run-in with another tourist. What would I say?

Hi. My boyfriend has been kidnapped by a murderer! I'm on my way to save him right now. When you get a chance, could you please let the rangers know we're up here? Also, a cheeseburger would be great!

Then again, there's always the possibility than any stranger I run into is no stranger at all, but my enemy. Without any idea as to who did this to us, I'm in a vulnerable position.

Shoots of determined grass push through the slush, fading as I climb higher. I stop and check Mike's phone for a signal every few minutes, but none appears. Something wet lands on my cheek, and all at once it's snowing again. This time, I'm not afraid. Dots of white sprinkle the world. They dust my hair, my hands, the tip of my nose. The valley quiets under the fresh powder, and so do I. It gets harder to breathe as the incline increases, but the floating specks of white comfort me. They signal that the Great Everything is still at work, and no matter what happens when I reach the cables, the world's clock will still tick.

Hours pass, and by now my feet have grown so used to walking that they barely notice the distance. By the time I see it, I've almost forgotten what I'm looking for:

The cables. Their origin point looms in the distance. Taut, steel ropes snake up the mountain, curving into a tiny pinpoint before disappearing on the horizon. It's a treacherous route; steep, made more hazardous than usual by the melting slush that coats the cables. But it's not the danger that makes me stop in my tracks. It's the man, standing at the start of the cable-walk, his back turned to me, hands wrapped tight around the steel ropes.

He's looking up the mountain— away from me— his face obscured. Through white streaks of snowfall, the outline of his body is barely visible. Broad shoulders are cloaked in bulky winter-wear. His posture is easy; not a care in the world as he leans up against the poles that hold the cables in place, like he's waiting in line at Starbucks. He's the man who turned my world upside down, and to him, today is an ordinary day. He waits for me with his backpack hanging off one shoulder, as if he can't be bothered to put it back in place. It's a lime-green backpack; hideous, with silver reflectors on the front. They amplify rays of sunlight, making him noticeable even in the drifting powder.

My breath catches in my throat. I've seen that backpack before. And even though every fibre of my being wants to deny it, I know who this man is. Maybe I've always known. My voice croaks out his name, but it comes out more like a scream than a whisper.

"*Mike?*"

Something in me shatters, and the earth breaks open. My cells divide, ripping me into a thousand pieces. My body is like the snow, and suddenly I know where snowflakes come from. They're pieces of a woman who lived in a cloud, so high up that the man she loved couldn't hear her scream. She tore herself apart to blanket the world in white, because it was the only way to make him sit up and pay attention. I'm standing in the middle of her beautiful, tragic remains.

So many things make sense now, and yet nothing makes sense at all. The jacket; Mike must have packed it after all, to leave as a clue. The fire; Mike disappeared because he was the one who set it. The horses; Mike insisted on the horse tour because he knew it would take us into backcountry, remote and far from help.

Mike's footing shifts; he's about to turn around, to look me in the eye. At eight thousand feet up, we've climbed to the top of the world together. Half-dome is a vacuum— a place to tell our secrets. Whispers and screams are one and the same in a place without air. Here, he will show me what kind of animal is he is.

His shoulders move. Another second and we'll be standing across from each other, teeth fully exposed, darkest selves released. It's a task other couples only toy with. They skirt around it at the dinner table, see glimpses of it in the car on the way to the movies. Sometimes a person's animal lurks in the shadows for a lifetime, emerging only briefly because a hint is all that's needed to keep a partner in check. Other times, the animal waits until the opportune moment to make its entrance— usually after a wedding, or a birth— a time when its partner has no means of uncomplicated escape. But no matter when it emerges, rarely is the animal revealed in its entirety. It's always offset by the best of a person. But not now. Not here. We will show each other our most secret selves, without pretense.

He'll want me to ask, "*why*?" But I won't give him the satisfaction. Maybe it's a game Mike likes to play with Cassandra, the woman he *really* loves. Maybe Ken was right, and they planned this together. Or maybe Mike just resented my inability to open up to him, and to test how much I cared, devised a twisted scavenger hunt. A hunt that — like so many others— will certainly end in death. If I have anything to say about it, it won't be mine.

The wind shifts again and my hair wraps around my neck like a scarf. The wilderness sprawls out beneath me, and I picture my body tossed off the side of the mountain, cradled by the trees like forest debris. If Mike tries to kill me, I'll fight to the death. I won't let surprise make me slow, or reluctance weaken my fists. He may be stronger than me, but even if he wins, I'll make him feel like he's lost. Fingers will gouge, teeth will bite— he won't walk away whole. I'll get at least one good shot in, if only because he won't expect my ferocity; shock tends to make opponents slow. But I am not one who wastes time asking, "Is he really going to hurt me?" Because, if I'm being honest with myself, I've been expecting it all along. The piece of me that looks for the worst in others, is also the worst in *me*— but it's about to save my life.

He's almost fully turned around now. I can see the edge of his ear.

Next up will be the freckles we can't explain— the ones that scatter asymmetrically.

The thought makes my heart ache, because— to do what I need to— I'll have to let go of a future I didn't know I was planning. One with Mike and I, in the home we'd buy together, its wood floors the exact color of maple syrup.

Our kids would be more like him and less like me, and I'd love that about them. They would trust the way he does, with wide, open arms and a sense of ease. At night, we'd all sit out on the deck, eating dinner under the summer stars, talking about how Mom and Dad met. She didn't think love was to be believed, and he proved her wrong. We'd have too many pets, our house a tangled mess of sticky hands and dirty paws; but everything about it would be beautiful.

It's the first time in our relationship that I've let myself acknowledge the depth of my feelings for Mike. He's the one.

It's too bad I'll have to kill him.

Stillness. A gap in the snow. The Earth stops turning; the Great Everything is preparing to catch me, in case I fall. Planets move in retrograde, and somewhere far away, a star explodes. Meteors thousands of miles wide collide with foreign moons, and none of it matters any more than what's here: two small people, on top of a rock, meeting each other all over again. My broken heart is only a piece of the vast cosmos, but to the Great Everything, it matters just as much as any sun, as any moon. Her eyes are large, and when the scale is infinite, even solar systems appear small. To her, I am the size of a galaxy, and just as important.

I want to stay in this moment forever— when the possibilities haven't collapsed, and everything is both true and false at the same time. But then it happens: Mike turns around. The moment is lost.

We stand across from each other, the divide between us caked in white powder. My boots leave footprints on the snow as I close the distance. Falling snowflakes blind me, but I continue my approach. The gap between us shortens. The figure of a man comes into sharp relief, all his features visible; a smile playing at the edge of his mouth; one eyebrow that drops lower than the other; a child-like, youthful roundness to his jawline.

Air fills my lungs. Planets return to their orbits. The Great Everything nods, because yes, she knew it all along, and was only waiting for me to find my way home. Just as quickly as it shattered, my heart repairs itself. The universe is set right again, all because of one undeniable truth:

This man isn't Mike.

My knees buckle— begging to sink into the snow— but I deny them and stay upright. Syrup pumps through my veins, sweet not just because I've admitted how I feel about Mike, but because I can *have* him. If we survive this, we can return home, together. Something sour pulls at the edges of the idea, but I bury it deep and plan to unearth it later. Now, it's time to face my enemy.

Relief gives way to nausea. I know this man. Seven days spill across the snow; Sue making eggs, a broken arm, hot chocolate, and Tums.

"Logan."

Logan looks off into the distance, tracing the outlines of the invisible trail behind me.

"You made good time," he says, as if nothing has changed between us. He absent-mindedly scratches his cheek, his gloves digging into the side of his face, leaving red streaks behind.

I search for possibilities— for any explanation that negates Logan's involvement— but then my inner wolf howls and I know he's the one.

"That backpack is Mike's," I tread carefully, feeling out our strange new dynamic. Logan just nods, and doesn't volunteer any more information. "He isn't—" I can't bring myself to use the word *dead.*

"Not yet," Logan answers, and we leave it at that.

"You killed Brock." The words tumble out involuntarily. My heart races, and suddenly I'm thinking of Sue, and Ken, and the way Sue looked at me on the night I left. "The Hardingers—" I start to ask about them, but Logan puts a finger to his lips and makes the *shhh* sound.

"We won't talk about them. Not now," Logan says, his eyes placid like the surface of Tenaya Lake. The corner of his lip twitches a little, but not in amusement. It's a spasmodic motion, like his mouth is trying to run away from his face in protest to its assignment. Suddenly, I notice a million tiny quirks in Logan's exterior. The red splotches on his neck that hint at unexpressed emotions. The whistling sound when he exhales. The constant fidgeting, his body always in motion. All of it hints at a well-hidden instability.

"How did you do it?" I ask, still trying to piece together this new version of Logan. "Mike would've beaten you in a second..."

Logan flushes, and suddenly the red spots on his neck congeal, coloring his throat auburn. "I made the hot chocolate that night," his voice shakes a little, and now I know where his weakness lies. "It was simple enough to drug him. Despite what you might think, brawn isn't everything. Sometimes brains win out. If more women realized that, they'd end up with better men."

I don't say anything, and the color leaves Logan's neck—he takes my silence as agreement. He scans the horizon, thoughtful, mentally reviewing his work. "It was well-planned overall, except the last clue was too easy," he adds, pulling at the edge of his coat, his fingers always moving, always fidgeting. "But I didn't think you'd make it this far. It wasn't supposed to end this way."

"How was it supposed to end?" I whisper the question, not so much to him, but to no one in particular. My legs resist the urge to pace. The wolf within me yearns to attack, but I'm waiting until he tells me where Mike is. I can't destroy him until I know where Mike is.

"You were supposed to give up," Logan shrugs. "To leave him in the wilderness."

"I would never do that," I answer, but before the words have left my lips, Logan's talking again.

"Wouldn't you?"

His jawline looks different in motion, and I realize now that what I took for a youthful roundness is actually just the product of a little extra weight. He isn't a college-kid on spring break; he's a grown man. He sees himself as a victim, deprived of what the world owes him. It adds a sulky affect to his features, making him appear younger than he really is. Why didn't I look closer, when I had the chance?

"All people look out for themselves, Zoe. You know this, yet you fail to behave accordingly," he's pacing now, lecturing, his words tumbling out with ease, as if he's practiced this exact monologue many times before. "You're careful, yes. You moved in with him but put the lease in your name. That was excellent. You keep him at arms length, a guest in your life. And yet, there are moments when you look at him, and you soften," he adds, creases appearing by his eyes. "This is a very dangerous thing. I'm here to help you, Zoe. You need a partner who understands true human nature. I've been watching you for some time now, and I have to say, you and I— we're the same."

Suddenly Logan is a mirror, and my reflection is my adversary, bouncing back the worst of me in fractal pieces.

"It's ironic, you chose a butterfly as your picture," he continues, rapid-fire, almost frenzied in his delivery. "That's what I see you as. A caterpillar becoming a butterfly. You know somewhere deep inside that you can never really trust another person. They won't understand, not the way I do.

Butterfly. The word triggers something, a memory of the final clue. *"So come get Mike! At least, you'll try. I'll be waiting, butterfly."*

"This was your chance, Zoe. By leaving Mike to die in the wilderness, you would have finally come to terms with the basic nature of human beings: selfishness. You could have freed yourself. You and I could have tried again, as equals."

"Again?" The word makes my skin prickle.

"You still don't remember?" he asks. His tone isn't sad—

it's angry. His gloved hands curl into fists, the fidgeting momentarily interrupted.

"Let me help you," he spits, his voice tinged with disdain. "Stood anyone up lately?"

My pen-pal from the dating app. The one I cancelled on when I met Mike. The cute rhymes we shared back and forth. The clues were clues in more than one way— they rhymed so I would remember.

"My profile picture on the app," I think out-loud. "It was of me on Halloween. I was wearing—"

"Wings."

"Josh?" I ask. He nods.

"You don't look like your photos." I feel stupid as soon as I say it. Of course he wouldn't use his own pictures.

"Those aren't of me. I like my privacy," he smiles at me, as if my current predicament proves his point.

"Is Josh even your real name?"

"Could be," he shrugs, making me sure it isn't. The mystery he shrouds himself in casts a shadow down the spine of the mountain. This man's refusal to tell me who he is makes him less of a man, and more of an idea. There is no Logan. There is no Josh. Just this shape, this body, this amalgam of the philosophical nothingness I fear most.

"How did you find me? I didn't use my full name."

"Your work," he answers. "You said you were the manager at the Delune hotel. I stopped by once. You were annoyed when I asked you how to get a room, like you couldn't be bothered. You should really work on that, Zoe."

He was the customer who complained about me.

"You had a beard then," I remember aloud, images of the strange, bearded man superimposing themselves over Josh's face. The man followed me around the lobby for an hour, always staring, always asking, but never booking a room. I recognize him now, but only by his eyes— creaseless, narrow, calculating, but somehow still forgettable.

"I hated to shave it off. I look like a kid without it. But I couldn't have you recognizing me, at least not right away," he answers.

His hands grip the cable as he steps forward. We're nose-to-nose now, every pore on his forehead made visible. He grabs my chin and pulls my face close to him. I want to bite him, but something in me whispers, *not yet.*

"All I wanted was for us to try again," he says, his breath hot on the side of my cheek.

"We're the same, Zoe. You have no idea what your messages meant to me. And then, finally, when we were about to take the next step, you stood me up. And when I held you accountable, you cut me out of your life. Do you understand what that does to a person? To a man? You owe me. I gave you plenty of chances to turn things around. I sent you *signs*, Zoe. So many signs..."

There must be a question in my eyes, because he presses on, his voice urgent, seeking. "Didn't you think it meant something when the flowers you planted at your new place were destroyed?"

I can still smell the sweetness— broken pink and purple petals spread across the stoop— flowers Mike and I had planted only days earlier, pulverized, their flailing roots covered in earth, homesick for carefully dug holes they'd never belong to again. My gut churns with guilt. We blamed Cassandra, but nothing she ever did was violent. I should have known it wasn't her.

"And the mail? I took it from the box for you month after month. I left it by the door, so you wouldn't have to walk to the mailbox," he continues, his speech quickening, as if remembering the deed gives him a rush of adrenaline. "I was trying to show you the kind of partner I'd be, the love we could have. His I threw away of course— you shouldn't even be sharing an address with him."

The mail. We thought Cassandra was stealing Mike's mail out of obsession, or devotion. How wrong we were.

"You *need* me, Zoe," he continues, his gloved fingers digging into the side of my face. "I can show you the kind of person you need to be to function in this world. I can *save* you from being hurt ever again. I let you explore— let you get the bad guys out of your system— but now it's time for you to come back to me, especially after everything I've done for you. I thought you were tiring of him— thought you were ready to give into your true nature— but then I saw him buy the ring, and I realized you might say yes. And what would I do then? I had to stop you from making the worst decision of your life."

A ring? Mike bought a ring? There's no time to process. I have to stay focused.

"Because the truth, Zoe, is that no one really cares about you enough to give you what you need. No one besides me. I planned all of this for you. To show you your true, inner nature, and the nature of all beings. By leaving Mike behind in the forest, you would have realized that love is a name we give to physical, chemical reactions. Nothing more. There's no one in this world worth dying for. There's only people who can keep you safe, and people that can't. I can keep you safe. I can teach you how to protect yourself from the worst of this world."

He runs a finger over the edge of my mouth, and I shiver. "I thought you'd leave him, but you surprised me," Logan whispers, and I almost think he's going to tell me he's decided to call the whole thing off, now that he's seen what real love looks like.

"Clearly, you're more lost than I thought," he adds, shattering any hope of a stalemate.

He lets go of my face with a shove, pushing me further away from the cables. We're standing on ice, a thin level of frost above the soil. My feet slip, and without the ropes, there's nothing nearby to grab onto. I fall onto the ground, my ungloved fingers going numb.

"You and I belong together, Zoe, if only you can let go of fantasy, let go of illusion. I'm sorry it's come to this, but I'm afraid I have to push you to the brink to help you grow," he smiles at me. "You have a choice to make. Mike's at the top of the mountain, at the end of the cable walk. We can hike up there together, and you can die by his side," he opens up Mike's pack and pulls out a handgun he's stored in the back pocket. He points it at me, but I don't flinch.

"... or, you can take my hand. And we can leave here, together."

He holds out his other hand, waiting for me to take it. He crouches down to my level, whispering like he's talking to a child.

"I would never take the choice away from you, Zoe. You have to be the one to decide. Is your love for Mike so real you're willing to die with him, or do you recognize that it's nothing but a biological illusion? If it helps you in your decision-making process, you should know that Mike's been lying to you. He didn't tell you, did he Zoe? He didn't tell you about Cassandra, or what he did to her."

My eyes must give me away, because Logan's runaway mouth curves upward into something between a frown and a smile.

"It's his fault she's the way she is. He broke her. He destroyed her, and then he walked away. One day, he'll do the same thing to you. Somewhere inside, you know it's true."

His words pull me under like heavy anchors, dragging me deep into the place I try not to go. Boxes unpack themselves. Glass sculptures of the Mike I know shatter. His unwillingness to disclose why they broke up, the fact that he never got a restraining order— all of the blank spaces in his story bubble up, ending my game of mad-libs where I fill in answers I think I can live with. Cassandra's message to Mike replays in mind; *"It was your fault."*

"You'll never be safe with him" Logan continues, still holding out his hand. "He didn't ask me about you. Not once. You're right, not to trust anyone, Zoe. Except me. Let me help you. You're tired. Let's go home."

My arms shake, and my stomach churns, because he's right— I *am* tired. My body is weak with hunger, burnt from the cold. It's a sickness worse than anything I've ever felt, as if every piece of me is shutting down at the same time. Darkness swallows me and I can't resist it. The truth I've always known grows like mold over my skin, taking the dirtiness within and externalizing it into flesh. My blood runs brown and dishwater grey, pounding in my ears, confirming the thing I've resisted for so long. No one is to be trusted, and everyone is alone.

Mike's been lying to me.

My inner ogre stirs, standing face-to-face with my wolf, and the two of them look at me, waiting for me to decide. It's a moment I've been avoiding since the day I met Mike, but now it's here, and something needs to be done. I'm either all in, or I'm out. I either trust him, or I leave. I look out across the vast expanse of the world, which drops off at the edge of half-dome, taking in the light one more time before turning to face the comfortable darkness.

Slowly, carefully, I reach toward Logan, my fingers trembling. My red hand slips into his, and he pulls me up to standing. The gun slacks by his side. He leans in to pull me closer...

And that's when I elbow him in the face.

The sharp edge of my forearm connects with his eye, and I put whatever strength I have left into it, watching as his jaw flies upward.

The motion makes him lose his footing. He's not holding onto the cables anymore, and he skids backward, landing on the snow.

If I hesitate, he'll shoot me, so I move without thinking.

My boot slams into his nose. A crunching sound echoes across the mountain as it breaks. Red splatters of blood drip onto the Earth.

I want to try to wrestle the gun from him, but he's clutching it with both hands, and could shoot me in the struggle. Instead, I grab onto the cables, running as fast as I can up the mountain. My inner wolf howls, a wild thing set free, searching for her partner.

Hand over hand, I push my way up the mountain, relying on the cables to keep me from tumbling down the trail. The hike is a forty-degree incline, the ground solid rock. Puddles of melted slush have frozen solid, creating pockets of ice over the surface of the mountain.

As my speed increases, so does the chance of slipping. A single misstep could send me careening over the edge of half-dome. The valley sprawls out beneath me, dotted with green trees the size of pin-heads and rivers as thin as thread. Should I fail, an eight-thousand foot fall awaits me.

There's no time to be overly cautious. Maintaining my head-start requires speed, and depends on how quickly my adversary recovers from a blow to the face. A glance over my shoulder reassures me: he's not behind me. There's nothing in my wake but snowfall and my own boot-tracks.

Upwards, upwards— the ascent never ends. Steel cables rub my hands raw. Blood coats the wires, and it takes me a moment to realize its mine. My head spins, but it isn't the elevation— I'm dehydrated, malnourished. Everything in me wants to quit, but I've come too far.

Finally, my hand moves to grab the next spot on the cable and meets nothing but air. The cable-walk ends, and the ground levels out, revealing horizontal rock.

I've made it to the top.

The mountain's peak is other-worldly. Coated in snow, it's so tall that standing in certain places reveals nothing but sky, creating the illusion that half-dome is the world's end. It's a two-color palette of white and blue, familiar and strange all at once, as if I've landed on some alien planet that's the inverse of our own. Gravity wields less power here, and my boots pad over the undisturbed Earth like it's nothing but moon-dust.

Up here, the snowfall is thicker, and my eyes strain to see against the blinding shower of white. Then, a figure emerges in the distance, crouched against a rock. The planet's spin slows, and the mountain waits; still, breathless. All events leading up to this moment have happened in real-time, but now, Time stops counting, abandoning her post to watch. Clouds lean in, listening. The wind ceases to blow, preferring to lie stationary. Everything in the natural world inhales and steps aside— for us.

I move closer, and the figure comes into focus. He's been so beat to hell he's barely recognizable. Purple bruises mar his eyes. His cheek is swollen, and a deep cut on his arm burns with infection. He's lashed to the rock by too many ropes to count, tied up by someone who deeply fears his escape. Dry lips and crows feet by his eyes— lines I've never seen before— signal dehydration that's as bad as my own. He's in bad shape, just like me. But is he alive?

"Mike?"

He doesn't stir.

19

*P*lease *be alive.*

Careful steps on undisturbed snow. My own hands reach out across the rock, detached from my body as if they belong to a stranger.

I tell myself a story, not caring if it's true. I tell myself that love makes it impossible to lose someone. When you love a person, they become a piece of you, and you become a piece of them. The sound of his voice. The way he folds the laundry. The infinite, tiny mannerisms that build a person— all of it weaves its way into your being, leaving indelible traces behind like veins beneath the skin. No worldly separation can remove the imprint, and even when he's gone, the reflection of him remains, like a nuclear shadow after a flash of light. I remember the tree, its roots wrapping themselves around Brock's body, and I know that Mike will always be a piece of me. Even if he's gone from this world, my cells are entangled with his, and I'll find him across any distance, no matter how wide. In the deep, empty spaces of the universe; in the hollows so tall and the holes so bottomless; in the places where there is no up or down, no

North, or South, or East, or West; love is how we find each other.

As I reach out to him, I tell myself that even if he's not alive, he'll still be with me.

But please let him be alive.

Our hands touch, the numbness in my fingers making it hard to gauge where I end and he begins. His skin is cold, and at first nothing happens, but then his eyes open. He recognizes my touch. He's alive. I silently thank the Great Everything, promising to marvel at her beauty— at her infinite complexity— every day for the rest of my existence.

It takes him a moment for him to place where he is. Whatever drug is in his system hasn't worked its way out yet. A discarded syringe by his feet signals consistent dispensing of some kind of sedative. When awareness comes, horror floods his irises.

"Zoe—" Mike's voice is strained, panicked. "You shouldn't— you *can't*— be here."

He's somewhere between sober and drunk, and I wonder how long it's been since the last time Logan drugged him. Mike tries to stand, but he's still tied up. The snow blankets us, falling thicker now than ever before, flakes of white resting on our eyelashes. The cascade of powder is so heavy that if we sit here long enough, undisturbed, we'll be buried alive like two statues, holding hands for eternity.

"Logan, he's been stalking you, he's—" Mike starts to say, but I stop him.

"I know," I answer, neglecting to mention that Logan could appear over the edge of the mountain any minute, gun in hand.

Mike rests his head on the boulder behind him, defeated. "You shouldn't have come. You have to go, Zoe— right now— it isn't safe." His speech is clumsy and slurred, but even through through the fog, some things remain clear. He scans my body the same way I scanned his, taking inventory of the shape I'm in, wondering if I'm strong enough to run.

"I couldn't leave you," I answer, and suddenly my body is heavy, as if it senses it's safe with Mike and can finally allow itself to feel everything I've been ignoring. The exhaustion, the hunger, the cold, the wound on my leg— it all hits me at once. I sink deeper into the snow, wondering how long it will take for us to disappear beneath the shreds of white. "You're part of my pack, so I couldn't leave without you," I continue, my eyes watering, warm tears spilling onto my hand, melting the frost off my skin. "I'm a wolf, did you know that?"

Mike manages a smile, getting more alert the longer we talk. I expect him to tell me that I don't make any sense— that I'm hallucinating, driven to insanity by too many nights in the wild— but instead, he nods.

"Of course I did, Zoe" Mike answers seriously, looking straight through me in that way he has about him, like he's met me in a thousand lifetimes before this one. "I've always known that."

He says it with so much understanding that it makes my ribs split open, and suddenly it occurs to me that maybe Mike's always seen me. He knew I was a wolf. Despite my attempts to hide the worst in myself, he's seen glimpses of my inner ogre, and he's loved me anyway. The desperate ache inside— the desire to be known— fades, replaced by something else.

Now, we're kissing, all danger forgotten. We're the only two people left in the world, battle-scarred and broken. Aware that death might come at any point, we kiss with a purpose: to say hello and goodbye all at once. If it's my last act, it's a perfect one.

When we part, Mike looks at me, and something in his eyes has changed. There's an unspoken, animal charge to the air. Electrons buzz. The forest quivers, delivering a warning.

"He's down there, isn't he?" Mike asks, even though he's already intuited the answer. I nod.

"Does he still have a gun?"

I nod again, wishing I'd tried harder to take it from him. Mike shakes his head, because he can see what I'm thinking — it's written all over my face.

"You're a hero, Zoe. You did great. Better than I did."

The silence settles. We both know this is it. We're going to die. There's no other way off the mountain, and the second we head down the trail, the man called Logan will shoot us— assuming he doesn't hike up here first to finish the job before we even attempt escape.

Mike scans my face like he's memorizing every detail in case he never sees it again. "You know, I believe I suggested we go somewhere *tropical* for vacation..." he says, defaulting to humor like he always does in times of trouble.

"You'd still be tied up and about to die," I remind him.

"Yes, but I'd have a margarita in one hand, and you'd be in a bikini. Not the worst way to go," he laughs, his eyes searching the mountain. A moment passes, and we fill it imagining all the things that could have been. Then, Mike's eyes harden. His posture changes— it's the movement of a man who's not ready to die.

"We're not done. Not yet," he says. "Hide here, Zoe. Let me go first. I'll try to get the gun away from him, but whatever happens don't come down until I call back to you and say it's safe."

I'm objecting before he's even finished the sentence.

"I'm a wolf, remember?"

Mike sighs.

"Besides, when one partner is weak the other is strong," I continue, satisfied that I have the opportunity to turn Mike's quote around on him. "We're both weak right now, which means both of us have to be strong, even though we're really... weak." The words spill out in a pile; the cold has scrambled my brain. "Do you know what I'm trying to say?"

"I do," Mike answers, somberly, the sedative working its way out of his system with every passing second. "Alright, let's get these off of me then—" he motions to the ropes around his sides. "I've been working on them over the past couple of days. I cut through one completely, but I couldn't reach the others..."

I get to work on the ropes. Two of the knots untie easily. The rest, though, are so tangled they require something sharp. I search for a rock with a sharp edge and find one a few yards away. After sawing for what feels like an eternity, I slice through the rest of the ropes, and Mike is finally free.

He stands, but wavers— he hasn't moved in days, hasn't eaten in just as long. We take inventory of our wounds. Together, we make half a person. We're both a mess, hardly fit to fight. But there's no other option. We've come too far.

We split the contents of my pack, devouring what little food is left, and sharing what's in the canteen. Mike insists on giving me more water. I don't want to tell him about the cascade, or that I've had enough water to last a lifetime. If we survive, there will be time to tell stories.

The food helps Mike's system rid itself of the drug, and he's fully alert, now. We keep watchful eyes on the ridge where the cables give way to the peak, but no one appears.

I'm not surprised. The man who calls himself Logan is a coward. He won't come to us and risk being disarmed. He'll wait until we start our descent; easy targets against the backdrop of a white, pristine mountain.

It looks as if it's to be a fight on the trail. We take stock of our assets, working as a team, formulating a plan that uses both of our strengths and avoids our weaknesses. We find a tactical use for every single item left in my pack, promising that we'll utilize everything we have to our advantage. Just because we don't have a gun, doesn't mean we're defenseless. Mike is an optimist with an eye for human behavior, and I'm a pessimist who tries to stay one step ahead of the worst case scenario. It's a pack effort, and together, we cover all bases.

After running through the finished strategy a half a dozen times, we're beginning to believe we have a shot. There's no sense wasting more time. We've eaten all our food, and the resulting surge of energy will only last so long.

It's now, or never.

We clasp hands at the head of the cable walk, united against the darkness. Then, we step over the edge, disappearing into the blinding, white unknown.

Mike's hand feels so solid in mine that I wonder how I could have been so quick to believe the worst in him, to assume the man I saw at the base of the mountain was him. The sour taste I swallowed earlier bubbles up in my throat. I start to think about Cassandra, and what Mike might have done to her, and those dark spaces— the ones in the corners of the universe that are all anti-matter, where love is the only compass in a meandering labyrinth of infinite space. It makes me want to confess to Mike, to tell him that I'm broken, and to ask where his fractures are.

But then my fingers are wrapping around the cables

again, and I'm looking out across the iris of the Great Everything, assured that when you love someone, everywhere and nowhere, broken and whole, close and far, are exactly the same thing.

THE BULLETS FLY LIKE SPARROWS, beaks sharp, wings like knives on the edge of the wind.

Logan doesn't hesitate. From the moment we step over the crest of the ridge to the top of the cable walk, he opens fire, drowning us in poisonous metal darts rendered invisible by the snow.

The first bullet zips past Mike, tearing a streak in the shoulder of his jacket. He reels backward from the force of the blast, and I clutch his other arm, praying he hasn't been hit. He glances at his shoulder, and even though there's blood, it's just a flesh wound.

He pushes me toward the Earth, both of us crouched like crabs as we weave our hands around the cables, descending the icy causeway in tiny steps. Two more bullets streak past us, landing in the snow with soft plunks. One of them flies by my ear, the sound it makes a stage-whisper, a raspy shout.

"That's three!" Mike shouts at me, sounding like a soldier in the middle of combat. "We're almost there, and now we know," he nods toward the source of the bullets to indicate Logan's location— a cluster of trees at the base of the cable walk on the Eastern Edge of the dome, the last stop before the mountain becomes mostly rock, too devoid of soil for any plants to grow.

Another bullet buzzes past us. Four shots. It's almost time.

"Zoe, if you get to the bottom, and you change your mind, I can do this myself—"

"I won't," I start to tell him, but I stop when another bullet whips by, hitting the cable and severing it in two. It breaks apart in a shower of sparks, hissing down the mountain like a snake that's been stepped on, disappearing from view. We cling to the final cable. It's the only thing preventing us from sliding down the icy slope toward oblivion.

"Five," I count aloud, my heart pounding as it considers what I'm about to do. Mike must feel my heartbeat radiating through the palm of my hand, because he squeezes it tighter.

"There's still time. You can go!" Mike continues, his voice urgent. "That's what I want! Please— run as far as you can. Find a ranger station—"

I should've known Mike would try to change my mind in the heat of battle. It makes leaving him an even greater impossibility. I don't indulge him with an answer. Instead, my lips press against his, hoping it won't be the last time.

The sound of metal on metal. Another bullet. The cable I'm clutching severs. Mike and I scramble to grab onto the nearest post, steadying ourselves on the last remaining piece of the cable walk in our immediate range. The next post is five hundred feet down the mountain.

We lock eyes, and I want to tell him everything— about the wolf, and the universe, and the spaces I found— but I've never been good with words. Words are Mike's strong suit. Instead, I memorize the freckles on his face before whispering, "Six."

My hands release the post. I let myself fall, landing horizontally on the Earth, ripping off my jacket to reveal Mike's white, long-sleeved shirt. My backpack sits on my chest in reverse, and I cross my arms over it, hugging it tight to my body. I barely have time to breath before I'm picking up speed, sliding down the ice-covered trail on my back like a deranged bobsledder, a member of a luge team in the world's most dangerous Olympics. My jeans are a pale, watered-down wash, so light they're almost white. Combined with Mike's shirt, they help me blend into the landscape, impossible to see against the backdrop of the blizzard. A bullet plunks into the snow— Logan must have reloaded— but it's so far away that I know our plan to camouflage me worked.

I'm invisible.

A twist of the neck and I manage to glance over my shoulder for one last look at Mike, growing ever-smaller behind me. He's running full-force toward the Eastern edge of half-dome's curved bottom, where Logan hides in the cluster of trees that marks the beginning of the trail.

He's nearly halfway there, sticking to our plan to take advantage of the time Logan needs to reload the gun. Mike moves in zig-zags, but he's heading straight toward the cluster of trees, becoming an easier target with every second that passes. My task involves stealth and secrecy— things wolves are good at. Mike's taken the most dangerous job— the one that puts him directly in the line of fire.

Logan's words about being willing to die for love echo in my ears, but I ignore them, squeezing my arms tighter around my chest, focusing on the bumps in the Earth and going faster all the time, my speed increasing with the slope of the mountain. It's hard to estimate my fall-rate, but I've heard that Lugers reach speeds faster than sixty-five miles per hour, and that sounds about right. The ice beneath me is smooth, and there's little traction to slow me down between my back and the frozen trail.

The ridge on the far end of the dome disappears, opening up a view of the valley, the forest a miniature model inside a snow-globe from eight thousand feet up. The foreground is a blur, nothing but white and green streaks of light cradling me in my descent, whispering something about relativity, and forward motion, and laws of the universe that change when things are very big, or very small, and which one am I? Some moments it feels like I'm flying, as if I might break off from the mountain and be cast into the sky, where I'll meet the woman who tore herself into pieces to make it snow. I'll ask her if it was worth it, and tell her what it feels like to be seen, because now I know.

The mountain widens and the ice thickens. Mike's shirt is too big on me— kept heavy by melted frost— and it's starting to creep up my torso, revealing fragile skin begging to be burned. The trail changes from smooth to rocky— a signal that I'm almost there. My trajectory is uneven, now, and I try to ignore the searing feeling of hard rocks under melting ice, each one slamming into my back like a mallet.

My eyes scan the horizon, looking for the end of the cable walk. Then, it appears— a brown sign covered in powder, impossible to read but still there, a beacon in the night. If I were to wipe it off, it would tell me I've reached the base of the cable walk, the top of Mist Trail.

I tuck my head in and turn sideways, curling around the backpack that's resting on my stomach, letting the new roundness of my body slow my descent.

My joints groan as I tumble to a stop, remembering the thrill rolling down a hill brought me when I was a kid and wondering what I ever saw in it.

On my hands and knees, I scan the horizon for my marker, the one that signals the end of Mist Trail and the start of the cable walk. It comes into focus a few yards away, highlighting not just my geographical position, but two metaphorical paths, each leading to a different version of me. I could leave. I could continue to follow Mist Trail down the mountain and look for help. Mike told me not to stay. He would understand.

A part of me wants to continue down the mountain, but the wolf inside won't budge. I may be bruised, starved, nearly dead, but for all my mistrust— in spite of the ogre within, and my search for the monster in others— I'm a pack animal through and through.

I hike my backpack higher on my shoulder and make my way back up the mountain, heading this time toward the patch of trees on the lower Eastern edge, ascending as quickly as possible without the benefit of the cable walk. If everything goes according to plan, Logan will have fallen for our trap and believe I've escaped, allowing me to take him by surprise while Mike disarms him. Before revealing ourselves at the top of the half-dome, Mike and I discussed every moment of the altercation in advance, laying a trail for ourselves, planning each move with militaristic precision. It should give me comfort, knowing that we've thought this through, but my time in the wild has taught me that the Great Everything doesn't care about my plans. In fact, I think she enjoys watching them crumble, if only because it forces me to ask her to help me, to submit to the universe in a kamikaze trust-fall, arms wide, hair floating, relinquishing myself to whatever comes next. The destruction of my plans reminds me that I'm a thing of the wild, totally dependent on the Great Everything, no different from any other crea-ture relying on her for survival.

For a moment, I wonder what forests Logan has walked through, and if he's ever seen the beauty I have, in the way that I have, and if he did, what he thought of it. Maybe if he looked the Great Everything in the eye, it would change him. Or maybe he already *has* looked her in the eye— seen the wisdom reflected there, the infinite balance in her irises — all to no effect.

Maybe, he looked her in the eye, but felt nothing at all.

20

When I reach the trees, there's a magnetic charge in the atmosphere, invisible particles of energy settling on my skin like radioactive dust after an explosion.

The forest is quiet, as if the animals here can sense impending destruction. Birds stay close to their nests, preferring to lie in wait rather than attempt to soar in a windless sky. The snow has ceased to fall; its absence makes the air taste empty. Pine trees tower upward in a dense configuration, leaning over me, imposing, their needles sharp, weapon-like, ready to slice at any moment. I push deeper into the pocket of forest, searching for Mike in the stillness, searching for Mike in the silence.

At first, there's no sound except the soft graze of my boots on the snow. But then, the unmistakable smack of two people colliding echoes across the forest, followed by voices, two of them, angry like bears roaring into the mountain. A primal shout— guttural— rips through the trees, declaring that the creature who made it is alive, and intends to stay that way.

I cross toward the sound, keeping my head down, staying under the cover of branches whenever possible, but moving with speed, with efficiency. Images of a wounded Mike race through my mind, but I watch them from afar, experiencing them as an observer. There's no room for fear, only action.

I stop when I reach them, concealing myself about one hundred yards away behind a rock formation, close enough to watch but far enough away to avoid detection. The shouts I heard earlier double in volume. They are loud. I must be quiet.

Two figures circle each other in the distance— Mike and Logan.

Logan hunches over, holding his jaw. Blood hits the snow.

Mike shakes out his right hand, still stinging from the punch he threw. I notice a patch of red, sticky syrup on Mike's left bicep— he's been shot, and it looks like the bullet went straight through.

We knew this might happen when we formulated our plan, but I'd hoped he'd make it to Logan before he had a chance to reload.

Still, the wound is on Mike's arm, not his chest, meaning it's missed his heart. If he doesn't loose too much blood, it won't be fatal. I search the snow for the gun but I'm too far away to spot it— uneven terrain blocks the Earth beneath their feet.

Logan's about to stand, but Mike's on him again, kneeing him in the stomach, taking him down with a punch to the liver. Mike's left arm dangles by his side, useless because of the injury, but he's still a force to reckoned with. Logan claws at the air, trying to scrape at an eye or get a hand around a throat, but he's no match for Mike in size or skill.

Another punch and Logan hits the ground with a sickening cracking sound, making me think he's landed on a rock.

It's over. Mike's kneeling over Logan now, hand raised, fist clenched, about to deliver what will certainly be a death blow. I won't have to put our plan in place, because Mike's going to kill him. The brutality of it all makes me look away, just for a second, but when my eyes squeeze shut, the sound I hear isn't Logan's scream: it's Mike's.

Mike stumbles backward, moving onto higher terrain just long enough for me to spot a silver edge protruding from his calf. It's a pocket-knife; one Logan must have hidden somewhere on his person, easily accessible in a waistband or jacket pocket.

Mike reels, exhaling, summoning the strength to pull the blade from his flesh. He reaches down and wraps his hand around the handle, but the whole process is taking too long, and Logan's already recovering, swaying in place, look at Mike like he's deciding whether to run or attack.

I don't give him time to make up his mind.

From the moment it happens, I'm already reaching into my backpack, pulling out the fire starer, making my way across the snow like a predator stalking its prey. Logan is distracted, too busy to notice a white blur blending in with the landscape as she makes her way toward the trees behind him.

When I find my position— about twenty feet away, concealed by branches laden with snow— I click my fire starer. It breathes, coming to life, raging against the cold like it's been waiting, waiting for this very moment to bring sulphuric wrath.

The poetic justice of using fire against Logan isn't lost on me, and I want to talk to him about it, to tell him how the fire belongs to me— how it always has and always will— but I don't, because the most dangerous adversaries are the ones who wield their power in the shadows.

The fire roars, and I allow it to blaze over the wrappings of my powdered eggs, pieces of trash I saved just in case they might be useful. In my other hand, I stuff a tube-sock with the remains of the leaves Sue used on my head, which I now know to be Eucalyptus leaves. They've been drying in my backpack for days, protected from the elements, growing more dangerous all the while.

"Eucalyptus trees are antiseptic," Sue told me on our hike to Tenaya Lake. "Very pretty trees, but also difficult to maintain. They used to grow outside our house in Santa Barbara. Fire services would cut them down every three years or so. The leaves are highly flammable in the dry seasons." I can hear her voice so clearly it's like she's with me now. I don't know what Logan did to the Hardingers, but he's about to pay for it.

I head toward Logan, my steps swift and soft, padding over the earth. His back is turned toward me. He's managed to find a reasonable-sized rock to use as a weapon, and he's holding it in his hand, arm raised, preparing to strike Mike with it.

Mike's already removed the pocket-knife from his leg, lifting it into the air like an ice-pick. He tries to raise his left arm to defend against Logan's boulder, but the gun-shot wound won't let him, leaving him entirely exposed on one side. He can either defend, or attack, but not both at once.

The whole thing reminds me of a sick game of rock, paper, scissors: Mike with the scissors, Logan with the rock, and little old me, about to sneak up on him with the paper.

The distance closes and now I'm right on top of them. They're about to attack each other, but then Mike notices me over Logan's shoulder— one hand on fire, carrying the sun in my palm— and he can't help but smile, just a little bit, because we both know this is the end.

Logan notices Mike's face, and he's about to turn around, but I'm already reaching under his jacket, shoving the sock filled with dried eucalyptus leaves underneath it, letting its neck stick out like a tail before setting it ablaze, a makeshift stick of dynamite.

Logan turns, but it's too late. "Paper covers rock," I say, and before he can answer, the interior of his jacket catches fire. It's a waterproof jacket, so the inside is warm and dry, kept safely away from the snow— the perfect environment for my stick of dynamite.

Logan screams, running into the snow, rolling over, trying to unzip his jacket and stop the fire within from spreading. He shakes it off but the damage has been done. His undershirt is burned black, the skin underneath it already blistering, red sores forming under exposed, charred remains.

"You bitch," he tries to come at me, but Mike's already running for him, knife in hand, ready to finish it, to end it.

Logan stops, retreating as if he's just remembered something, and then he takes off, heading higher up the mountain toward the cable walk. Mike and I look at each other for a second, wondering why he would head for the least advantageous position, but then Mike groans, and I know why Logan's running.

"The gun," Mike says, and we both take off trying to reach the place where Mike disarmed him, further up the mountain. Mike's injuries are too debilitating— there's no way he'll run faster than Logan. He calls out to me, "Zoe, don't! Stick to the plan—" but I leave him behind, my legs carrying me as fast as they can into the distance to the spot at the edge of the trees, where the forest ends and the mountain begins.

It's not far, maybe eight-hundred feet away, and the landscape around it shows signs of a struggle— blood on the trees, cracked branches, disturbed footsteps in the snow.

Logan's figure comes into view, searching in the snow for the gun, but finding nothing. We're at the carved edge of half-dome now, and the side of the mountain drops off into nothingness, the end of the world in front of us, waiting. I look over my shoulder, but Mike's out of my line of sight.

We're alone.

Silence fills the wild again, as if every animal is watching, breathless. Logan turns, his back facing the edge of the world.

"Where is it?" He says, voice calm, steady.

"It was my job to get the gun," I answer, pulling it from my backpack, turning it over in my hand. "While Mike was distracting you."

"You could've shot me back there."

"I might have hit Mike."

"Yes," Logan says, pretending to be hurt, his tone dripping with manufactured sadness. "We wouldn't want that, seeing as you 'love' him."

"I do."

We wait for a minute, letting the stillness settle.

"Was this part of your plan?" Logan asks.

"No," I say, and it's true. This was not part of our plan. Logan looks out over the edge of the world, eyes unaffected.

"What do you see, when you look out there?" I ask him, wondering if he knows about the Great Everything, wondering if he's felt the depth of her love— love that isn't connected to biology, or chemistry, but just exists wherever the light goes. He doesn't answer. "You're going to keep coming after me." It's a statement, not a question.

"Yes," he says.

"If I turn and walk down this mountain, you'll follow me."

"Yes," he thinks aloud. "If I can make the trek. If not, I'll wait until the opportune time."

We stand there together, my finger on the trigger, Logan's life in my hand like the fire I palmed just minutes ago, flickering, unstable, a living question I can't answer.

"You're not a killer," he says, and even though I know he's right, I also know that sometimes fish fly, and some- times birds swim, and animals do all sorts of things under unusual conditions, just to go to that place where the sky and the earth are the same for a moment.

The gun's metal is crisp against my fingers, final and heavy, and holding it makes me think about all the time I've spent looking for the monster in others. The nights I've lain awake, worried about fangs. The sideways glances at a person I thought I knew. The careful orchestration I bring to situations that don't call for it. All of it, meant to safe-guard against the presence of the animal in someone else, when— maybe— the best chance at safety would have been to find the animal within me.

The world told me to hide my animal, to subdue her, but she is the one who protects me from harm. The Great Every- thing gave her to me. The Great everything made me wild, and to be anything but that misaligns the cosmic balance, throws universes out of orbit.

There'a reason I'm a hotel manager; there's a reason I took a job that requires me to be nice even to the rudest of guests. I'm an expert at hiding the sharp pieces of myself, the ones that aren't pretty to look at it.

But now, it's time to embrace all parts of me.

Yes, I am kind, but I am also mean.

I am warm, but aloof.

I have fur to soothe and teeth to bite.

I am bitter, and sharp, and I think too much, and there's pointy edges here, and barbs that might prick, and all of it needs to be allowed to take up space— to exist— because that's the grand design that keeps galaxies spinning.

Bang.

I shoot him.

Logan slumps to the ground, his eyes wide with surprise, and he's clutching his chest before he realizes that's not where he's been hit.

He looks down at his leg, and the new hole I've created there. It might as well be in the center of his forehead, because a shot to the leg keeps him from moving, and— in the cold— movement is life.

If we leave him here, he's as good as dead.

I step toward him, and the look in my eyes must be truly crazy, because he cowers, putting up an arm as if hands can stop bullets.

"Listen up you little fuck," I tell him, spit flying. "The person you've imagined me to be doesn't exist. Do you know who I really am?"

He shakes his head.

"I'm the bitch who's going to tear your throat out if you get within five hundred miles of me, or anyone I love. You know what I'm good at?"

Again, he shakes his head.

"Finding monsters," I tell him, and it's true.

I turn around, and Mike's behind me, with a look on his

face that says he's been here the entire time and watched the whole thing.

He takes my hand, and we head for the cable walk together, two wolves making sense of the wild.

We don't look back.

21

———

Logan is behind us, but hours later, and the danger remains. Mike and I side-step our way down the mountain, leaning on each other like two trees uprooted in a hurricane. I throw up three times on the way down, but it's not because I'm sick over what happened up on the mountain. Something's wrong inside me, a sharp pang in my stomach making me stop and hurl.

We reach the bottom of half-dome, and even though everything is spinning, I recognize this as the place where I felt small. The shadow of the mountain extends across the valley, eating its way across the landscape, consuming everything in its path. Half the day has passed, and we're both weak from blood loss and lack of food. We stop to bandage our wounds. Mike's lost a lot of blood, but compression seems to help. He's in better shape than I am, and the heavy fatigue pumping through my veins makes the world seems like quicksand. I'm too dehydrated. I try to drink water, but I can't keep it down. Mike checks for cell-service, but the batteries on both our phones have died, and even if they hadn't, it's unlikely we'd get reception anyway.

Mike stops to unfold my map, guessing at the nearest spot where we might find help.

"There's a road," he exhales, his voice heavy. "We're not too far from Yosemite Lodge. We can make it, Zoe."

He says the last part more for himself than for me. It's an effort to convince; as if only saying something out loud will make it true. I don't answer, and when Mike hands me the map, I pretend to glance at it before nodding in agreement.

We walk, and it's a never-ending journey, forest on forest spreading wider into the distance.

Sometimes, my legs give out, and my head slumps toward my chest, but I regain consciousness right before I hit the ground.

The world clicks in and out of focus, and my eyes can't help but shut every now and then, as if my body is trying to reboot itself.

The valley's beauty fades into multi-colored streaks of green, brown, and white. It's an impressionist take on the wild. Roughly brushed outlines of shapes I've seen before, but can't quite place. Everything blends together, soft and inviting. Something sharp inside my gut sends a shockwave across my mid-section, and I must have gasped out loud, because now Mike is looking at me.

"Zoe?" He puts his arm under mine, taking in my face, looking for what's written there. "Are you with me?"

"Yes."

It's all I can manage. His good arm is under my shoulder now, keeping me upright. As we walk, Mike points out a million beautiful things, trying to make me stay alert.

"The hawk. Do you see it? Way up there."

I don't see it, because I can't look up. My head is too heavy. I'm aware of some pain inside me, but at the same time, I'm detached from my body, floating around outside it.

Maybe if you ignore basics needs— hunger, thirst, companionship— for long enough, your body ejects you in retaliation, like a fighter pilot tossed from the cabin of his own plane. Another sharp pain cuts through my midsection, and I double over.

"Why does it have to hurt?" I whisper aloud, not actually meaning to say anything at all.

"It hurts? Where? Zoe, look at me," Mike answers, his voice dripping with something I've never heard in it before — panic.

I don't look at Mike, because I wasn't talking to him. I was talking to the Great Everything.

She answers in colors, shades of the forest, burnt and beautiful, as striking as they are overwhelming.

There's no way to directly translate her response into words, except to say that beaches come from rocks that are torn apart by the sea, and thunder always booms before the lightning, and nothing beautiful has ever been made without the soft edge of creation first being dragged across the blade of "to be."

No bird builds a nest without exhausting its wings. No seed becomes a flower without first breaking free from its shell, splitting itself open because it yearns for the sun.

The smooth interlocking of two hands in love is always preceded by the pain of reaching out into the unknown, braving the darkness in the hopes of finding light.

Growth rarely comes without pain, and to live is to sign a covenant of experience. Our existence comes in spirals; circles of attention that narrow in focus on one central point, the light that serves as the Universe's center and the only place within it where no speck of darkness can be found.

Every moment of our lives is spent trying to move closer

to the light. For the privilege of seeking the sun, we agree to allow the world to bring us to our knees, all so we can be two steps closer to the light of the Universe when we stand up again.

At times, we fear the darkness, but this is unnecessary, because darkness is only the absence of light. It's defined entirely by its opposite, allowed to exist only insofar as it serves its purpose of bringing us closer to the light, again and again, until one day we find our way into the infinite warmth of creation.

That's where I'm going.

I'm not afraid of dying. I'm not sad about it, either. I've spent seven days in the vastness of the world in its most primitive form. I drank the water. I watched the pine trees lean away from the wind. I smelled the flowers, opening wide in the morning only to shut tight at sundown. I've found my fangs, and made peace with myself, even the parts of me I learned to hide. I've stared straight into the eye of the Great Everything long enough to know that she'll send me where I'm meant to go. Even if there's darkness first, she'll guide me to the light. I don't have any regrets, except one:

Dying means leaving Mike, alone.

He'll be fine without me. He's too perfect not to find another. If I'm able to watch him from whatever lies beyond, I will, every day. When it's his time, he'll find me, because love is how we find each other.

I sink into the snow. I don't have any regrets about what happened on the mountain. At least if I'm leaving, I'm doing it as the real me, whole, complete, not partitioned so as to be made more palatable to the world. Maybe that was the plan all along. My life's purpose was to find myself, and now I have, so I'm leaving.

Mike's still trying to keep me alert, pointing out so many beautiful things in the wild, but I can't walk anymore. He pulls me into his arms. His mouth is moving, but I can't hear what he's saying. I glance up one final time, and the last thing I see is the look in Mike's eyes, his irises made from fractal shades overlapping in a way too beautiful to be real.

I should have looked at them more, when I had the chance.

The world turns black.

IF YOU'VE NEVER DIED BEFORE, you haven't lived.

When I died, a tunnel waited for me, but it wasn't vague, or ethereal, or filled with light. It was hard and tangible, like the cement semi-circle formed beneath a freeway overpass.

It was so real I could reach out and touch the walls. I felt my way through the darkness, pushing toward a pin-prick of light in the distance.

The tunnel's exit waited for me, there, a worm hole between the body I was leaving behind and the next phase of existence. It was a wrinkle-in-time calling me onward, and nothing about it was particularly dream-like.

It was scientific in its construction, almost architectural, or biological, a clock-work process as self-assured as gravity, ushering me onward to be born-again-backwards. As I walked, I felt no fear, no sense of strangeness— just an innate animal knowledge that forward was the way to go.

When I reached the end of the tunnel, the light grew so bright it burned through me, becoming a feeling more than a sight. In a single bite, the light ate me and spit me out in reverse. The tunnel's exit was its entrance; a quantum conundrum.

Now, I'm back in Yosemite Valley, familiar trees rendered strange from a new perspective. Whatever beauty the Earth held for me before is multiplied by a thousand.

The snow isn't just white— it's every shade from cream to eggshell, stacked on top of each other in infinite parts that make a whole. The wind doesn't just blow— it ripples across the valley in an orchestrated movement, millions of threads weaving themselves into an invisible blanket smothering the Earth.

My senses work together in a way I didn't know was possible. Synesthesia makes sight and sound one and the same. Colors are tastes. Green is my favorite, heavy and crisp, like an apple baked into a pie.

Smells are visible. The scent of the pine trees renders as wisps of smoke, wafting, soft on the winter air.

Nothing is hidden. The grand design is fully apparent, all its pieces revealed in vivid strands.

When I move, the world adjusts in a kaleidoscope shift, so many pieces rearranging themselves, briefly turning to streaks of light before settling back into place.

Every bird is a galaxy, every acorn a moon. Atoms on atoms reveal themselves, unfolding in infinite combinations we call "mountains" or "pebbles." Size is nothing but a construct— one I don't need anymore.

I always imagined dying as moving into some watered-down state of being, soft and muted, but I feel more alive than ever.

I don't realize I've stepped outside myself until two figures reveal themselves in the snow.

The man is Mike, but he's Mike like I've never known him before. No piece of him is hidden. Every feeling he has — every thought— presents itself as a color, falling from inside him and landing on the snow.

He holds a woman in his arms: the old me.

"Zoe!" his voice isn't a single sound, but an entire orchestra, so many shades of purples and yellows making up the tone that belongs only to him.

Mike shakes the old me, but she doesn't wake up. "Stay with me..." His feelings drip onto the snow in shades of red and blue, and the crack in his voice makes me want to leave all this beauty behind, to try again. But my body is so far away, I'm not sure how to get back to it, or what tunnel to take.

Mike picks the old me up, carrying her body across the endless expanse of the wild. The effort breaks the bandages on his arm, causing the wound to bleed again.

I want to tell him to leave her, and I half-try, but when I speak the words come out as a feeling, a golden ball floating from whatever piece of me is my new chest.

I push it toward Mike and it hits him in the ribs, but he doesn't react. He just walks on and on, step by step, leaving a single set of footsteps in the snow.

Hours pass by. The sun changes its angle in the sky.

I wonder why I haven't left yet. I feel like I'm late for a train.

I follow Mike and the old me through the forest, watching as he grows weaker in the cold, carrying two with the body of one.

Finally, it happens. Mike sinks to his knees, unable to go further.

He lays the old me down in the snow, taking his coat off and wrapping it around her shoulders. Arms shaking, he holds her wrist in his hand, searching for a pulse.

The look on his face says he didn't find one. He's crying, now, his tears making the air smell like cotton-candy, and Six-Flags, and that moment we had at the theme park. He puts a hand on the cheek of the old me, his fingers causing a clinking noise to chime across the forest; the sound of atoms connecting.

"Don't go," he whispers, but it's too late, because I'm already on my way.

Mike presses on the chest of the old me, trying to bring her back with CPR. Minutes tick by, but nothing happens. He checks her pulse again, but her pulse doesn't answer.

There's nothing he can do for me now.

I half expect him to leave the old me in the snow and keep heading for the lodge, but instead he lays down beside her, both of them on their backs. He intertwines his hand with hers, part of a pack, the fate of one the fate of both.

"Wherever you're going," he whispers, red and purple feelings spilling hot onto the snow, "that's where I want to be."

It's what he said to me by the lake, where the fish jumped high, bringing the worlds of air and earth together.

The words are an invocation, making me think of the bridges between people, the gaps that we fill and the chasms we cross to find each other.

I'm between two worlds, now, but something about what Mike said helps me find my way home, like Mike is gravity and now I know which way is up.

The entirety of the universe is at my disposal. Darkness to light, distance to distance. I peer into the Great Everything, searching in the space between moons, between suns, between us.

I leap across the chasms in the old me, weaving stardust over the canyons I couldn't cross, the ones where I hid my questions, the ones where I asked "what if he is a monster, too?"

I build causeways and swim in the tail of a comet, searching the vastness of the universe for a single pin-prick of light— the one that will bring me back to where I'm supposed to be.

When I find it, it's smaller than a marble, but more important to me than any planet.

I sieze it, and I know it's the right one, because I'm sucked backward into another tunnel, falling, falling, into a bright light that never ends.

My eyes open, and I'm back in my body.

It's a shock to my system, like being dunked in cold water after laying in the sun. The beauty I experienced earlier is gone, and an animal grief floods my chest. The world is washed in bland sepia, harsh and angular.

A sharp pang in my stomach hurts, but even pain is so dull it barely registers. I try to speak, but my breath just rattles in my throat.

"Zoe!" Mike sits up, leaning over me, running his hands over my face like he's not sure I'm real. "You're going to be alright. Stay with me."

I try to answer him but I can't speak. All I can do is inhale and exhale.

Mike scans the forest for something— anything— useful. Trees dot the horizon, their leaves perfectly arranged in a cross-hatch pattern.

"Help us," Mike prays into the emptiness.

He's asking the Great Everything, and relief washes over

me; whatever is meant to be will be, now. At first, nothing changes, but then there's a sound, the rustling of leaves somewhere far off in the distance.

"Oh my God," Mike whispers, his voice dripping with disbelief. "It can't be. Zoe, look. Over there, by the ridge."

He points at something I can't see. It's a shadowed outline against the horizon. It moves, but when I reach out to touch it, I realize my hands are too far away. I'm alive, and I can't stretch my fingers across galaxies anymore.

"I'll be right back," Mike touches my shoulder, and then he's gone. I'm not sure how long it takes him to return, but when he does I'm tired, and my eyes are heavy, and the world is going in and out of focus.

"We're going to be alright now," Mike lifts me up, putting one hand under each arm, raising me into the air. He leads us toward that shape in the distance, growing bigger all the time. We're right up against it now, but I'm still not sure what it is, and the last thing I see before I black out again is a soft, blonde head of hair.

It was Molly who saved us.

Molly, with her fawn-colored mane, her hooves wide like terror, bottomless but somehow still filled with power. The rippling in her haunches, the soft lashes framing her deep-set eyes, the whip of her tail— all things I used to fear, coming to my rescue, plucking us from oblivion.

After I blacked out, Mike loaded me onto her back, keeping one hand on my shoulder to prevent me from slipping over Molly's side. They walked together across the snow for miles, keeping each other company under the cold, winter sky. Mike said he got so weak from blood-loss at one point he had to wrap a hand in Molly's mane to keep from falling over. But she waited for him. She never stopped walking, never panicked and ran away, never threw me from her back. She stayed with us until we made it to the lodge. A quick radio call to the ranger station revealed that every other horse went straight back to camp, except Molly. No one could explain how she got so far from where Brock set her free, except me.

I woke up to the prick of a needle in my arm, the red lights of an ambulance frosting my bare legs in a strawberry glaze. The concerned face of a male EMT loomed over mine, the scruff on his chin framing his mouth as he asked me my name, my age, the date. Zoe. Twenty-eight. I don't know, I don't know, I don't know.

The medical staff tried to keep us apart to assess our injuries, but Mike pushed his way into my ambulance, refusing to move until they stabilized me. They've re-bandaged the wound on his arm, and the wrapping looks official, more professional. He told me about Molly while they hooked up my IV. Now, he's distracting me while another EMT looks at the wound on my leg, muttering about frost-bite and shaking his head.

"It's bad, isn't it?" I ask Mike.

"No," he answers, squeezing my hand. "It's fine. Don't think about it now."

"What if they have to take it?"

"Then they take it," he says it like it's nothing, on purpose, so as to avoid scaring me. He keeps his voice even, like we're deciding where to go for dinner, not predicting the future of my leg. Mike pauses, adding, "Did I tell you about what Molly did when we got to the lodge?"

"No..."

"She knocked on the kitchen door. I swear to God, she dropped us off, walked right around the side of the lodge, and knocked on the back entrance to the kitchen with her nose. It was like watching you, waiting in line for Chick-fil-A."

"Was not," I'm laughing as I say it, and my voice repeats like it's an echo, not an original sound. Whatever they put in my IV is good. It must show on my face, because Mike's looking at me with a smirk.

"That IV kicked in, huh?"

"No," I lie, scanning his eyes again and taking note of the fractal patterns there, the ones I wished I'd paid more attention to when I had the chance. I lean back, sighing. "I'm glad you have eyes."

"You wouldn't prefer a boyfriend without them?"

"I like them," I add, serious. "Not just regular eyes. Handsome eyes."

"Me? Handsome? Now I know the drugs are working." Mike runs a hand over my forehead. One of his fingers has changed color, stained dark purple and red. One of the EMTs working on my leg notices it too, and nods to his partner, a woman with straight, stringy hair and perfectly groomed eyebrows. She clicks her tongue.

"Wish you would let us look at that," the female EMT says, her voice dripping with annoyance.

"Her first," Mike says, and that's that.

Someone knocks on the side of the ambulance, sending a rippling across the metal exterior. It's a man in a khaki shirt and flannel jacket. He looks official in some capacity, like maybe he owns the lodge, or at least manages it.

"Rangers radio-ed in from down the road. They managed to clear a path through the snow."

The female EMT nods. "We should go. Don't want to get stuck overnight."

It occurs to me that I have no idea what time it is.

"How long have we been here?" I ask Mike.

"A few hours," he says. I must look confused, because he squeezes my hand tighter. "You were asleep for most of it."

The man in the flannel jacket turns back to the EMTs. "You've got a decent gap in the weather if you hurry. I'd take 'em now." He makes it sound like we're a set of packages being picked up for delivery instead of two people who've been through hell and back.

The ambulance doors close as it reverses, and the change in angle reveals a new view through the back windows: yellow tape, microphones, and dozens of camera lights flashing.

"Are those—"

"Reporters," Mike nods.

After spending a week alone in the wilderness, the idea that anyone would care about our situation strikes me as strange, until I remember Logan.

"Have they found him?" I ask.

Mike shakes his head. "I told them where we left him. But not yet."

The ambulance pulls away from the lodge and starts the rickety journey down the mountain. I don't know if it's the drugs, or the way the metal inside the van reflects the light, but suddenly there's a sour taste in my mouth, and I feel the need to confess.

"I have to tell you something," I say to Mike, palms sweating.

"Sure," he answers, keeping it simple, making room for me like he always does.

"I thought it was you."

"You mean the EMT? You thought he was me when you woke up?"

I shake my head. He doesn't understand. Of course he doesn't. He isn't broken like me.

"At the top of the mountain," I'm talking too fast now, and my words are slurring, but I have to get this out. It's poison, and I need to suck it from my veins while I'm weak enough to be bothered by it. Otherwise, I'll leave it there forever, slimy and subtle, spreading between my fingers and toes. "I'd walked so far, I was tired, not thinking straight. And Ken said it was strange you disappeared when the fire happened. We called for you, in the forest, after the fire. You never answered. And then — Logan— he had your backpack. It was so hard to see in the snow, and for a second I thought, maybe, that you, I thought—"

I don't say anything else, because the look on Mike's face says he understands now.

"You thought I did this to you."

The fractal pieces in his eyes seem to break apart for a second, and now he's looking at me like he's never seen me before, like I'm a stranger, a person he doesn't know at all. My ribs split open, because suddenly I understand how it feels: Mike's looking at me the way I've always looked at him.

He doesn't say anything, and I dive into the silence, trying to fill the void.

"There's something wrong with me," I'm crying, and now Mike is holding me. "I'm broken."

The female EMT with stringy hair leans in, clucking her tongue again like a sensible aunt. She inserts herself unapologetically, as if our conversation is a medical matter, not a personal one.

"You aren't broken," she fiddles with some dial on my I.V.

"Been doing this job twenty years. I've seen anything and everything. Lotta bad things happen to women. Makes it hard to trust anyone, doesn't it?"

There. Just like that. In ten seconds, this total stranger just explained the thing I couldn't say to Mike. She pointed out that the monster under the bed— the one I'm always looking for— is real, and hunting, and sometimes hides within the people you love most.

Mike scans the roof of the ambulance like he's searching for some secret code written there. Then, he runs his hands through his hair, his face the face of a man who's agreeing and discovering something all at the same time. "Remember what you told me? About the wolves?"

I nod, replaying the story aloud, my head swimming in a chemical cloud. "The wolves told me I need to end up with someone who can live in the wild with me."

"I'm here, Zoe. I'm in the wild with you. We can make our own rules."

The EMT glances at me cross-eyed and Mike jumps in, offering an explanation. "She saw a pack of wolves while she was out there. Four of them."

The EMT frowns. "That morphine *must* be working if she thinks she saw a wolf."

"What?" I ask, trying to sit up even though my arms won't let me.

"It's a shame," the EMT shakes her head, as if she's missing out on something really special. "Wish we had 'em. We've got everything else— bears and mountain lions. Can't tell you how many tourists come out here hoping to spot a wolf. It's a waste of a trip. Have to go further North to see some. There's no wolves in Yosemite."

Mike squeezes my hand. The look in his eyes tells me he

understands now. The gap between us closes. The fish and the bird can finally build a home together.

He smiles, and without breaking eye contact with me, answers the EMT.

"There's at least one."

22

Mike and I are finally alone, the wheels of our little rental car bumping against the pavement.

It took two weeks for the hospital to discharge us. By the time we were allowed to make the long trek back to Silverlake, the linoleum floors and spotted ceilings had started to feel like home. It was strange putting on ordinary clothes, and not just because they were donated by someone who had seen our story on the news. My body had grown so accustomed to the looseness of an open-backed hospital gown that the scratchy waistband of a pair of jeans felt confining by comparison. Mike— outfitted in someone else's flannel shirt— agreed. Leaving the hospital and returning to the real world was like being thrown off the side of a pirate ship that had taken us prisoner. We were happy to be free, but unsure what to do with ourselves, floating in the middle of the ocean, without our captors presiding over every waking moment.

The doctors couldn't identify a sole cause for my temporary demise, except for a combination of dehydration, starvation, hypothermia, and gastrointestinal parasitic infection that prohibited the absorption of nutrients. Ironically, the least serious of them all might have been the most insidious.

"You probably picked the parasite up from drinking contaminated water," a male nurse in scrubs told me while changing my I.V. "Did you swallow any unfiltered water out there?" I didn't answer, because there was no way to explain to him that I swallowed everything out there, including fear, self-doubt, and basic human dignity.

It struck me as poetic that the parasites were the thing that almost killed me. Not Logan. Not a massive snowstorm. Just tiny little bugs invisible to the naked eye. A course of antibiotics managed to wipe the parasites out— small warriors doing battle inside my body, the scope of my insides an entire universe to them. My leg turned out to be fine, too. The redness we noticed in the ambulance was a bacterial infection, not frost-bite, so the antibiotics killed two birds with one stone.

Mike wasn't so lucky. The frost-bite on his finger couldn't be treated with a drug, and there was talk of amputation. The Doctors said we'd have to find a specialist in Silverlake to monitor the tissue, and it could take a few months to see if it healed or not. Mike says he doesn't care— he doesn't use that finger to make his furniture, anyway— but sometimes I catch him looking down at it with a question in his eyes.

We told them where we left Logan, but inclement weather delayed the search. When they did look for him, they didn't find anything on the mountain. No body. No backpack. Just some broken tree branches and a burned sweatshirt. They've assured us he's probably dead— it's difficult if not impossible to last long in the wild, wounded, without help. When I pointed out that we were living evidence to the contrary, nobody said much.

The news coverage of our escapades spread so fast that apparently it was the highlight of the 24-hour cycle for days. When the hospital called my Mom to let her know we'd been injured, she'd already seen what had happened on the news and was in her car, speeding down the highway, halfway to Yosemite in record time. Before she got to the hospital, she stopped at a CVS and picked up all kinds of supplies, leaving with a giant bag filled with Kleenex, cough drops, and two cans of chicken soup, one for Mike and one for me. When I pointed out that we didn't have colds and nothing in the bag would help, my Mom just shrugged and said, "One day when your kid almost gets herself killed, let's see what *you* come up with!" Then, she hugged me. Mike actually really appreciated the soup, and made a big deal about how much he preferred it to the hospital's offering. At my Mom's insistence, he called his aunt and uncle to let them know what happened. They said they hoped he felt better, and to let them know if he needed anything. He didn't let them know, because what he needed, they couldn't give him. They never came to visit.

The Hardingers made it out alive, too, albeit more unscathed than Mike and I. They came to see us in the hospital, and they brought balloons with them. Big, round, multi-colored balloons tied to thin pieces of ribbon. I didn't ask where they got balloons in the middle of nowhere, because I'm learning not to question the small miracles in life.

Sue told me about what happened after we parted, sitting half-on, half-off my hospital bed like a kid sharing ghost-stories at sleep-away camp.

"I can't believe I didn't see it until it was too late," she whispered, tapping at the bed's metal sidebars. "And to think, we were with him that whole time."

At the other end of the room, Ken waved a hand in the air, re-enacting a scene for Mike. "And then he hit me with the butt of the gun, nearly knocked me out. I was almost down for the count. Thought I'd die for sure, but managed to get back up and push him backwards off the boulder where we'd all made camp. He was climbing back up, and he'd have gotten me for sure, if it weren't for my brilliant wife..."

Sue's cheeks burned a ruddy red as she turned toward me. "I decided to swim to camp rather than walk through the woods so Logan wouldn't hear me stepping in the brush. I signalled Ken from the lake with the flashlight. He jumped off the boulder right into the water and we swam into the center. It was too dark for Logan to spot us out there."

Ken leaned his crutches against the wall, motioning to the white cast around his foot. "Broke it on the fall. Water was too shallow. Knew as soon as my heel hit the bottom that something was wrong."

"We wanted to warn you, Zoe," Sue said, playing with a tassel on the edge of her purse. "We talked it over for hours, trying to decide what the best thing to do was. We didn't know where you were, how to find you—"

"You did great," I told her. "Really. I wouldn't be alive if it weren't for you."

"As soon as we got to the lodge, we shouted for them to call search and rescue. We came off like a couple of crazies, saying your names over and over, describing what you both look like, muttering about Logan. Wish we'd gotten to the lodge sooner, but the trip took longer than we thought it would, what with Ken's broken foot..."

The Hardingers stayed until the nurses kicked them out, but came again the next day, and the next day, and the next. Between the Hardingers, my Mom, and the medical staff, there was always someone in our small, curtained room, and Mike and I never felt truly alone during our stay at the hospital.

Now— inside a car that feels too small, headed toward Silverlike— we're on our own again, wearing too-big clothes that aren't ours, trying to step back into lives that aren't familiar. We drive in silence for the first thirty miles, watching the wild streak by, unbridled asphalt stark against the green backdrop, hinting at a destination yet reached and a talk to be had. Words don't come to me, so I don't say anything. Instead, I let the white lines click past, wishing I could see Mike's feelings again, imagining red and purple thoughts dripping onto the steering wheel.

Suddenly, the trees turn to buildings and the world is inhabited once more. Mike lets out a sigh, as if he's been thinking this entire time, and the sudden density of our surroundings has made him remember there's someone else in the car.

"What a mess," he says, eyes creased, hands tight on the wheel, mind still sorting through everything we left behind.

"I have to ask you something," I answer, making him look at me, taking his eyes off the road for just a second.

I used to think a relationship was a question; one to be asked again and again, one that requires the asker to measure fangs and guess at the sharpness of teeth. But now —sitting in this car with Mike— feeling like I've met him in a thousand different lifetimes and am about to introduce myself again, I'm starting to think that a relationship is really just a series of introductions made over the course of a lifetime. *Hello, how are you, I'm the new me. Are you the old you?*

"You can always ask me anything," Mike says, eyes back on the sprawling asphalt.

"No, I can't."

"What do you mean?"

"There's one thing I can't ask you about." My tone is smooth and two-sided, the vocal equivalent of a pair of scissors held wide open, ready for action. "It's an unspoken rule."

"Who made the rule?" Mike asks.

"Both of us. You set it up early on, and I agreed to it every day after that," I pause, trying to find a way to explain the new me. "But I'm not that person anymore. I can't keep seeing you without knowing everything."

Mike chews on the inside of his cheek, but he doesn't get mad. Instead, he turns the heater down and closes the vents, as if preparing to be interrogated by a police officer with a spotlight. "Well then," he says, careful. "Let's break the rule. Ask me the thing you think you can't ask."

"What really happened between you and Cassandra?"

There's a long silence before Mike answers, and when he does speak, all he says is, "I'm going to need a piece of pie first."

We pull over at the next twenty-four-hour diner we stumble on. It's the kind of place where the mugs don't match, and the waitresses still wear heels, and there's a tired sort of fatigue clinging to the air, like the diner itself would like to be euthanized, if only the owners would just-let-go-already. We pick a booth in the corner, sliding over tomato-red seats upholstered in a plastic-like fabric, fraying at the corners, patches revealing the foam interior in the most unfortunate spots. We settle in, and, after ordering a slice of pumpkin pie and a cup of coffee— black— Mike shows me the worst of him.

~

RELATIONSHIPS ARE MADE OF SPACE, big empty caverns waiting for two people to fill the gaps, empty rooms in a large tract home, begging for clutter, yearning for kitsch. A partnership is an invisible vacuum, an empty stomach longing for the feeling of fullness. Mike stirs his coffee, peering into it as he tries to explain the phenomenon, searching liquid oil for the right words.

"Our entire relationship was about me, not her," he says, scratching the scruff on his chin. "We knew she had a problem. It was always there— but they were treating it. She had her family in San Francisco. Friends. Her entire life. She was stable. But I had always wanted to start my furniture business in LA, to get a warehouse in downtown, source materials cheaper. I would make pieces for the rich and famous, Cass and I would get a beautiful place on the West Side. I had this idea— this vision— to build a home there."

He picks the mug off the table, swirling its contents around like someone reading tea leaves, divining the future.

"What I didn't understand is that when you love someone, they become home, and whatever you make, you make together."

He glances up at me, looking for some reaction, but I don't give him one. Instead, I swirl my fork in the whipped cream on the apple-pie I'm not eating, spreading it around the plate to make it look like I've had some.

"If life was a house, I'd already built it, without asking Cass what she wanted. I picked out the shutters and the doors. I chose the floors and the windows. And then I expected her to move into it. I was young, and stupid, and when it came time to head for L.A., I packed her up like just another thing I was taking with me."

"Did she tell you she didn't want to move?" I try to ask it in a way that doesn't sound judgmental, but not because I'm not judging him— only because I want the truth, and making him feel safe is the best way to get it.

Mike folds his napkin into squares, an origami shape shifter, part bird, part triangle.

"She did. I think she knew she wasn't going to fare well away from everything that kept her in the right head space. If I'm being honest, I probably knew that too, on some level. But I—" he clears his throat, ashamed, a sign he's about to tell me the worst part. "I didn't care. I didn't make room for her. Our relationship was ninety percent me, and what I wanted, and Cass let me do it because..." a waitress with permed, red hair walks by, and Mike waits for her to be out of earshot before finishing, "... because I told her we'd have to break up, if she wouldn't move with me."

"Did you love her?"

Mike pushes his plate to the side, sending crumbs over the smooth surface of our table.

"I loved her, but I wasn't very good at love. I don't have a family, Zoe," he makes eye contact with me for the first time since we've sat down, and the pain there makes me want to leap across the table and tell him we don't have to talk about this, not now, not ever. But I don't, because I deserve the truth.

"You know how it is, with my aunt and uncle, and I act like it's not a problem but it bothers me— it bothers me more than I let on. When I met Cass, I was nineteen. We got through college together, and when school was over I felt like an adult orphan with no idea what to do. I set my mind on a plan for my life, and was too scared to deviate from it because it was the only thing that made me feel like I knew what I was doing. All I cared about was making the fear going away. Do you know what I mean? The fear— the vague kind that keeps you up at night even when there's no good reason for it? It's different for everyone, but for me, it's the idea that I'll die alone, an old man, with no one in this world who cares whether I'm here or not."

Yes, I think. I'm familiar with that one.

"It was that fear," Mike continues, "that caused me to pressure Cass into the life I imagined. I wanted my vision, exactly as I saw it, but I wanted it with *her* because I was just out of school, and scared shitless to try to take on the world by myself. A less selfish person— a man, not a kid— would have moved on his own, but that wasn't me, back then," he looks up again, searching my face for some reaction, but I don't give him one.

"We moved to L.A., and I started my business. Cass was fine, for the first couple of months, but then the distance got to her. She didn't know anyone in the city, and I wasn't —" he stirs his coffee again, seeking more answers, "— I wasn't as supportive as I should have been. I didn't help her make friends. I didn't help her find a new Doctor. I expected her to give up her entire life, move into mine, and be completely fine. We were so young, we weren't equipped. As the months went on, her behavior got more erratic. She'd have these episodes. Once, I came home and she'd taken all the kitchen cabinets off their hinges. Just unscrewed them for no reason at all. Every other week a window would be broken, and she'd claim someone threw a rock at it, that people were after us. I begged her to let me call her parents, but they didn't support her moving with me in the first place, and when she didn't listen it caused so much tension that we were basically on our own. We were alone, and she was combusting from the inside out."

"What did you do?" I ask, stacking my plate on top of his — a signal for the waitress to take it. I've done a fair job smearing the pie around, and it looks like I at least made an effort.

"We went on that way for a few years," Mike answers, sipping his coffee even though it has to be cold by now.

"I got older, and wiser. I tried to get her help, and sometimes we'd go months without an episode. It wasn't all bad. There was a lot of love between us. At one point— when I realized she might never get better— I told her we should move back to San Fransisco and try to start again there, together. But she wouldn't budge. She never told me why, but I think it had something to do with fear of change. She'd already made a move once, and it completely untethered her. Facing a second was too much."

"What made you break-up?"

"It was a car accident," Mike downs the last of his cold coffee. "Cass was driving, and she had an episode. She took us from a side-street, heading the wrong way down a freeway exit, going sixty miles an hour against four lanes of traffic. We slammed into a barrier. It's a miracle we didn't kill someone."

"That's why you're such a careful driver."

Mike nods. "After that, I realized I wasn't doing her any good, that I'd only stayed with her so long to appease my own guilt. I was still being selfish, only in a different way. We broke up. Her parents came back into the picture— even got her to move back up North a couple times— but without fail, it happens again. She goes off her meds, comes straight back to L.A. and tries to pick up where we left off. It's ironic, that I pushed her into a life she didn't want, and now she won't let it go."

"Maybe it wasn't the move. Maybe she would have been the same," I say, thinking aloud, "If you'd stayed in San Fransisco and never left."

Mike gives me a sad smile before pushing his mug to the side of the table, the final addition to our collection of dirty dishes, yet to be picked up any one of the five bored waitresses milling around the diner.

"I used to lie to myself and say the same thing, but there's a truth here, Zoe, and it's one I took ownership of the day Cass and I broke up. I made someone I loved uproot her entire life, even though I knew she wasn't completely stable. I *knew* she wasn't well, and instead of doing what was best for her, I pressured her into what I wanted, because I was afraid to be alone."

Finally, a waitress stops at our table, her silver hair pinned back in a bun. "Get you guys anything else?" she asks before taking our plates, barely giving us time to shake our heads.

"And that's it," Mike says once she's gone. The table looks empty without plates, the distance between us wide when not interrupted by mugs and napkins, forks and knives. "Now you know everything. I could tell you I'm not that person anymore, but I'm not sure you'd believe me. Maybe, if I'm lucky, you'll let me show you who I am, every day, in small pieces, until one day you don't have to ask anymore."

Mike waits, letting the silence sit heavy on my shoulders as I think about empty rooms, and the space we take up, and the line where needs end and love begins.

We've introduced ourselves again, meeting each other all over, and now I have to decide if I like this stranger, this new version of Mike, fractured and damaged, not a princess in a field but an ogre just like me.

A few seconds pass, and then I'm on my feet, and I'm stepping out of the booth, walking over to Mike's side and holding out my hand.

He shakes it, and we're officially starting over, the two of us brand-new and broken all at the same time.

THERE'S a kind of love story— you've heard it before— where the princess is trapped in a castle, and the prince comes to save her. She knows at once he's the one, and they live happily ever after.

Ours is not that kind of love story.

In our story, two ogres meet at separate ends of a bridge, each carrying ratty old suitcases, heavy with fears. They wait on either end, wondering if it's safe to cross, inching forward a little bit each day, until one day they meet in the middle, and build a home there.

When we get back to Silverlake, Mike and I take inventory, looking not just at where we've been, but where we're going. We re-decorate the house. Mike builds us a new bookshelf, and two coffee tables for either side of the couch. He's careful to make sure they're the same size, and he asks me what color stain I want. I paint the accent wall in the living room orange. We plant new flowers.

In each moment, we pay attention to the space in the relationship; who chooses where we go for dinner, what show to watch that night, how much of the vacuum we fill with ourselves. Logan was wrong about love. It does exist, and not because of chemicals, or biology, but because we were made to find each other, to seek the only permanent thing in a world of impermanence.

Love isn't perfect— it's marred and a little unsteady, just like the people who feel it— but it's there. It's only perfect when we get it from the Great Everything, and in the meantime we all just stumble along, doing our best to love others while meeting ourselves all over again, in diners and in forests, in mirrors and in enemies.

Little by little, I stop looking for fangs in Mike's mouth, because something has changed inside me. My time in the wild reminded me that I have my own claws, my own teeth.

I've spent so many years looking for the animal in others — a glimpse of a tail, a growl in the night— that I forgot about my own power, the piece of me that defends, the part that bites back.

There will always be space for me in this home, because I require it. I've found my fangs again. And if, one day, I find myself shoved into a corner— by Mike or anyone else— I'll flex my claws and leave. Not because I don't love him— I will always love him— but because I love me, too. The animal I was taught to hide has emerged in full, and her favorite refrain is, "I want, I need, I must have."

In the darkness of night, my laptop glowing in time with Mike's snores, I search for wolves in a Google deep dive. The EMT we met was right: there are no wolves in Yosemite. I keep reading about them anyway, and learn that at least one part of my encounter with the wolves was real: the idea of an alpha male is a myth, nothing more. Wolves live in pairs, in equal partnerships, in families. They lean on each other to make sense of the wild.

One day, when we're putting new curtains up, it suddenly occurs to me that if I am a wolf, Mike must be something too. "You're a golden-retriever," I tell him, without explaining it at all.

"Yes," he says. "That sounds about right."

When Mike asks me to marry him— pulling the ring from his worn-out pack, one of three he took to Yosemite— it's easy to say yes.

Mike is a golden-retriever; one who sees the best in

others, but the worst in himself. I am a wolf; aloof, but willing to go to the ends of the Earth for the people I love. Together, we make a rag-tag pack, different, but committed, ready to meet each other again and again, always making sure we know one another, strangers and partners all at the same time.

The gap between us changes each day— varying in size from moment to moment— but whether it's big or small, we've learned how to cross it, what bridges to build. We ventured together down a dangerous trail of obsession— Mike obsessed with not pushing me away by revealing the truth. Me, obsessed with figuring out whether I could trust Mike. And Cassandra, unable to let go of the memory of who Mike was to her. But now, we're free. I'm not afraid to marry Mike, because now I know where the teeth are hiding, where the tails are twitching.

Now, I know what kind of animals we are.

C *assandra.*

MY HANDS ARE HOLDING pig-meat when the story comes on the news: Mike's face projected on the little TV screen in my kitchen.

My apartment is a one-bed, one bath, carpeted, cock-roach-ridden mess in Van Nuys. The only nice thing about it is that I've put a small television set in every room. It makes me feel like there's another person around the apartment, even when there isn't. "Cassandra," I'll say out loud, liking the way my own name tastes in my mouth, "it's important for a home to have a *busy* feeling." It's my go-to excuse for watching too much TV.

The toaster jumps right when the morning show pops on. It's one of those exhibitionist talk shows that combines the most horrific events of the week with a panel discussion by people who are totally unqualified to comment. My hands stop pulling bacon from the pan when his face appears; Mike has that affect on me.

I don't usually eat bacon, but was feeling particularly low while at the grocery store and decided to go for it. Mike hadn't answered my texts for almost a week, and even though I'd camped outside his house every night, I hadn't seen him once. I was beginning to wonder if he'd picked up and moved, but a peek inside his living room window proved all their stuff was still in place, exactly as it always is. Maybe Mike and Zoe changed their schedules, just to avoid me.

It was an upsetting thought, to be sure, and it still gnawed at the corners of my mind when I headed for the grocery store. So, when I saw the bacon, I threw it in my cart without pause. It had been a tough week.

Now— as my hands trace the ripples of the sliced comfort food— seeing Mike's face on the TV doesn't feel like such a surprise. I see him everywhere. Someone with Mike's broad shoulders gets on the bus? I do a double-take. A friendly barista passes me coffee, flashing a kind, wide smile? For a second, he's Mike, too. They're all Mike in one way or another, aren't they? Unattainable.

My head whips back around to confirm that my first impression was wrong, but Mike's face is still on the screen. He looks terrible. Two black eyes, a busted lip— it can't be him, but it is. Blinking doesn't help— Mike won't disappear. He's wrapped in an aluminum blanket, sitting on a stretcher as an EMT takes his vitals. He looks angry. He's yelling at the EMT, but I'm not sure why. He glances over his shoulder like he's waiting for someone.

A female talk show host with big lips and wide eyes— God, I envy those eyes— is commenting on the original news footage, which plays on a floating insert. The remote clicks as I turn up the volume, still holding the bacon in one hand.

"Two campers were rescued from Yosemite backcountry last night," she says, her dark hair perfectly shiny as she whips it over her shoulder. "Reports state that the couple was pursued through the wilderness by an unknown attacker."

Another panelist— a man in his late forties wearing a bland suit— laughs, tagging onto the discussion. "I've had some bad vacations," he adds, sounding too pleased with himself, "but this is something else!"

The panel continues their roasting, but I'm laser-focused on the insert, which is still blasting footage from the original news story. Ambulances surround the scene. The cameraman zooms in on a woman— Zoe— laying on a second stretcher, being wheeled into one of the trucks, its red lights flashing. Mike tries to stand— to follow her— but the same EMT he yelled at earlier holds him down. Mike pushes the EMT away, practically ripping the stethoscope off his chest, then follows Zoe into the ambulance.

Her face is obscured by the angle, but as they wheel her inside, her hand falls over the edge of the stretcher, reaching out for someone.

Mike.

He intertwines her fingers with his, holding onto her like he'll never, ever let go.

But you do let go, don't you Mike? As soon as things get hard — that's when you disappear.

"Yosemite personnel have requested that all hikers stay away from the area until further notice," the male talk-show host continues.

"A murderer on the loose and the worst snow-storm in a

decade? You don't have to ask me twice!" The female host adds, practically patting herself on the back.

Sorry, Yosemite Personnel. No dice.

Staying away is the last thing on my mind. A desperate, urgent need to see Mike churns in my stomach. Even though I know he'll be upset. I just need to see him with my own two eyes, to confirm he's okay.

The bacon drops on the kitchen floor, sticking to cheap linoleum tile. The stove clicks as I turn off the gas, commencing a search for my keys. They're not on the hook, not in the fridge. Finally, I find them under a cushion on the couch. Typical.

I'm double-checking that my bus pass is still in my wallet when an unfamiliar sound emanates from my entry-way: three loud, urgent knocks at the front door.

Placing the noise makes me pause, if only because no one ever knocks on my door. I don't have many visitors. Slowly, tentatively, like a cat greeting a stranger for the first time, I undo the security lock. The door creaks as it opens, revealing a man I've never seen before.

He isn't very tall; maybe 5'6" at most. There's a youthfulness about his round face, even though faint lines by his eyes hint that he's not in his twenties anymore. His energy is that of an object in motion— he's invigorated, cheeks flushed like someone who just came back from the gym. Something about him reminds me of the frat guys that used to wander the classrooms of UC San Fransisco. They always looked plush and alive, despite bleary-eyes that hinted at a party the night before.

He holds out his hand, waiting for me to do something with it. He tries to put weight on his right leg but cringes, shifting to the other side instead, making me wonder how he hurt it. There's a long, uncomfortable silence, and for awhile, neither of us fills it.

"Well?" I ask, trying not to sound too defensive or too inviting.

"We have some friends in common," he says. When he smiles, his teeth shine at me, and I don't like how pointed they are. His mouth makes him look like he has a secret he won't share.

"Who are you?" I say, hating the way my voice shakes at the end of the word "you."

His smile gets bigger, like he's about to tell me a joke even though he knows I won't understand the punchline.

"You can call me Logan."

THE END.

~

TO STAY WITH THE ADVENTURE, order the second book in the Predator/ Prey Thriller series, "Lies Run Deep."

Available now in ebook, paperback, and audiobook!

MORE FROM VALERIE BRANDY

LETTER FROM THE AUTHOR

Dear Reader,

Thank you for dedicating your time to the world of the Predator/ Prey thriller series! I'm a screenwriter and film-maker coming to books from Film & TV, but one thing I love about books in particular is connecting directly with a community of readers. It's very special to be able to speak with you and hear what you want from characters in our novels.

I hope you'll reach out to me by joining my mailing list at the link below! I love to keep my readers updated on new releases, offer advanced copies, free giveaways of novellas, sneak previews, and more.

If you liked this book, I hope you'll finish the rest of the Predator / Prey series, which contains three books. Also, check out my Annie Hudson Real Estate Mystery Series by starting with Book One, "Murder Behind the Gates." And if you want to read more from me in general, please keep in touch at the links below! I love hearing from readers, which makes all the work of writing worthwhile.

Warmly,

Valerie Brandy

Join the author's mailing list at:

www.valeriebrandy.com

ACKNOWLEDGMENTS

To my Mom, Sharon Lennon-Mehlschau, for teaching me what a courageous woman looks like by being one. Thank you for your endless support, and for encouraging me to listen to the still, quiet voice within.

To my Grandma Valentine Lennon, one of the three musketeers. We miss you, but we know you're still with us, and we think about you everyday. To my Grandpa, John Lennon, for making me feel like I'm part of a pack, even from the other side. And to the rest of my family, with love, unconditionally.

To Irene "Rambo" Sperling, for help with marketing and rebranding. To Hope Jaymes, for always being there, not just with words, but with actions. To Linda Triol, who graciously proofread an early version of this book. To friends who entertained me and pets who are the best writing assistants.

To all the producers and development executives I've worked with this last decade, who have taught me how to ask the right questions about story. I'm obviously a very lucky person, because there's too many of you to name individually.

Finally, to God, for guiding me in difficult times and speaking to me when I need it most. Thank you for the Great Everything. Everything I do— and everything worth doing— comes from you.

ABOUT THE AUTHOR

Valerie Brandy is a writer, direc-
tor, and actress based in Los
Angeles.

She began her writing career by
selling a feature length screen-
play at just 20 years old,
becoming one of the youngest
members of the WGA west at
the time. She's since written for
numerous film studios and television networks, most recently
serving as a full time staff writer at Walt Disney Studios live
action feature department, where she continues to develop
new projects. Her work has been acknowledge by the Nichol
Fellowships in Screenwriting, run by the Academy of Arts &
Sciences.

Her directorial feature film debut, *Lola's Last Letter*— which
she also wrote and starred in— was released in 2016 by
Random Media and Sony's "The Orchard" after a successful
festival run, premiering at the historic Chinese Theatre in
Hollywood. The film received a five-star review from the
Examiner, a special feature in Huffington Post, and a Best
Principal Actress nomination from Los Angeles Film
Review. Valerie shot the film in seven days with a cast and

crew of just seven people. In their review of the film, Huffington post stated that, "... the key word in describing Brandy is *unflinching*..." Starpulse called the film, "... breathtakingly real and raw... Brandy is an important voice for her generation." *Lola's Last Letter* is currently available OnDemand at iTunes, Vudu, Googleplay, Comcast, Youtube, and many other platforms.

Brandy's second feature film, "A Unified Theory of Love," stars Richard Karn (*Home Improvement*) and Eric Isenwhoer (*Parks & Rec)*, and is due to hit the festival circuit in 2024.

As an actress, Valerie recurred on FX's Emmy-winning show "Justified" as the manipulative Trixie. She received her B.A. from UCLA in three years, graduating as a prestigious Alumni Scholarship Recipient, and holds an M.F.A. in Film & Television Production from Asbury University, where she graduated Magna Cum Laude.

Brandy lives in the greater Los Angeles area with her smush-faced dog and snow-white cat. "Trail of Obsession" is her debut novel.

www.ingramcontent.com/pod-product-compliance
Lightning Source LLC
Chambersburg PA
CBHW030129010826
48973CB00002B/482